MAXWELL'S
ZOOM

MAXWELL'S ZOOM

M. J. TROW

www.blkdogpublishing.com

Other titles in the Mad Max series

Other titles by M. J. Trow:

Author's Note

People often comment on the Maxwell series – very generously as a rule, thank you – and say that Metternich may possibly be the oldest cat in fiction. When a series is a long-running one, authors have a choice. They can kill off characters one by one as they naturally age, or they can forget all about the passage of time and just write about the people whom readers have come to love as if they were immune to it. Ngaio Marsh, creator of the great but never late Roderick Alleyn was asked why he hadn't aged and she said she decided he didn't have to – a wise decision, as he would have been almost one hundred years old at the time of her last book if he had aged naturally. He begins as forty-something and ends that way, having had a son late in life and seen him grown up and leave home in that time. It is necessary to suspend belief when it comes to fiction of any kind and so I ask that you do that for the Maxwell family, who all love spending time with you and love being ageless too!

The other point to make about this book is that it is set in lockdown. Something that in March 2020 was to be with us for a week or so still is with us in many ways and has changed the world we live in probably forever. The Maxwell series is light-hearted, as all readers know, but please don't think that Maxwell or any of his family treat the pandemic or its ramifications lightly; to all who have lost anyone to covid, my heart goes out. The details of every stage of the lockdown may be smoothed out a little for the purposes of the narrative, but I hope I have managed to capture the roller coaster that has been our lives since, to quote Nolan Maxwell, 'it says on the news that bats are giving people colds.'

Enough from me. I don't usually poke my oar in, but on this occasion, there were just a few things which needed to be clarified. On with the book!

The Sons of Mary seldom bother, for they have inherited that good part;
But the Sons of Martha favour their Mother of the careful soul and the troubled heart.
And because she lost her temper once, and because she was rude to the Lord her Guest,
Her Sons must wait upon Mary's Sons, world without end, reprieve, or rest ...

Raise ye the stone or cleave the wood to make a path more fair or flat;
Lo, it is black already with the blood some Son of Martha spilled for that!
Not as a ladder from earth to Heaven, not as a witness to any creed,
But simple service simply given to his own kind in their common need.

And the Sons of Mary smile and are blessèd---they know the Angels are on their side.
They know in them is the Grace confessèd, and for them are the Mercies multiplied.
They sit at the feet---they hear the Word---they see how truly the Promise runs.
They have cast their burden upon the Lord, and---the Lord, He lays it on Martha's Sons!

The Sons of Martha
Rudyard Kipling, 1907

ONE

Peter Maxwell had survived more school terms than any man he knew. The boys who were boys when he was a boy had either seen the light and gone into rather more lucrative employments than teaching – mowing lawns, traffic wardens, things of that nature – or they had taken early retirement with both hands and run off into the sunset, laughing. All terms had their own flavour. There was the mixed anticipation and dread of the Autumn Term, when any sane teacher had that feeling in the pit of the stomach that the complete wastes of space from Year Eleven had somehow inveigled the Powers That Be that they would reform if only they could stay into the Sixth Form and, worse case scenario, those same wastes of space would end up in their set for advanced something-they-couldn't-manage-in-its-simplest-form. After half term, most of the dead wood would have wandered off to work in Morrisons, so that found its own level. Then there was Christmas, with the tinsel being wound round the heads of the flightier girls – and the occasional boy – from late October. The least said about that, the better. And then, there was the Spring Term, hilariously named as it began in the dreariest, dankest, most unpleasant time of the year. At least the Half of that term usually coincided with the odd crocus trodden into the mud of the narrow strip of what was laughingly called lawn along the approach to Leighford High and sometimes, if rarely, there was just the whiff of hope of sunny skies. But the thing that Peter Maxwell hated the most, was the uphill slog from the end of February until Easter, with all the fear of forthcoming exams, with white-faced swots and insouciant idiots who had no idea how bad they were in front of him at every lesson. But this year, something was different …

Two

'Dads?'

'Yes, mate?'

Maxwells fils et pere were breakfasting alone that Saturday morning and Nolan was in a questioning mood. Ever since he could talk, he had wanted to know the reason why and he knew his Dads was the man to ask. Except about maths, and even then he would have a brave stab.

'Bismarck and the Count don't catch bats, do they?'

'Bats?' Maxwell scratched his head and flicked an errant Coco Pop off his boiled egg. 'I shouldn't think so. They inhabit pretty different spaces, I should think.'

'But if a bat was ill and was on the ground, perhaps. Would they then?'

'Well ... bats are mice with wings, I suppose.' Maxwell was pretty fearless, as men went, but bats were his Achilles heel. He had always worried they might get caught in his hair, still as mad and wiry now as when he had been young and fancy free.

'But they would know, wouldn't they, not to catch them.'

Maxwell put down his egg spoon and looked at his son. 'If you're planning to have a bat as a pet, you can forget it. You managed to squeeze in a kitten and that's enough.'

Nolan looked at him, wide-eyed. If a bat phobia was a genetic thing, then he had definitely inherited it. 'No, Dads.

3

Ugh! You can't have a pet *bat*!'

Maxwell was relieved – he had come to love Bismarck, who had grown from a very small scrap of stripe into a worthy confederate of the black and white behemoth that was the Count, but there were limits. The original Count Metternich and Otto von Bismarck had never met, but they were of sort of the same German persuasion, so that was good enough.

'So, why all the bat talk, then? Have you finished with that?' He nodded to the bowl in front of his only son.

'Hmm? Oh, yes, thanks, Dads.' Nolan pushed the bowl across. There was occasional talk of making him do more around the house, but somehow, the cleaning up after the cleaning up never seemed worth the effort. 'It says in the news that bats are giving people colds. And I didn't want the Count or Bizzy to catch it.'

'The news?' Maxwell was a little puzzled. They didn't keep Nolan wrapped in cottonwool, but they weren't great news-watchers either. He had been vaguely aware of bats being in the news, but hadn't equated it with cats. Or with anything much, really. Chinese bats could stay in China, if he were given a choice.

'And Bizzy's little brother isn't well. He's at the vet. Do you think he caught a bat?'

This was heavy stuff for breakfast time. Bismarck's brother – called Frank, after the combine harvester in *Cars* for no reason Maxwell could ascertain – lived with Plocker and had always been a bit of the runt of the litter. But Plocker had been adamant that he wanted that one and so it had come to pass. Maxwell wasn't totally amazed he was at the vet, but made commiserating noises, nonetheless. 'I don't think Frank is really up to catching bats, mate. What with the squint and everything.'

Nolan took a slice of cooling toast off the pile in front of him and gouged about a pound of butter out of the dish to squish onto one corner, as was his wont. 'Well,' he said, indistinctly, butter running down his chin, 'it's a worry.'

THREE

'So he said,' Maxwell told his wife as she sprawled on the settee next to him having a foot rub after a busy day, '"it's a worry".'

She wiggled her toes. 'He *does* worry,' she said. 'Do you remember that time when he was about three and I asked him what was the matter and he said he was worried that he didn't have anything to worry about?'

Maxwell laughed. 'Yes, I do remember. But where is he getting all this? It can't be Plocker, surely?'

Plocker was a lovely child, with eyes as blue as the sky and a head as empty as the great outdoors. He and Nolan had been inseparable almost since the moment they met, but he would never be a watchword where great thinkers gather. Maxwell had predicted he would be prime minister one day.

'Well, it might be. If it's come across a bit garbled, then it has all the Plocker hallmarks. But I think he's just picked it up in general conversation. And there *is* a lot going around about some nasty bug coming out of China. Wuhan Province to be precise. We've just had a briefing about it this very afternoon.'

Maxwell's eyebrows rose sharply. 'A briefing? Really? What will you be doing? Arresting bats?'

Jacquie smiled at him, the smile she used when she was going to be serious and really wanted him to be the same. He saw it and dialled the levity down a notch.

'Really, though. A briefing? How can it possibly affect the police?'

'There's been a meeting of Sage.' She looked at him, daring him to make a stuffing comment so he didn't. 'They are talking about a lockdown.'

'A *lockdown*?' This time, Maxwell was the serious one. He was the historian, the one who knew where things like lockdowns could lead, even in the year of people's Lord 2020. 'Do you really think it will come to that? Do you think … well, do you think people will comply?'

She snorted down her nose and felt behind her for her gin and tonic. 'No, of course they won't. Why do you think we had a meeting?'

He nodded. 'Fair point. And this lockdown. Is it …?'

She pulled her feet from off his lap and with one movement was sitting on his knee, head tucked in to her special place, warm against his neck, in the place where she felt safe, no matter what the odds. 'Yes,' she whispered. 'Yes, Max. It's coming.'

FOUR

Detective Inspector Jacquie Carpenter-Maxwell switched off the television and turned to face her husband, sitting deep in thought in his favourite chair. Neither spoke for a long minute.

'Well,' Maxwell said at last. 'I didn't think I would live to see the day.'

'Nor did I,' Jacquie said. 'And that's speaking as a police person, not a historian.'

'I was just speaking as a human person,' he said, 'but yes, that too. I … I don't really know what to say.'

'There's nothing, is there?' she said. 'We're both in odd situations. You are going to have to learn how to Zoom, for a start. Video teaching doesn't just happen, you know.'

'I'm going to have to learn how to *what*?' This sounded as though it might be even worse that it had appeared to be at first blush.

'Zoom. But that's something for later. For now, you know what you have to do.'

He looked at her, eyes searching for clues.

'I can't do charades right now,' she said, sitting down. 'One of us has to go and see if Mrs Troubridge is all right. She's going to have to take extreme care, more even than the rest of us, and one of us is going to have to make sure she understands.'

'One of us?' Maxwell said. 'You, surely.'

'In normal circumstances, I would agree,' Jacquie said.

'But this needs someone with a bit of gravitas.'

'Yes,' he said. 'You.'

'No, not me,' she said. 'You. You're the teacher around here.'

'And you're the woman policeman.'

'Exactly.'

He sat back. 'Sorry, you lost me somewhere around "exactly".'

'Exactly, she needs someone to make it very clear to her, that she can't go letting in every Tom, Dick and Harry who knocks the door. She had a Jehovah's Witness trapped inside for four hours last week.'

'Well, that's a bright lining to the cloud, isn't it?' Maxwell said, chirpily. 'No more Holy Joes. No more charity fundraisers. No more dropping off bags for jumble.'

'Stop trying to change the subject. Off you go.'

'It's late.'

'It isn't.'

'It's late in Troubridge Land.'

'She'll have been watching the announcement. She likes that young Mr Johnson. Apparently, he reminds her of Mr Troubridge in his prime.'

'Really?' Maxwell had seen pictures of Mr Troubridge and a prime was difficult to imagine.

'Yes, yes, I know. Mr Troubridge looked a lot like Rudolf Hess, but memory can gild any lily. But she'll be frightened, I would think. She'll be worrying about getting groceries, all that. So, just pop round, there's a dear.'

'You don't call me dear.' He was clutching at straws. 'Are you well?'

'Go. Meanwhile, I'm going to go and have a look at how much loo roll we have.'

'Er ...'

'Just. Go.'

Maxwell negotiated the front path to his own house easily enough, but had only gone a short way down the corresponding one to the Troubridge residence before he felt a sharp pain in his shin. Looking carefully, he saw a wire stretched across the path and, beyond it, several more. He picked his way past the obstacles and rang the bell then leaned on the wall, rubbing his leg.

The door flew open and revealed an unusual sight. A woman stood there, swathed in black bin liners, a broom extended in one hand, a bottle of bleach in the other. Behind her, in the shadows, was a smaller apparition but no less startling. That one had a balaclava pulled down over her face, made, unless Maxwell missed his guess, from the leg of a pair of lockknit directoire knickers, last sold from market stalls circa 1955. Only one eyehole was in the right place but from behind it gleamed the baleful eye of Mrs Troubridge. The first woman turned her head and spoke to her companion.

'It's all right, Mrs T,' it grated in a thirty a day growl. 'It's only Mr M.'

'Spray him, spray him,' the small woman howled, poking her in the back.

'Hold on a minute, Mr M.,' the black clad figure said. 'Let me just …' she turned round and spoke to the old lady. 'Now look, Mrs T.,' she said, firmly. 'This isn't going to work if you don't show no discernment.'

Maxwell always had to give himself a mental pinch when Mrs B, cleaner extraordinaire, came up with a big word. The woman was an IT geek of some repute and clearly had a head on her shoulders, but several rounds of Mr Bs of various character had rubbed off her intellectual gleam somewhat. But she was a woman to be reckoned with, as everyone found to their cost, sooner or later. He waited patiently, listening with a smile.

'You know we can't really spray people,' she was saying patiently. 'I explained …'

'That nice Mr Johnson,' Mrs Troubridge said, drawing herself up to her full five foot nothing, 'said we have to wash more often while singing Happy Birthday.'

Mrs B glanced over her shoulder and shrugged, not an easy trick to pull off. Years of hoovering had given her an unusually strong upper body. 'Sorry, Mr M. Won't be a minute. It's been a lot to take in,' she continued, bending slightly to be nose to nose with her charge. 'I don't mind wearing the bin liners until I can find something better. But I will not be spraying either Mr Maxwell or anyone else with bleach. As soon as we find out more, we'll get something in place but until then, Jessica, please …' she took the old lady's hand and squeezed it, 'can we just wait and see?'

It was a side of Mrs B that Maxwell had not often seen and he was impressed. He was even more impressed when he saw Mrs Troubridge squeeze the woman's hand in return and give her the smallest of nods.

'I'm sorry,' she said, a word that seldom left her mouth. 'But …' her voice shook, 'that nice Mr Johnson …'

'I know,' Mrs B said, 'I know, love. Now, just go upstairs now, slow like we promised, and I'll just see what Mr M wants.'

Slowly and with great care, the little woman grasped the handrails which Maxwell noticed for the first time were now on both sides of the stairs and made her slow way up. When only her feet were visible, Mrs B turned to Maxwell and rummaged in her pocket, through several layers of plastic. She stepped outside and pulled the door gently to, waving Maxwell ahead of her.

'Six foot, Mr M, please, if you don't mind. Not that I hold with rules, as you know, but I have Jessica to think of. She's going to need all the help we can give her. Now,' she tapped a cigarette out of the packet she had unearthed and lit it with a single use zippo she never seemed to have to replace, 'what can I do for you? We've got no spare loo roll, if that's what you're after.'

'Um … no,' Maxwell said, feeling the world was slightly tilting. He wasn't used to Mrs B limiting herself to only one idea at a time, though if there was a time for concentrated thought, this surely was it. 'I .. well, Jacquie … Mrs Maxwell and I were worried about Mrs Troubridge, whether she had understood how careful … well …' His thoughts just petered out and he stopped.

'That was very kind of you,' Mrs B said, formally. 'How is Mrs M? And little Nolan? Must be worried, I expect. I hope he hasn't heard about this cat flu that's going round, he'll be worried about Bismarck, I expect. And Mrs M, the police'll be on alert, I expect. How's she going to cope? Have to do a lot more at work, I daresay. I won't be able to give you any hours for the foreseeable, I've got Jessica to think of.' She pulled on the cigarette and Maxwell saw it grow a whole inch shorter.

This was more like it. While she let the smoke dribble luxuriantly down and over her chin, he said, 'Not at all, just being neighbourly. She's fine. So is he. Just the same as everyone else, I suppose. He has heard, yes. He is a bit. She'll manage. They are. Don't worry. I quite understand.' He took an extra step back while she wafted the smoke away.

'I'm moving in for the foreseeable,' she said. 'Mrs T isn't too good on her pins these days and she gets a bit confused. She should be in somewhere by rights, but a home won't be the place to be with all this going on. Old ducks carking left and right, it will only depress her.'

'Won't … er …?' Maxwell could never keep track of the Mr B situation, which came and went in a random pavane that no one but the dancers understood.

Mrs B raised an eyebrow in an interrogative gesture.

'Won't … the family …?' He decided to keep it vague.

'Oh, them.' She took another drag on the cigarette, finishing it and throwing it down in one gesture. She ground it out savagely and spoke almost to it as she did so. 'I doubt they'll notice.'

'Until they run out of loo roll,' he suggested, to lighten the mood.

She glared at him. 'Hmph,' she said, giving it as much venom as she could. 'I doubt they'd notice even then.' And on that fragrant idea, she stepped back inside and closed the door.

'That was quick.' Jacquie was on the sofa with her legs pulled up, watching a man going by the inappropriate name of Chris Whitty tell an agog nation that they were all going to die. She wondered why, as he clearly knew he was going to be on television, no one had thought to make sure he was wearing the right size collar. She pointed to Maxwell's drink waiting for him on a side table. 'I started without you – I hope you don't mind.'

'No, not at all.' Maxwell sat and swigged in one well-practiced movement.

'So. Wasn't she in?'

'No, she was in.'

'So … why so quick?'

He took another drink and smiled, a little tensely. 'Mrs B has moved in with her. She is going to keep her safe.'

'Blimey.' Jacquie looked at him wide-eyed. 'That's a tall order, especially if you listen to this clown. According to him, unless my grasp of English has slipped a mile, we're all doomed, people will be dropping in the street, the NHS will be overwhelmed by week Wednesday and the devil take the hindmost.'

Maxwell looked at the screen. He had been vaguely aware of this man already but had never noticed how like a tortoise he was until tonight. He looked over at his wife, sitting in the lamplight, her hair shining, her cheek as smooth as silk, her hands clasping her glass just a little too tightly. He raised his glass to her. He knew what she was thinking, as surely as if she had had it tattooed on her forehead.

'We'll be fine,' he said. 'All of us, from little Bismarck to me. I am an old git, we all know that, but I don't have anything underlying to worry about, if madness can be excluded. And so please, please, my love, don't worry.'

Her eyes filled with tears. Having your mind read was a relief sometimes. It saved having to work out the words. Eventually, she spoke. 'Of course it will be fine,' she said. 'After all, we've got loads of loo roll.'

FIVE

The jogger did a double-take. Standing sturdily right in his path was a policewoman who looked to his eyes to be about twelve and also about four feet high. Since his heart attack and his born-again attitude to exercise, one which drove at least his wife to distraction and, had he but known it, almost everyone he knew, he had also come to terms with his chronological age, something he had tried to forget for years with the use of hair-dye, Spanx for Men and a liberal dose of other women, applied as required. He now allowed himself to agree that policemen looked young and so he was happy enough with that, but why was she standing right in the way? His technique demanded that he ran in straight lines at a regular speed, dictated by his iWatch. He glared at her as they got nearer, but she didn't flinch, just held out a hand to stop him.

'Can't stop, dear,' he said to her patronisingly as he swept past. 'I have a program.'

'So do we, sir.' The six foot policeman built like a brick shit house who stepped out of hedge was less easy to avoid. He was covered head to foot in dark blue PPE and to add to it he had a night-stick and a very conspicuous camera on his chest, which he swivelled to bring the jogger into focus. 'I'm afraid I must ask you some questions, if you could just stop bouncing up and down on the spot.'

'I'm afraid I can't, officer,' the jogger said. 'I can't cool down or I could sprain something.'

'If you could just step back, sir.' The policeman whipped a digital tape measure out of his pocket and pointed it at the man's feet. 'Back … back a bit more … yes, that's it. Now, sir, if I could just have your name, please?'

'My name?' The man's face was becoming an unattractive purple. His cardiac rehab mentor would have a fit. 'I'm just out for a jog. Surely, that isn't a crime?'

'That would depend, sir. Where do you live?'

The jogger's eyes bulged and he became almost incoherent. 'Where do I *live*? What's that got to do with the price of fish? I live in Leighford. The Brighton side.' Even in his fury, he didn't want to be taken for some oik from Tottingleigh.

'I see, sir. Postcode?' The jogger rapped it out and the policeman tapped it into his tablet. 'This app,' he flashed the tablet briefly at the jogger, who couldn't see what it said from a precise two metres away, 'says that you live 3 miles and 147 yards away from this very spot.'

'And?' The jogger was still bouncing but was now looking murderous.

'Well, sir, as you doubtless know, having watched the broadcast yesterday evening and read your newspaper this morning to keep up to date with current legislation,' the policeman drew in a desperate breath. Long sentences were certainly more difficult through a mask. 'Travelling more than three miles to take exercise is now an offence.'

'What?' The jogger leaned forward and the policeman stepped back, brandishing his digital tape measure. 'So, I can't get in a decent jog now, is that it? Bloody Whitty and Vallance are so keen to stop me dying of sodding Covid that they'll kill me through lack of exercise?'

'I don't think 3 miles and 147 yards is lack of exercise, exactly, sir, is it? That's if you have jogged from home?'

'Of course I haven't.' The man was bouncing less enthusiastically now but was rather tentatively lunging on alternate legs and pushing up off his thigh. 'I drove. There's a bloody dual carriageway between here and there.' He stood up, not bouncing or lunging, as he saw the policeman's eyes narrow. He couldn't see it, but he knew that behind his mask the man was displaying an evil grin.

'Really, sir.' A few more taps on the screen almost made the policeman laugh aloud. 'By road, we are, yes, as I thought – we are almost four miles from your place of residence, sir. So if you would like to just go back to my colleague there and give her your name and address, we will be in touch.'

'In touch?' The jogger was snarling the words between his teeth now. 'Why?'

'To arrange payment of your statutory fine, sir. Now, if you could just step aside; I need to chat with this lady walking her dog …'

Maxwell sat at his desk in the study at home and looked uncertainly at the keyboard of the computer. He poked it randomly and fortunately, nothing happened. The screen in front of him was live, with squares dividing it, some with faces in, others with small snapshots of other people's bedrooms, kitchens, lounges and, in one case, a shed. At the bottom corner, there was a scene he thought he knew, then he recognized it – it was the wall behind him and slightly to the left. He moved across and loomed into view, rather disconcertingly reversed, as in a mirror, his glasses askew on the top of his head. He put a tentative hand up to check on them and became more disoriented still.

Jacquie lurked to his right, ready to step in with some timely help if needed. For example, currently, he didn't have the sound up; there was no background babble as she would have expected. She leaned in low and moved the bar so that he could at least hear his pupils. She mimed taking the register, pointing at the clock. He looked at her, puzzled. There was no microphone as far as he could see. He had seen microphones, big jobs with 'BBC' in them in big letters. Or else the little ones attached to a lapel that angry guests tore off before leaving chat shows in a huff. She read his mind and pointed to a tiny hole at the top of the screen.

'Really?' he said and all the heads in the squares spun round to face him. 'Oh, clearly it is,' he said, and they all looked around, puzzled. It seemed that Max was as Mad on Zoom as he was face to face. 'I'm going to take the register,' he said. 'And because I can't possibly use two keyboards at once, I'm going to do it on paper and fill it in later. So any of you who are in earshot had better get into your little square PDQ or I shall mark you absent.'

A few more heads popped into view.

'So … who's missing?' He scanned the screen, which looked like an American game show on speed. 'Chantal. Any one know if she's all right?'

A face loomed a little nearer in its square and Chantal's BFF said, 'Her and her mum got stuck at her gran's in Wales, cuz of lockdown.'

'Aha, though,' Maxwell said, also looming nearer. 'I happen to know, yes, Ten Zed Aitch, even *I* happen to know, that she could be on Mars and she could still be here.'

'She ain't got a compu'ah,' her BFF chimed in.

Maxwell was yet again staggered that the girl could be bothered to go to all the trouble it took to miss out the 't'. Jacquie nudged him and mimed being on the phone.

'Phone?' he said, acidly.

'Umm …' BFF was stumped.

'Don't say she doesn't have one, because I have confiscated it on an almost daily basis since September. In a candy pink cover with a unicorn in sequins if memory serves. I suggest, Britney, that you get on the old blower and have her in one of these squares in the next half a minute, or I shall want to know the reason why.' He cast his eyes over the rest of the screen. 'Anyone else … David?'

A girl in the top line, middle, cleared her throat. 'Mr Maxwell, sorry, he did ask me to tell you. His mum is … well, she's got Covid, ain't she, and he's looking after his sister.'

Maxwell decided to ignore the grammar and nodded. 'Tell him hello and wish his mum better soon. Right … oh, hello, Chantal. Nice to see you.'

She grunted a greeting and tossed her green hair over her shoulder. Green hair wasn't allowed at Leighford, but she was at her gran's in Splott, wasn't she, so they couldn't do nothing – it was a long phrase to be expressed in a single hair toss, but nonetheless, she managed it.

Maxwell made the last tick in the last box and beamed at his class. He had not been keen when the Zoom suggestion had first been mooted, but now he could see the advantages. No smell of gum, feet and cheap perfume. No texting under the desk, a skill he had yet to perfect. No giggling and passing notes. There they all sat in their little squares, some of them in rather well-planned bedrooms, with – saints in heaven be praised! – books on the wall, real ones, not the ones you could buy pictures of by the yard from Amazon. Others were in the kitchen, as the occasional passing figure of a harassed mother could attest. The one in the shed would need checking on – that was just weird. It was a warm spring, but … Maxwell made a small note in a margin and looked up again. 'Right, Ten Zed Aitch, before the world went mad, where were we? Ah, yes, Kristallnacht, I believe.' And, as the lesson gathered pace, he hoped that none of them would see the connection between what was happening in Germany immediately prior to the outbreak of war and what was happening here. Because he would have to tell them that this was all for their own good, that the nice Sage gentlemen were not rabid loonies who wanted to cage the world and Mr Johnson was not a Reichsmarschall in mufti. And he would have to try to make it sound like the truth.

An hour later, in the kitchen, he sat opposite his wife, cradling a coffee in both hands. 'That went well?' The statement became a question.

'You're a natural.' She sipped her coffee and nibbled her Hobnob.

'It's very quiet. Where's Nole?'

'You're not the only one who can Zoom, you know. He's doing maths in his bedroom on your phone.'

'Ah. You found my phone, then.'

'You can run, but you can't hide, Max.'

'I suppose at the moment, I shouldn't really do that kind of thing. Stay off the grid, that kind of jolly jape.'

She looked at him and after a moment stretched out a hand and held his. 'Right now, I would say we need all the jolly japes we can pack in to each day. It's not exactly a laugh a minute, is it?'

'True. But we'll be all right, Mrs M. I promise.'

'But *do* you, Max? You're just the sort who won't wear a mask, who won't … well, obey the rules. And … it worries me. It worries Nole. Even the Count has had a word, you know, on behalf of them both.'

Maxwell took a deep breath. This woman had made his world complete and although it went against every fibre of his being, he would obey every single little cockamamie rule that the dynamic duo of Whitty and Vallance could throw at them. Every single one. He told her so and felt her relax.

'Really?'

'Really.'

'And … you won't make fun?'

'Oh, God yes, I'm going to make *fun*. You can't have everything, woman, can you?'

She laughed and slapped the hand she had been holding. 'No, I suppose not. Have you got any more Zooms today?'

'No.' He stretched and yawned. 'I've done some lesson plans which include a questionnaire.' He pronounced it like Angela Rippon, with a ringing 'k' at the beginning and no 'w'. 'So I'll have marking to do later when they send them in. Then tomorrow, I'm going to do a question and answer on Zoom and when they get the questions right, I switch them off and let them go.'

'Surely, it's when they get them wrong … oh, I see what you did there.'

'Indeed. Four Pea Enn are cunning as weasels. If once they spot a wrong question gets them sidelined, I'll be getting gibberish from all over. After that … actually, I wanted to talk to you about after that.'

'Me?'

'I'm doing Victorian crime with the thickies and I was hoping …'

'No. And should you call them thickies?'

'Not beyond these walls, no. And perhaps not even here, but these are strange times. But, couldn't you …?

'Max!' She stood up and tilted his cup to see if he'd finished. 'Are you done with that?'

'It's full of Hobnob. They're not the same as they were, dratted lockdown Hobnobs.'

She walked to the sink and rinsed the sludge away. 'I can't help you because I'm at work tomorrow. So you will be in charge of Nolan's home schooling – he doesn't have any Zooms tomorrow. So I don't actually think Jack the Ripper is on the menu anyway.'

'Hmm.' He picked up a few Hobnob crumbs with a dampened forefinger. 'Perhaps not. I'll think of something else. This could be a blessing in disguise, though. If we home school Nole, he could be degree level by May.'

''Oh, for pity's sake, Max,' she said. 'This nonsense will all be over by then and we'll be back to normal.'

'Hmm.' Maxwell was not a historian for nothing. He knew how these things went. He left the room, singing softly under his breath, to the Gene Pitney tune, 'When Whitty and Vallance rode to town, the women folk would hide, they'd hide. When Whitty and Vallance rode to town, strong men would step aside. Cos keeping everyone locked well down was all they understood, and when it came to talking a load of drivel, they were mighty goooood!'

Jacquie sat in her office later that afternoon and looked at the whiteboard which some kind soul had marked off in squares. In each square was a name and a quartet of boxes. The boxes were marked I for in, H for home, SI for self isolating and an X, which meant anything from feeling a bit poorly to being in hospital. Fortunately, so far, there were none of those. Most of the admin staff were working from home, with mobiles fitted with a system no one understood which would ensure that calls were taken in order as they came in. It meant that speaking to the same person twice was next to impossible, but waiting times were, if anything, shorter than before. A skeleton staff of senior officers was always on duty. The first idea was that teams would be created so that everyone worked alongside – if being in different offices and wearing PPE in meetings could be called alongside – the same few

people, but Jacquie and Henry Hall had leapt on that and
strangled it at birth. Without a second thought they could
both name at least three people who, if they had been stuck
on the same team with them, would have driven them both to
drink. So the rota was complex and arcane, but it seemed to
be working. Today, Jacquie was on with Henry – their offices
being opposite, it was easy to communicate as long as they
kept the doors open and the voices loud.

There had been meetings – oh, so many meetings –
but the only thing that everyone agreed on was that there was
no telling what was going to happen. It was easy enough for
those who had hold of the microphone to say that everyone
must stay at home, only going out for essential food and
medicine and one lot of exercise per day, but how was that
going to be policed? What was 'essential' food? What was
vital for one person could be just a frippery for another.
Jacquie could name a handful of kids in Nolan's class who ate
only certain brands of certain foods and indeed, Nolan
himself didn't consider a day started if it hadn't started with
Coco Pops. So were they essential? The long and the short of
it was, they were going to have to suck it and see. Genghis, a
beat policeman of unusual severity, had been put on desk
duties. He had been known to arrest a nonagenarian who
accidentally dropped a handkerchief which she couldn't bend
to pick up, for littering. He was about to put her in a cell
when she couldn't pay the spot fine when Henry had
intervened. Tempers were going to be on a knife-edge; no
one needed Genghis loose and lethal in a situation like this.

The IT geeks were in an excited twitter. They had
been requisitioning for drones on a weekly basis ever since the
first one came on sale and had always been turned down. But
now, they saw their chance and pounced. What better way,
they argued, to keep tabs on people breaking lockdown, than
flying above their heads, checking on their every move?
Taking too much exercise; nabbed. Shopping more than once
a week: gotchya. They spoke of face recognition software,
body-shape mapping – their little eyes glowed with
excitement at all the fun they could have. The icing on the
cake, as far as they could see, was that they could do all this

from *home*! No need to dress, even. They could be playing *Resident Evil* with one eye, watching the drone cam with the other. A quick call if they saw any transgressions and some other poor sod could go and mop up the mess. The other poor sods in question had looked at them with undisguised contempt and, with a collective grunt, dismissed the idea as so much hot air.

The police at the sharp end had, indeed, the sharp end. They would be policing breaches of lockdown and would sometimes have just seconds to decide whether it was deliberate or inadvertent. An old lady having the usual three friends round for Bridge of a Tuesday afternoon was just as much a lockdown villain as the four students getting legless in the quad, and yet … and yet … Jacquie sighed and pulled some more paperwork to the space in front of her; this was not going to be easy.

Nolan was lying on the sofa, his legs up the back and his head dangling off the edge of the seat. It was his go-to position when Zooming with Plocker and although Maxwell had vague misgivings about blood rushing to the head and similar medical emergencies, the child seemed to like it, so he left well alone. Bismarck was on the windowsill, playing with Nolan's trailing laces in a desultory way. Count Metternich was sprawled upside down in Maxwell's chair, his stomach exposed in the way only a cat who knows he is in charge will risk. Maxwell felt himself suddenly a little superfluous and took himself off to the kitchen to mark the results of his latest online quiz. He chuckled as he took the top off his pen. Eight Eff Oh – named, despite protestations from most of the staff, following the random algorithm designed by a long-ago maths department – were rising to the occasion and the answers were getting fuller as the term ground on, with some of the wits and wags taking advantage of the lack of face to face to unleash their wilder flights of fancy. But the way Maxwell looked at it, learning was learning, no matter how it happened and the main aim was to keep them engaged. If it didn't happen to be strictly about the Factory Act of 1833 was a bit moot at this particular stage of the game.

The sun poured in through the kitchen window and threw sparkles off the taps. The dishwasher hummed happily to itself and the fridge gave the occasional gurgle. The birds were singing their socks off and somewhere, someone happily working from home was mowing the lawn. It struck him that it was idyllic – was this lockdown some plan by the universe to make everyone take stock? If so, it seemed a bit draconian. With hardly any travel happening, even the skies were quiet. It had come as quite a shock when Maxwell had ventured out on some essential shopping earlier that week to find that suddenly the bicycle had become the method of travel de jour. Where once he would be almost alone, White Surrey's tyres hissing against the tarmac the only ones to be heard, now he was just one of a gang of cyclists, most hunched over the handlebars like something from the Tour de France. It seemed to Maxwell to be a little out of place when simply out to buy some milk and a loaf of bread, so he kept to his usual style of sitting bolt upright, his trousers kept in place with clips but otherwise no special clothing. In particular, no Lycra. He had spent an unsettling half an hour surrounded by more tensed buttocks than he had ever seen before in his life, so now, when and if he ventured out, he went on foot.

In the background, he could also hear Nolan talking to Plocker on his phone. The gadget had never had so much use in its life – he had been staggered at the things it could do. It had been acquired after a long fought battle to which Maxwell had given every fibre of his being. Anything called 'smart' that was nevertheless a small rectangle of plastic and glass would never really have his vote, but it had come into its own over the last month or so, it had to be said. Nolan and Plocker had even had a virtual Easter Egg hunt, which was declared a draw, the first time that had ever happened since the boys were still in nappies.

But for now – Maxwell drew a deep breath – a Zoom with Ten Zed Aitch, the Set From Hell.

Jacquie coo-eed across the corridor and she heard the scrape of a chair as Henry Hall pushed himself back from his overladen desk.

He stood in the doorway, masked and gloved, leaning against the doorjamb.

'There was no need to come over, Henry,' she said, looking into the tired eyes above the mask. 'I could have shouted.'

'No, no,' he said, muffled by the mask. He raised his hand to remove his glasses and rub his eyes in the gesture she knew so well, then stopped himself. 'I needed a change of position.'

'Are you all right, Henry?' She looked more closely. His skin was looking quite grey these days and she doubted his working from home slots were spent outside, as almost everyone else's were. 'No problems at home or anything?'

He shook his head and then nodded. 'Margaret has … well, she's become a bit obsessive about the news. Death rates. That kind of thing. Variants. She hangs on Whitty's words as though he's God.'

'Well, he does rather look as if he agrees, doesn't he?' Jacquie made sure her smile reached her eyes. Sympathy was hard to do in a mask, even if the mask had Wonder Woman on it. It wasn't issue, but at her desk it just made her feel a little less like a number, more like a free woman, with apologies to Patrick McGoohan.

'Excuse me,' he said, leaning forward and dragging her spare chair into the doorway. 'It's that kind of thing, isn't it?' he said. 'Getting us all down. Having to apologise for leaning forward a foot or two. Stepping into a room.' He slumped down as if his legs had stopped wanting to carry him. 'She has made me move into the spare room, you know. I have to undress in the garage. Shower before I can go into the sitting room and then we sit at opposite ends.'

Jacquie frowned. 'Why? You're not high risk here. She doesn't have anything underlying, does she?' It would be so like Henry not to say.

Again, the exhausted shake of the head. 'No. She's just …' He threw caution to the winds and rubbed his eyes after all. 'Exhausting, to be honest. She believes everything she sees online and she's online *all* the time. And it doesn't matter if they contradict each other. If I could find Neil Ferguson, I'd like to … well, let's just say, it wouldn't involve social distancing.'

'I'd forgotten he had already buggered up foot and mouth. Max reminded me.'

'I don't know how they keep their jobs … but, enough of us. You coo-eed?'

'I did. Although, now you're here …' she sifted some papers about, trying to look as though she knew what she was looking for. 'Ah, yes. I've had quite a few reports on this address,' she pushed it forward but with the best will in the world, Henry was never going to be able to read it from two metres away, or, as Maxwell would have it, six feet, nine and six tenths inches, or two cloth-yard arrows, Medieval archers for the use of, so she read it out. 'Broadgate Avenue. It's out on the Brighton Road.'

'Yes, I know it. What number, do we know?'

'Well, that's the thing. The reports are coming from dog walkers along the footpath at the back. There are no numbers on the gates and in fact not every house has kept access to the path, because of burglars and things, I expect. It's quite secluded out there and dark at night. Semi-rural, almost.'

'Vague idea?' Henry had perked up. A non-lockdown problem was just what he needed.

'About halfway along. We've had,' she riffled the pages, counting under her breath, 'eight calls but they are not all for the same thing. That's why I had put it aside. One woman said she heard screaming. Another said there was a man shouting, just the same name, over and over, shades of Alan Partridge.' She saw a light die in Henry's eye. He wasn't a man for TV comedy. Or, indeed, any comedy at all, really. She pinched the top of her mask to stop it slipping down. She wished sometimes she had a more substantial nose. 'Dog barking, this one says. Umm … this one is different again. A light flashing on and off. The trouble is, guv,' in the newly woke world of Leighford Policing, that wasn't something he got called much these days and Henry smiled behind his regulation PPE, 'there's nothing to it really and as a rule, I would ignore it. But … eight reports. What do you think?'

Henry Hall lounged back in the chair, crossed his ankles and shoved his hands in his pockets. 'Calls to the station have gone up by God knows how many percent since all this insanity began,' he said. 'People dobbing in their neighbours for having a party and when someone goes round, it turns out to be a rerun of *Eastenders* being played too loud. A mad old trout had the desk on the phone for nearly twenty minutes yesterday with a complaint of abuse, turns out she couldn't get a Tesco delivery until next Wednesday, which apparently interferes with her human rights. So …' he looked at the ceiling, 'I don't know, Jacquie, to be honest with you. It could be they are just eight lonely people who want to hear a human voice.'

'All in the same place, though?'

'As you said, it's semi-rural. And given that you can't … shouldn't, anyway … drive to walk your dog, then they are all from reasonably nearby. I don't know that path, so …'

'We walk it sometimes,' Jacquie said. 'Actually, it joins a playing field at one end to a patch of woodland at the other. It's a kind of shortcut. So anyone who is a goodish walker could come from a mile or two away without going to great lengths.'

'Oh, right. So they might not know the road, from the front, as it were.'

'No. Not necessarily.'

'Tell you what. Make a bit of a plan of where the callers' home addresses are. See if there's anything in that. Sometimes people make calls to make trouble, as you know. Have a squint at the CYP reports, see if there are any vulnerable kids out that way. Why not ask Max?' Hall laughed into his mask and made himself cough. 'He can probably save you hours of work.'

Jacquie tried not to show her surprise. 'He doesn't have access to any of the details – he's working from home.'

'Yes, of course he is. Sorry. Now the boys are not at home, I've lost track. See if he's worried about anyone, though. You could check the names, perhaps – I don't know. It's something and nothing, isn't it? But we can't let things slip through the cracks just because every bloody man and woman in the station is out measuring how far apart people are standing in the park.' He blew his cheeks out and regretted it when his glasses steamed up. He waited until they cleared, having got fed up with wiping them all the time. 'Was that all?'

'Yes.' It wasn't much of an all, when it was said and done. She glanced at the clock. 'Time to go home, I reckon.' She reached down for her bag. 'Come on, Henry. Time for some down time. You're ...' she looked at her plan, '... ooh, you're off for four days now. Try to get some rest.'

Henry Hall looked hunted. 'I think I'll see if anyone wants to swap,' he said. 'Anyone isolating, needs covering?' His eyes were hopeful but he knew the answer.

'No,' she said, shooing him in front of her. 'We're covered. Go home. Have a talk with Margaret. Get drunk, both of you, why not? I'll tell you what, I'll Whatsapp you Sylv's number. You remember Sylvia, the nurse at Leighford? Well, she's become a bit of a debunker, if you like. People who are finding it a bit much, she talks them down off the ledge. Literally, in one case, apparently. She puts the facts and figures into perspective.'

He looked at her doubtfully.

'No, honestly, Henry. Anyone who can deal with the girls at Leighford can deal with anything. She doesn't make you feel silly, just reassured. Even just on the phone.' Jacquie suddenly realised how much she missed hugging people. She should be hugging Henry now, he looked so woebegone. But of course, if there was no ban on hugging, he wouldn't be needing a hug. Bugger Covid. Bugger battered bats or whatever it was they ate in China. Just ... just bugger.

Maxwell looked into the sitting room and noticed that Nolan was in his second most favourite position, on his stomach in front of the telly, Bismarck curled up in the small of his back, Metternich tucked under his chin.

'Comfy, chaps?' Maxwell got a wave from two of them, so that was all right. 'What are you watching?' He and Jacquie had decided not to go for the Parental Controls option, on the basis that they always made sure they knew what Nolan was watching. But it never hurt to make sure.

'Storybots. It's our assignment for today.'

Maxwell went further into the room. That sounded a bit too much like fun to be schooltime watching. On the screen, some cartoon characters were explaining how electricity was made. After thirty seconds he was completely lost so just made random parental agreement noises and sidled out of the room. With any luck, he wouldn't have to call the kid to come and help him with his Zooming.

Today was going to be a good day, he could tell. He remembered how to log on and almost all the squares were full. Chantal had brown hair again and was looking moderately engaged. David was back – Maxwell had had an email from Leighford office that his mother had been taken into ICU, so please try not to dwell on death; she was pretty serious. He wasn't going to find that an easy task, given that they were at that point in the syllabus when the Holocaust was rearing its inevitable head, but, thinking on his feet, he thought he could probably rejig a little, just for today. The poor child did look haunted and no wonder. His eyes swept the screen. The usual mix of bedrooms, kitchens, the occasional garden now the weather was warmer and … yes, there it was. The shed. He really must find out more about the shed.

'Mr Maxwell?' Chantal's whine had always grated with the Head of Sixth Form. How could anybody put at least thirteen syllables into 'Maxwell'?

'Yes, Chantal?' He was reasonableness itself.

'Why do we have to have all these laws?'

'Laws?'

'Yeah. All this stuff about we can't go to school. Or see our friends. Or …'

There was a chorus of agreement from the other squares, as if the mob were lighting its virtual torches and preparing to march. This, Maxwell ruminated, was how it started. The sans culottes marching on the palace of Versailles screaming at the Austrian woman, Marie Antoinette 'Why can't we get out of our bubble?' Lenin's Bolsheviks attacking the Winter Palace, shouting 'Bugger you,

Kerensky, we don't want to wear blue masks. We want red ones.'

'Yes,' he told the rising masses that were Ten Zed Aitch. 'Laws are a nuisance, aren't they? Unfortunately, we can't do without them. Jake.' He picked on the Brightest Boy in the Class, predictably sitting framed by a bulging bookcase.

'Yes, Mr Maxwell?'

Chantal tutted loudly. Even on Zoom, the Swots had it all their own way.

'Think back to Year Eight.'

'Blimey,' Jake was heard to mutter. That was two years ago, nearly a seventh of his life; but of a tall order, really. But Maxwell was more hopeful – he'd just heard the lad mutter a word that Jake's great grandfather would have used.

'That nice little island in the Thames, back in 1215. What was it called again?'

'Oh.' It all came flooding back to Jake. 'Runnymede. Magna Carta.'

'And where did King John sign it?' Maxwell asked.

'He didn't!' the entire class chorused.

Maxwell clapped, far more vigorously than he had for the NHS of a Thursday evening. 'Well remembered, Ten Zed Aitch. Where did he stick his seal, then?'

'At the bottom!' they bellowed as one.

Maxwell laughed. Once this lot got to university, there'd be no more jiggery-wokery, no more cancel-culture, just a new batch of intelligent, questioning young people. But he hadn't answered Chantal's question.

'When the barons decided that the king was pushing his weight around, they drew up a list of sixty-three complaints, if you remember, and John was forced to agree to changes. Some of those changes became law. And they gave us freedoms; things that kings couldn't do any more. Jake, does 1832 ring any bells?'

'Umm …'

Chantal sniggered. The Swot had ballsed it up. Maxwell's blue-eyed boy had blown it.

'Anybody?'

'Great Reform Act,' somebody said and Ten Zed

Aitch held its breath.

'Well done, Archie,' Maxwell said, trying to keep the astonishment out of his voice. It was the first time he'd ever heard the lad speak. Chantal sniffed and tossed her hair. Not *another* smartarse! 'The Reform Act doubled the number of voters – still all men, of course, but it was a start. Anybody heard of James Keir Hardy?'

Nobody had.

'First working-class MP.'

'What? Like Angela Rayner?' It was Chantal, of all people, making the analogy.

Maxwell suppressed his astonishment yet again. It was so much easier over Zoom, long may it continue, if only for that reason. 'Yes,' he agreed. 'But with a better beard. What about Mrs Pankhurst?'

'Votes for Women!' three or four of the Baby Zoomers yelled.

Maxwell winked and clicked his fingers. 'Now you're firing, Ten Zed Aitch. All these people and many more changed the laws and made the laws that we still live by today. Without these laws, Chantal, it would be chaos. People would drive the wrong way down roads, park on the pavements. They'd help themselves to food in supermarkets without paying. They'd break into premises, smash windows, pee in the nearest corner ...'

There were howls of revulsion and laughter in equal measure.

'Now, I know what you mean, Chantal,' Maxwell quietened them down. 'These Covid regulations are tough, aren't they? But they're there for a purpose. They're there to protect us, keep us all safe. That's what most of our laws are for. We've all got to remember that and soldier on. And ...' he harnessed his inner Vera Lynn, 'There'll be bluebirds over the non-existent white cliffs of Leighford, tomorrow, when the world is free.'

Six

'**M**ay I ask you a few questions about your domicile, please, sir?'

The policewoman was very polite, but the dog walker still looked at her with hostile eyes above his mask. 'My domicile?'

'Yes, sir. As you may know, there is legislation currently restricting people from travelling too far to take their allowed exercise and so we are doing spot checks to see that there are no infringements.'

'Infringements?'

'To see that you have not travelled too far, sir.'

The dog walker looked down at the rather overweight cockerpoo on the end of its lead. 'Does Vlad look as if we have travelled far?'

'Vlad?' The policewoman looked around.

'The dog. Vlad.'

'Ah. Yes, I see.' Anything less like a Medieval murdering despot or even Christopher Lee the policewoman had yet to see, but names usually had a private meaning. 'Fan of *Twilight*, are we, sir?'

The dog walker looked her up and down. 'It's four o'clock. Why should you assume that?' He was hard to assess, being well masked and gloved, but she had him for mid-fifties. Probably a bit on the elderly side for teenage vampires, now she came to think of it, but it took all sorts.

'Not to worry, sir. Just making conversation. Did you

drive to this location to walk your dog today, sir?'

'No.'

She tapped a box on her tablet. 'Are you domiciled locally, sir?'

'I live up the road, yes.'

'May I ask where?'

'You may.'

She tilted an eyebrow. She was learning on a steep curve how hard it was to let someone know what you were thinking with most of your face covered up. It did no good, so she asked outright. 'May I have your address, sir?'

'I've seen this on the telly. Got drones, have you?' The dog walker looked into the sky, innocent of vapour trails with most planes grounded. 'Eyes in the sky, that kind of thing?'

'No, sir. We're hoping to avoid those measures. If I could have your address, that would be very helpful.'

'I just live on the Brighton Road. I mean, look at this dog. How far do you think he can walk in the average day?'

The policewoman was an animal lover and in her short sojourn on this popular path had been frankly appalled at the state people allowed their animals to get in. 'He is rather … portly, sir, isn't he?' She had been hauled over the coals only that morning for calling a labrador fat the day before.

The man seemed to soften. 'He is a bit broad in the beam.' He looked down fondly at the dog who was taking the opportunity for a breather. 'We're hoping to slim him down a bit while we're working from home.'

'Oh, I see,' the woman said, tapping a few more boxes. 'Are you furloughed at all?'

'Self employed,' the man said. 'Simply doing it from home now instead of just working at home.' He saw her confusion. 'Just my little joke,' he said. 'I'm a genealogist. I help people track their family trees.'

She stepped back. 'Is that a job?' As soon as she spoke she saw another coal-hauling in her immediate future.

'Well, I think so,' the man said. 'Anyway, must get on. We don't want Vlad here to stiffen up. It plays merry hell with his joints. Keep up the good work.' And with a nod and a click of the heels which she decided to ignore, he was gone.

It was only as she cross-examined the owner of a rather sprightly whippet that she remembered he had not given her his name.

'Good day?' It seemed strange to Maxwell to always be the one at home, asking his wife about her day. As a rule, in what they had taken to calling BC, Before Covid, it had been random chance who was at home before who.

'I had a good day, yes. Henry, not so much though. Margaret has got herself in a bit of a twist.'

'Did you give him Sylv's number?' Maxwell knew what was good for what ailed ya.

'I did.' Jacquie kicked off her shoes. 'He's home for four days now, so hopefully that will help. She has too much time to worry. You housewives …' she kicked out with a stockinged foot but missed him by a mile, 'you have too much time to think. How's Nole? Come to think of it, *where's* Nole?'

'He's in the garden. One of his assignments for today is to find ten different plants, list them and find out one fact about each.'

'Crumbs.' The Maxwells were not horticultural geniuses. 'Do we *have* ten plants in the garden?'

'They can be weeds, happily. So, yes.'

'I think there's an app …' Jacquie rummaged for her phone.

'Done and done,' Maxwell said, smugly.

Jacquie collapsed in a mock faint. Then, recovering, said, 'How on earth did you do that?'

'Cheated, of course. I rang next door, Mrs B answered. I told her what I needed to do and she talked me through it.' Maxwell looked up at his wife through his lashes. 'No, actually, I put my phone in a plastic bag and left it on the step next door. Next time I saw it, it was in another plastic bag on our step, but with an app on it.'

'Clever,' Jacquie was impressed. 'Lateral thinking at its best.'

'And even better than that,' Maxwell said, proudly. 'It was Nole's idea.'

'This home schooling thing is suiting him,' Jacquie said. 'I don't suppose …'

'No. We are not home schooling him forever. He needs company. He needs Plocker. Zoom calls are all very well, but …' he smiled at her. 'It is fun, though. I watched a Storybots with him this afternoon. How music works. Amazing!'

'It's like Sesame Street, but for the Twenties,' Jacquie said, and went off into the kitchen searching for a snack, humming the Planets song, and not the Holst one.

Maxwell raised his voice a notch. 'I need to talk to you, though, about one of my kids.' He listened to the answer but it was round a mouthful of sandwich, so he wasn't quite sure what she said. 'I didn't catch that.'

She resumed her seat and threw him a Tunnock's teacake. She liked watching him trying to save the fluffy bit till last. 'I said, I need to talk to you, about one of your kids. Potentially. What did you say?'

'Much the same.' He unpeeled the foil and looked lovingly at the chocolate dome. 'Different pronouns. No potentially.'

'You go first, then,' she said. 'My situation is much more uncertain than that. I don't even know if there's anything wrong. Just some dog walkers getting in a stew. We've seen a huge rise in calls since lockdown.'

'The couple opposite,' Maxwell said, carefully biting the biscuit base away from his treat, 'rang your lot this morning to rat out their neighbours.'

'Really?' Jacquie's eyebrows shot up. 'What for?' Columbine wasn't exactly a hotbed of crime. And the couple opposite had not lived there long but the rumour had it they had met online and lockdown had trapped them. They had exhausted the obvious avenues of amusement and were clearly looking around for something new.

'Stockpiling.' Maxwell set his lips and raised a knowing brow then popped the chocolate-covered fluff into his mouth in one go.

'What is this? 1940? Stockpiling isn't a crime.'

'And you should know, of course, heart,' he said

through a mouthful of Tunnock. 'Anyhoo, apparently, their garden shed is full of loo roll.'

'I know this story,' Jacquie said. 'It came across my desk. Nothing to it. Apparently, all that was in the shed was a ton of Amazon packaging, waiting for a recycling pick-up that never came.'

Maxwell blew out his cheeks. 'Boring. But sheds do bring me round to what I was going to ask you.'

'No.'

'No, what?'

'No, you can't have another shed. You haven't been in the one you've got for … well, I don't remember when you were in there last. The door has all but healed up.'

'No, no, I don't want another shed, although it's true a man can't have too many. I'm a bit concerned about one of my zoom kids. He seems to be doing it from the shed.'

'That's okay, isn't it?' Jacquie could think of worse places to Zoom from. It was a well-attested story around the nick that one of the traffic co-ordinating staff always zoomed while on the loo.

'Well, I suppose it isn't the worst thing in the world. It's just a bit odd. As is the kid, to be fair. Never speaks in class or on Zoom. Turns in perfectly adequate work but nothing to set the world on fire. Doesn't seem to have any friends. Just one of the bland ones, I suppose.'

'What are the parents like? Do they seem like the kind of people who would consign their kid to the shed for the whole of lockdown, for example? Does he smell? Is he thin? Does he wear long sleeves or high collars when the weather is against it?'

'I know all the flags,' he said, not unkindly. 'I've never met the parents, but no to the rest. He's just … he's not a shed kid, if you know what I mean? I was expecting a bedroom, perhaps with a model aeroplane on a string – or is that too Fifties? A lounge with curtains with the patterned side facing out. But not a shed.'

'Is it a posh shed?' Jacquie knew that in these days there were sheds and sheds. There were competitions, for goodness sake!

'No. Just a shed. Lawnmower in the corner, spade, that kind of thing. And it's not as if they live in a tiny house, with no room. I checked. They live in Broadgate Avenue. It's …'

'Along the Brighton Road. Yes, I know it.'

He looked at her. 'Do I get the impression it's crossed your path already today?'

'It has. Or, I think it has. We've had calls from dog walkers along that path at the back.'

'I know the one. We've done it sometimes.'

'Yes. So you know that you can't tell what house you're behind. So we don't know where the calls refer to, not really. Just somewhere in the middle, we think. Henry asked me to see if you might know something. And it turns out, you do.'

'I might.' Maxwell didn't want to put himself forward, though he would be up front and central when the time came.

'It's a tricky situation, isn't it?' she said. 'If you were in school, you could check on the database …' She looked at his face and corrected herself. 'You could get someone to check on the database and then you could see if the child in question lived in the middle of the road.'

'Dangerous place, the middle of the road, but I know what you mean. He does,' Maxwell said. 'Number 67. The side with the footpath. What are your calls about?'

Jacquie shrugged. 'Flashing lights. Dog barking. Shouting. Nothing to add up, really.'

'True,' Maxwell agreed. 'But it is something to bear in mind.'

They both fell silent, thinking their own thoughts.

'I could send someone round,' Jacquie said. 'Just to see if everyone's all right. Number 67, you say?'

'Yes. I shouldn't have their addresses here, not really. But I got Thingee to send me the roll, so I could tick off for the register. Nole printed it out for me.'

'You're getting quite the IT team assembled, aren't you?' she said. 'In house and virtual.'

'All I need now is catering and secretarial and I may never go back to school. Any news, by the way? On how much longer this insanity is going to go on for?'

'We don't get updates every day any more,' she said. 'So I just know what you know. Which is wait and see. Face, hands, space. The usual bollocks.' She sighed. 'Poor Henry. He looks like nothing else on earth. And there must be thousands more in his position.' She pulled a rueful face. 'I wish …'

'You wish you could fix it,' Maxwell said, getting up and going over to plant a kiss on her nose. 'But you can't. And, if I am not mistaken, our very own Capability Brown is on his way up the stairs with assorted vegetation. Let's hope there's nothing poisonous. Apparently, casualty is a bit of a no-go area right now.'

The door crashed back and a beaming Nolan, Bismarck rubbing around his ankles, stood there, with armfuls of plants, some of them still shedding soil. With one voice, his parents yelled 'Kitchen!' and he trooped out to spread his spoils on the table. There were some plants they didn't even know they had and Maxwell suspected that this was the one and only time they would see them. One he knew was bindweed, so full marks to the boy for pulling that one up. The pansy would have to go back, perhaps not the nettle … but all in all, not a bad haul. With the ease of long practice, Nolan flicked to the camera app and laid out his plants to their best advantage. There were gold stars to be had and one could ever have too many of those.

'I'll just make that call …' Jacquie said, edging out of the room.

Maxwell nodded and turned back to his son. 'Do you know all the names of these?' he said.

'I used the app,' his son told him. Maxwell looked down at his slightly tousled head and smiled. He never thought a son of his would be using language like that. But, then again, once upon a dark, wet night, he thought he would never have a child again, so he wasn't going to stand on ceremony.

'Now,' Maxwell said, bending to the task. 'What can we bring to the table to get the star? Alphabetical order?'

'Nice one, Dads,' the boy absent-mindedly high fived

in his father's general direction. 'Weeds and flowers mixed, or seprate.'

There were some words that the lad had never really come to terms with and separate was one. He could spell it, on occasion, just not say it. But they let it go – sometimes, a reminder of babyhood was no bad thing.

'Hmmm … mixed, I think.' Maxwell had no imperative to let the school know that the garden at Columbine was more weed than not. He could hear the murmur of Jacquie's voice across the hall and tried to tune it out. He really, *really* didn't want number 67 Broadgate Avenue to be the epicentre of anything other than some shed zooming. But some little voice in his head told him he'd be lucky. And he wasn't feeling very lucky. A worm dropped on his slippered foot and he stifled a small scream. Thank goodness for Bismarck, who had not yet got the refined palate of his mentor. Nolan looked down.

'I wonder what worm tastes like?' he asked.

'Spaghetti?' Maxwell suggested. 'Noodles?'

'I think probably worm,' Nolan said, as Bismarck deftly threw up the partly-chewed annelid onto Maxwell's other foot. 'Bismarck doesn't like it, anyway.'

Maxwell looked down. He'd stepped in worse.

The muttering from across the hall had become more intermittent, a series of hmms and uh-hus which meant that Jacquie was taking notes. That rarely ended well and Maxwell concentrated on the plants. 'What's this one?' he asked, holding up a sad looking specimen with toothed leaves and indeterminate flowers.

'Hmmm.' Nolan consulted the app. 'It says here it's common fleabane.'

The Maxwell men looked down at Bismarck who tried to look innocent.

'It's a weed,' the boy added.

Maxwell was relieved. He wouldn't like to think he had shelled out good money at the garden centre for that sorry excuse for a plant.

'It can grow to six feet tall, it says here,' he said. 'That's if it's tall fleabane.' They both looked at it. 'I'll say it's that and then that can be the interesting fact. That it grows as tall as you, Dads.'

As interesting facts went, Maxwell had heard better, but with nine more to discover, any old port in a storm was his motto. The kitchen door opened and Jacquie's head poked round it.

'Nole, can you spare Dads for a minute?' she said.

'Of course. I'm at the picture stage now anyway and …' he paused, for he was a kind child, 'I can manage by myself.'

Maxwell dropped a kiss on the top of the boy's head. The lad was a diplomat already – probably something to do with having pets called Metternich and Bismarck. 'Back in two shakes of a worm's tail,' he said, pausing only to grab a sheet or two of kitchen roll to remove said tail from his slipper.

Jacquie had gone back into the sitting room and was standing by the window, a notepad in her hand. Maxwell perched on the edge of his chair and cleaned his slipper over the wastebin. 'Something of interest, I assume,' he said, looking up.

'Yes and no,' she said. 'Someone at the nick is ringing up the dog walkers and getting back to me. The check on the address is interesting, but I don't know where it gets us. I just didn't want to talk about it in front of Nole.'

'Right.' Maxwell folded the last of the worm into the kitchen roll and sat back. 'Nasty?'

'Very. But … well, let me give it you verbatim. Number 67 has a rather chequered history in our records. Domestic abuse, child taken into care, intermittently but over a reasonable period …'

'That's bad,' Maxwell interrupted. 'We don't seem to have had any communications on that score.'

'Wait, though. I was surprised until they told me the dates.'

Maxwell felt a tiny trickle of ice down his back. 'Go on.'

'The last reported occurrence was in 1987.'

'1987? Well …'

'Exactly. There are some records missing, apparently.'

'Do tell.'

'Filing cabinets are no more foolproof than digital, no matter what you say, dinosaur. But the child remained in the system, was fostered long term and now … well, who knows? We haven't had time to follow it up, but … why would we?'

Maxwell still felt chilly. 'So,' he said, hopefully. 'Just a coincidence, then?'

'Hopefully. But … I got the shivers.'

Maxwell did a whole body shudder, the way Metternich did when they tried to give him medication. 'With you there, heart. What a horrible thing.'

'The house was empty for ages. I don't know whether the parents did a runner or what, but they didn't live there any more and I don't know how it all panned out. Anyway, some of our beat guys are going round there, just to see how everything is. They'll ring when they get there, but as you can imagine, we're swamped right now.'

'Checking on stock piled loo roll?' Maxwell suggested.

'And making sure there are no illicit games of football in the park, no fraternisation on the beach. The big stuff, you know how it is. But when I know, you'll know. I promise. I suppose I had better go and help Monty Don with his plants – those gold stars don't win themselves, you know.' She closed her notebook and slipped it into the back pocket of her jeans. She wasn't being secretive. She was just being Detective Inspector Carpenter-Maxwell, a different person altogether from the Mem, heart, Mums, she-who-opened-tins. And he loved her for it.

SEVEN

Much, much later that same night, so much later, in fact, that it was early the next day, Maxwell nudged his wife in the ribs.

'Hmph?' Jacquie's grunt was more in sorrow than in anger.

'I was just wondering … did you hear back from the guys checking on number 67?'

In the dark, the sound of stirring, of bedclothes being pushed back, pillows being thumped and rearranged told him that she was not planning a long chat. Eventually, she spoke.

'No. They got a bit snarled up with keeping people off the beaches. Apparently, they were coming from miles around, pretending they were walking dogs. Shitting in front gardens.'

'The dogs?'

'The people. They'll go tomorrow.'

'As long as …'

'They won't forget.' Another pillow got a darned good thumping. 'Goodnight, Max.'

And peace descended again on Columbine.

In Broadgate Avenue it was, if possible, even quieter. Although it was always described as being on the Brighton road, being on *a* Brighton road would have been more accurate, in that, should you follow the road slavishly for long enough, you would indeed reach Brighton. But the road was not exactly direct, being more of the Chestertonian variety, rambling and rolling, so it saw very little traffic. And in lockdown, it had all but healed over. The footpath got some traffic but after dark even that was deserted.

If there had been anyone listening, they would have heard a faint rustle in the undergrowth at the side of the path, about midway along. In the rustling and almost hidden by it was the click of a forgotten latch and a creak of a hinge long ago rusted shut. In the silence, it sounded like a scream. Soft footsteps made their way up a path, sunk an inch or two below the level of a patchy lawn. It had once been bowling green perfect, but that was long ago. Now, divots were missing, and moss had colonised it under a laburnum tree just beginning to look the worse for wear now its spring glory was passing. The footsteps paused and a shadow slunk into the lee of a shed. Another noise was making an impact on the silence, a grunt and a squeak. A fat hedgehog laboured down the shallow bank from under the hedge and, jostling and whining, sounding like an asthmatic nanny, she nudged her little skein of babies up towards the dark house. She knew there would be dog food there, sometimes bread and milk. She told her babies, as best she could, not to be afraid. The dog couldn't get them. It was inside the house, behind the glass, and was anyway all mouth and trousers.

Right on cue, the dog erupted from the dark of the kitchen where he had been sleeping, chasing rabbits fleeter than the wind, catching them in his steel-trap jaws while all the most beautiful bitches of the neighbourhood watched in amazement and clustered round him, presenting their most interesting parts for him to sniff and, ultimately, to mount. It was a fruitless dream, poor neutered creature that he was, but if he was disappointed, scaring some hedgehogs shitless was a good second prize. He stood there, feet planted, lip drawn back, as the little family dipped their pink noses into the milk, pulled at dog food with their needle teeth. His growl didn't make it through the newly-installed double-glazed patio door, but it wouldn't have mattered anyway. A hedgehog, as all Erinaceus europaeus know, can outsmart a dog any day of the week.

Down in the shadows, the amorphous darkness made a note by the light of a small torch and quietly disappeared.

There was something innately peaceful in a breakfast with no timescale. No inhaling Coco Pops, no tearing at toast gone rubbery with waiting until its recipient came running in from having a quick shower before work. There was no tipping of half-drunk coffee down the sink because it was too hot to drink in the thirty seconds remaining. In fact, chez Maxwell, breakfast was fast becoming the favourite meal of the day.

'Pancakes?' Nolan's eyes were like saucers. He had forgotten that during their year in America, he had had pancakes for breakfast every day, just because he could.

'I thought we'd have some for a change,' his mother said, pushing the maple syrup across the table. 'There were blueberries needed using up and … I just fancied them, to be honest.'

Maxwell shoved his bacon to one side to make room. 'There's a lot wrong with the good ol' U S of A,' he remarked, 'but breakfast isn't one of them.' He slathered his plate with maple syrup, then looked down at the result. 'Not healthy, though, I'm thinking.'

'Maple syrup is good for you,' Nolan suggested. 'It comes from a plant. It's vegan.'

Maxwell sketched a brief take-off of Edvard Munch's oeuvre but even so sopped up some of the lovely Canadian goodness with a forkful of pancake.

'I think the bacon probably cancels out the vegan,' Jacquie reassured him. 'And I won't tell if you don't. This is nice, though, isn't it? Just a leisurely breakfast, no one rushing.' She sipped her coffee. 'I don't remember the last time this happened on a weekday.'

There was a brief silence, broken suddenly by the shrilling of her mobile phone. She glanced at it. 'It's the nick. I'll just be a minute.' She slipped out of the kitchen into the hall. Her men heard her say, 'Carpenter-Maxwell,' and they knew they had lost her for a while.

'Dads?'

'Yes, mate.' What was it about breakfast time that made his son want to set the world to rights, Maxwell wondered?

'You know lockdown?'

'Yes.'

'Is this going to be forever, now?'

Maxwell swallowed his pancake and bacon, mainly to play for time. 'Not forever, no.'

'How do you know that?'

How indeed. 'I don't,' Maxwell said. Honesty was the best policy. 'But I've been alive for a long time now, mate, and I have learned that everything finds its own level, in the end. And anyway, I don't think people would stand for it.'

'But the policemen would make them, wouldn't they?' A policeperson's child, thought Maxwell, and yet so trusting.

'They could try. But we won't get to that, it will all be over soon.'

Nolan looked down at his plate and moved his bit of pancake back and forth. A fat tear splashed down on his hand and he wiped it off quickly.

'Are you missing Plocker, matey?'

Nolan nodded and the tears came in earnest. He slid off his chair and into his father's arms, possibly the safest place in the entire world. Nothing could hurt him there. Maxwell leaned his cheek on his boy's bed-haired head and rocked him silently. Sometimes, even Maxwellian words were not the right thing. Eventually, with a great sniff, Nolan released his python-like grip and muttered into his father's pyjamaed chest.

'I've never gone this long without Plocker, not for ages. And he misses me as well, I know. I worry about him.'

Maxwell kissed his boy and had to fight back a tear. 'He's all right, he's with his mum. She'll make sure …'

'But will she?' It was almost a howl. 'She doesn't do pancakes, I know she doesn't. And Frank isn't well, still. And the tortoise has gone missing. And he can't do his sums. And … Dads,' the little tear-stained face was upturned now, 'he *needs* me!'

Maxwell patted his back and let him go back to his

seat. 'How about this?' he said. 'What if I ring Mrs Plocker and see if she fancies going for a walk. And we'll go for a walk and perhaps it will be in the same place at the same time. How would that be?'

Nolan's face lit up. 'Is that allowed?'

'Strictly speaking, no. But I'm sure we can make it work. Shall we do that? Where are you going?'

Nolan had shovelled in the last mouthful of pancake and was off out of the door. 'Getting dressed.'

'But …' Maxwell shrugged. All it needed now was to persuade Mrs Plocker and it would work like clockwork. Probably.

Jacquie, coming in from across the hall, only just avoided being bowled over by her son. 'He's keen,' she said. 'Where's he off to?'

'Getting dressed. We're …' in retrospect, it was probably better she didn't know. 'Busy day, you know how it is. Any news?'

Jacquie sat down and ran her finger round her plate; no point in wasting maple syrup, even if it was vegan. 'They went round, lovely couple your boy's parents. Doing loads of work on the house. They're both furloughed and so they are making the most of it. Decorating, making a vegetable garden, conservatory of course, kitchen extension, even; he's a builder by trade, so all done properly. That's why … what's his name?'

'Marcus.'

'That's why Marcus is in the shed. The house is in uproar.'

Maxwell sat back in his chair and looked at his wife with relief. 'What about the dog walkers?'

'Well, their reports make sense. They do have a dog, which is a softie – yes, yes, I know they all say that! – but they feed hedgehogs and he goes nuts when he knows they are outside. And the husband – Roger, I think his name is – does tend to work into the night if he's doing something that can't be left, which accounts for the lights.'

'Screaming?'

'Foxes.'

'Shouting?'

'The wife was a bit embarrassed, but apparently, on nice evenings when Marcus is in bed, they like to … well, let's say they enjoy a little al fresco.'

'That must annoy the hedgehogs.'

'I suppose someone shouting Roger over and over could be taken more than one way. But essentially, the team were happy that everything is all right at Number 67.'

He blew her a kiss. 'Thank you for following that up, heart,' he said.

She looked at him closely. 'You're not happy, though, are you?'

'Yes, yes, I am. Only … don't you think that those excuses are a bit pat. An answer for everything?'

'Max,' she got up and gathered up their plates. 'Sometimes, if it quacks like a duck and walks like a duck and looks like a duck, it is just a duck.'

'Sometimes, even a duck tries a bit too hard. Look at those Mandarin jobs – who do they think they're kidding?'

Before she could answer, Nolan crashed in, fully dressed for every meteorological eventuality. 'Ready,' he said, and went to stand next to his father who was not.

'Ready for what?' Jacquie asked.

'Nothing to bother your pretty little head over, heart,' Maxwell said with just the right amount of levity to stop her braining him with a jug upside the head. 'Nole and I have plans. We'll tell you all about them later, won't we, Nole?'

'Oh, yes,' the boy said, smiling beatifically.

Maxwell went in search of something to wear that would be suitable outside the house. It had been long enough for that to be something of a novelty – he knew that the big secret would be common knowledge before he got back downstairs but so be it. A little espionage was fun for a while, but the bottom line was, there was no keeping anything from Detective Inspector Jacqueline Carpenter-Maxwell for more than a moment or two. But she wouldn't stand between a boy and his Plocker – not if she didn't want to be trampled in the rush. In the bedroom, with the wardrobe door open Maxwell looked at his shirts in serried rows. Despite what he had told

Nolan just moments before, he wondered whether he would need to wear them, with associated bow ties, ever again.

Mrs Plocker was almost as grateful as Nolan had been when Maxwell suggested their totally separate and yet contiguous walk. They decided the beach was probably a non-starter, as everyone within a good many miles would be there, all pretending they lived three miles away and had a dog which could only walk on sand. The playgrounds were closed, for fear that the dreaded virus, all claws and teeth, would be lurking to leap upon the unwary. Maxwell fought down the urge to meet at the footpath behind Broadgate Avenue, because for a non-driver it was almost insanely hard to get to and also so narrow that they would have had to walk one in front of the other to maintain the social distancing. Yelling social inanities to the back of someone's head was not his idea of a fun walk. So they decided on a walk in the park – which was by definition easy – also likely to be crowded but simple to get to and nice and wide. Shouting at someone's ear was so much more friendly than shouting at the back of their head. It didn't take long to discover that lockdown didn't make small talk with Mrs Plocker any easier. She had been doing a lot of gardening – meaning that the gold star for ten plants was Plocker's by a country mile – and was doing some mindful decluttering, which as far as Maxwell could tell was much the same as any other decluttering, except that you stopped every now and again for a herbal tea and a bit of deep breathing. Frank had been finally given a clean bill of health by the vet, though the visit had been stressful. Rather like the exchange of spies on a Cold War bridge, Frank had been placed, in his carrier, on the ground and Mrs Plocker had backed away. The vet had then approached, looking not unlike an extra in *Contagion* and had examined Frank. The vet had shaken his head, as far as it was possible to tell, and Mrs Plocker had started to compose consoling talks with her son. Apparently, the vet was yelling, Frank had a twisted gut and the kindest thing would be … and then suddenly, there was an appalling stench, a stream of shit had hit the vet in the middle of his outer mask and … at this, Mrs Plocker had had to stop walking for a moment, to laugh like a kookaburra … Frank could be seen to visibly relax. And he had been fine ever since. The tortoise had been found, under the rhubarb, and all was right with the world chez Plocker.

Maxwell had even less to impart. He had never been able to share amusing anecdotes about school, although, God knew, there were plenty to be had. He couldn't share stories of Jacquie's day for much the same reason – confidentiality and the knowledge that as soon as you opened your mouth, you would discover that the amusing story involved the recipient's aunt or at the very least someone up whose alley the cat had once run. So, it was easier to say nothing at all. Gardening – short of mowing the lawn – was not something that happened at the Maxwell-Carpenter abode but there was a whole slew of amusing cat stories to be told and that seemed to fit the bill.

But none of it really mattered. Nolan and Plocker were a whirlwind, leaping and playing so close together that sometimes they looked like just one boy. Mrs Plocker's phone camera whirred and clicked as she promised to WhatsApp them to Jacquie later. Maxwell smiled behind his mask, hoping it reached his eyes. He was as fond of pictures of his boy as the next man, but there was such a thing as too much. After two circuits of the park, both parents decided that they had pushed their luck enough – the Covid police were everywhere in the guise of little old ladies with binoculars and, from time to time, actual police. They were breaking no laws, but were pushing envelopes left and right so, with difficulty, they separated the boys and promised to do this again sometime soon.

On the walk home, Nolan was full of news. Apparently, things happened in the Plocker house of which the boy's mother was totally unaware – and probably just as well. But one way and another, just seeing each other, being able to run, fight a little and generally re-bond, seemed to have scratched the itch. Maxwell looked down at his son, prattling happily by his side, and wondered whether the rest of the world would heal as easily as the hearts of two small boys.

The morning was not such an idyll for Detective Inspector Jacquie Carpenter Maxwell. Lockdown, to everyone's surprise, had not been the cause for armed insurrection and piles of blazing furniture barring the way from one conurbation to another. Most people, like Mrs Plocker, had reacquainted themselves with a garden or the decorating or both. Breadmaking had become almost a national obsession, at first through necessity and then because who wants to be the only person in the street not knocking out perfect soda-bread for the newly-instituted ceremony of afternoon tea with one's nearest and dearest. The sun shone, the gardens flourished and the grim tally of the dead and dying became a pavane that the whole world danced to, sadly but accepting.

But then, slowly and with increasing frequency, the calls began. First, it was because the neighbours were stockpiling loo roll and bread. Then, the neighbours were neglecting the hastily acquired lockdown dog. And then – and this morning's call had been one such – the neighbours were fighting.

'Sorry, guv.' The desk man was truly sorry. This was not the kind of work a detective inspector should be saddled with, especially a detective inspector with eyes and legs like those belonging to DI Carpenter Maxwell. 'The old dear next door was almost hysterical. Apparently, it all started in the garden when he …' there was a pause while he checked his notes '… when he apparently cut back a syringa vulgaris at the wrong time of year.' He paused. The name had caused much hilarity in the canteen but he could see in the cold light of a phone call to the DI that perhaps it wasn't that funny after all.

'And?' Jacquie really wasn't in the mood for *Gardener's Question Time.*

'And he threw the loppers at her and then chased her into the house. It went very quiet and then there was screaming.'

Jacquie had heard this sequence of events before. It usually ended up with some red-faced community police officer facing a couple in the throes of make-up sex. 'Are you sure they're not just … come on, Derek, help me out here! You know what I'm asking!'

'Apparently not. She isn't a screamer, by all accounts. I did ask.'

Jacquie began to warm to the story. She would have loved to be a fly on the wall when he put the question to the neighbour. She sighed. 'Do we have name, address, phone number?'

'No landline, as usual these days. No mobile we can track. People just have cheapies they pick up in the supermarket these days if they don't get fancy ones provided at work. We've only got one name registered at the address, which is Katherine James. She works for a bank in town, but is working from home at the moment, nothing unusual there.'

'Does she have a work phone, then?'

'Apparently, the way it works is when calls come in, they are just routed automatically to the next in the queue. In a way, they all have the same number and I'm blowed if I'm going to call a Santander helpline on the off chance I get someone who has been assaulted by a set of garden loppers.'

'Good point, Derek. Look, I'm feeling a bit desk bound just now, so I'll pop out myself, see what's occurring. Log me in as out, if you see what I mean. Where am I off to?'

'Umm … let's see … Broadgate Avenue. Number 65. It's out on the …'

'Brighton Road. Yes, I know.'

EIGHT

As she drove, Jacquie Maxwell mulled over what to do. In a way, this was Max's pigeon; he had alerted her to a potential problem and had put Broadgate Avenue on her radar. One of his pupils lived there and there had, worryingly, been no mention of a child. The story of the shed being the only sane place in a house which had become a building site may have held water at the time, but was it actually true? She toyed with fetching Maxwell, just in case, but then dismissed it. For one thing, social distancing made it all but impossible even with police credentials. Dragging in a complete outsider, albeit one who could make a world of difference, would only make a tricky situation worse. Soon, she was pulling up outside Number 65, a neat detached villa, slightly smaller than either neighbour, with the obligatory bay window to one side of a glazed porch. The garden to the front was mostly drive, brick paved and without a weed in sight. The beds had been ruthlessly stripped of bulbs which had been replaced with pansies, primula and some embryonic geraniums, waiting for the summer. The curtains at the windows hung straight as knives, all pulled back to leave the regulation six inches on either side of the frames. In short, it was the home of a Nosy Neighbour.

Before ringing the bell, Jacquie donned her mask and listened carefully for the sounds of any arguments or general disharmony, but the whole road seemed sunk into the torpor that comes with an unseasonably warm spring day. Bees were buzzing, birds twittering. In the far distance, traffic noise was just discernible, though a fraction of its usual. Jacquie had always been a fan of John Wyndham and occasionally revisited his dystopian worlds when having a nice wallowy bath. She would not have been at all surprised had a triffid lurched across the drive, tentacles flailing, but all she heard were slow footsteps shuffling up the path that led between the house and the garage.

The sight that met her made her jump. As a long-time neighbour of Mrs Troubridge, she had almost come to think of nosy neighbours as being default little old ladies, with their voices set to twitter. The woman who hove into view was if anything the complete antithesis of Jessica Troubridge, being built like a docker and wearing a pair of enormous dungarees and a rather startling wide brimmed hat, shoved down on a mat of springing hair. On her nose she wore a set of spectacles so thick that they actually pressed the skin down, giving her a look of an extremely short-sighted shar pei. She had a mask around her neck, but made no attempt to put it over her mouth and nose.

'Oh,' she boomed, finally getting Jacquie into focus. 'I thought you were the police.'

'I am the police,' Jacquie said patiently. She sometimes wished she had kept track of how many times she had said that phrase. It must run into the thousands. But she had never allowed the allied phrase from Sly Stallone – 'I *am* the law!' – to cloud the conversation, however much her husband would have liked her to.

'Oh.' The woman wrinkled her nose even more and peered closer. 'Oh, yes, I see that now.'

Jacquie wasn't quite sure how to take that.

'Is it about the shenanigans next door?'

Jacquie smiled. 'Yes. Shall we go inside? Just in case, you know, the gentleman with the loppers comes out? We don't want to …' she gestured and the woman nodded, suddenly appreciating the possibilities.

When they were settled on the hardest chairs Jacquie had ever encountered in the neat living room overlooking the back garden, Jacquie took out her notebook. She had no way of telling, but judging simply by eye, she would have bet good money that the chairs were an exact two metres apart. 'You don't mind if I just jot things down, I hope,' she said. Some people got quite spooked by a simple notebook and pen.

'Not at all,' the woman said. She had brought her voice down to a dull roar now they were indoors, for which Jacquie was grateful. She wondered how these measured and stentorian tones could ever make the desk sergeant think she was hysterical.

'First of all,' Jacquie said, 'could I just have your name, for the record?'

'Tchah!' the woman said. 'I gave every single detail to that moron on the phone.'

'Oh, come now,' Jacquie said, quietly. Derek wasn't the brightest apple in the barrel, but that was a bit strong.

'He seemed to think I was being frivolous. Frivolous, I ask you, when murder and mayhem are happening under your very nose!'

This was something that Jacquie was a little concerned about. That the woman was extremely short-sighted was beyond doubt. Her description of what had happened was very detailed and looking out into the back garden, she couldn't see how she would have had a clear enough line of sight to see what was going on next door. A large conservatory extension took up at least a third of the garden as it ran down to the lane behind and the rest of the plot was given over to mature shrubs and a big, swooping laburnum. The shed, which had in a way piqued her interest in the first place, was tucked unobtrusively in the bottom corner, right by the fence which bordered the lane.

'I do need the details from you, Mrs …'

'Bencher. Amelia Bencher.'

'Mrs Bencher. Is there … a Mr Bencher?'

'There is indeed, though I struggle to understand why that is relevant?'

'I simply ask,' said Jacquie, trying to stay calm, 'in case of a serious incident next door. In which case, corroboration of your version of events would be helpful.'

'Are you accusing me of *lying*?'

There it was. The stentorian yet high pitched whoop which had led Derek to assume she was hysterical.

'Of course not, Mrs Bencher. But in every case, as I am sure you know, the more witnesses we can muster, the better. Some quite serious miscreants have gone free for lack of corroboration.'

Mrs Bencher looked darkly at her, her nose wrinkles taking on a serious mien. 'All right, then. As a matter of fact, and not something for public consumption, but Mr Bencher happens to be in Scunthorpe at the moment.' She folded her hands in her lap and stared at Jacquie as best she could.

Jacquie chose her words. 'Scunthorpe. Gosh. Is he … is he there on … business?'

Mrs Bencher snorted and Jacquie felt her hair move in the breeze. 'I suppose you could say that. If you count that peroxide tart business.'

'Ah.' Jacquie felt a momentary twinge of fellow feeling with Mr Bencher. Life here at 65, Broadgate Avenue could hardly be a bundle of laughs.

'He thought I didn't know. He thought I believed him when he said he was going up north to play golf with some old business friends, but I knew. Unless Duncan from accounts wore pints of Opium – and where she gets it is a mystery to me, she must have a barrel in the shed – I knew he was seeing another woman. Then one day, I found a picture in his wallet and I knew. He was on a golfing break – obviously it takes him more than a weekend to slake his lust these days …' Jacquie was sure she saw a line of drool snaking down Mrs Bencher's chin, '… when lockdown happened. So he chose to stay there in Scunthorpe, with Little Miss Nineteen Nineties and leave me down here. Well, good riddance to bad rubbish,' she snapped. 'I doubt she had the foresight to get in four hundred rolls of toilet paper like I did.'

She leaned back and looked at Jacquie triumphantly.

'I … see.' It was all beginning to fall into place now. Mrs Bencher was taking her revenge on neighbours because she couldn't reach her own husband. 'I don't need to make a note of that,' she reassured the woman, who was beginning to look a little wild-eyed. 'So, what did you see? Or did you hear it first?'

'Well,' Mrs Bencher was calmer now and sat back ready to regale this nice sympathetic policewoman with the events of the morning. 'Like everyone, I suppose, Those Next Door have been doing more in the garden. They both work from home, if you call taking the occasional phone message working,' she huffed. 'Anyway, She was doing a bit of work along the boundary, none too soon in my opinion. Their Nelly Moser has a tendency to encroach.'

Jacquie nodded. That seemed clear enough.

'After a while, He comes out, with a pair of loppers in his hand. He starts snipping at this and that and nothing said. I could hear them chatting, a bit near the knuckle for my taste, but they're young and haven't known each other long, so I gave them some leeway.'

Jacquie looked up, puzzled. She hadn't heard there was a step parent situation next door – that might make a difference. She put an asterisk in the margin of her shorthand notes and looked encouragingly at Mrs Bencher.

'After a while, he started being a bit silly with the loppers, sort of snipping at her with them and she laughed and told him to be careful. Then, whether intentionally or not, he brought down quite a significant branch of their syringa vulgaris. Not a particularly valuable plant, of course, but very pleasant in the spring and you really shouldn't prune at this time of year.'

Jacquie repeated, 'Syringa …?'

'Vulgaris, yes. Lilac.'

'Oh. *Lilac*. I see. Well, she was probably right to be annoyed.' She hoped that was the right thing to say.

'Of course she was. I must say, I would be too, in her place. It isn't even as if it's his garden. It's hers. She got the house in the divorce. He's just some oik she met in a bar and got stuck with in lockdown.'

Jacquie put down her pen. 'Mrs Bencher. Can I just clarify something? Which garden did this all happen in? Number 67 or Number 63?'

Mrs Bencher looked at her as if she were insane. 'Number 67? Whyever would you think this would happen at

Number 67? A nicer couple never drew breath and a lovely little boy, though getting a bit teenaged now, for my taste. They help me with my shopping and all sorts. No, it's that couple at Number 63! No better than she should be, I've always said it. And as for him – eye to the main chance, it's as clear as the nose on your face!'

Jacquie closed her notebook with a small but decisive snap. 'I think I have all I need, Mrs Bencher. I'll pop next door now … no, really, don't get up … and see what's happening.'

'Will you report back?' The woman's eyes, piggy behind her lenses, were avid.

'Confidentiality, sorry,' Jacquie said, making her way to the door. 'But keep watching. I'm sure you will be able to work it out.'

'So,' Jacquie said to Henry Hall as he lounged in her doorway in what was fast becoming his default position, 'it was the usual thing. He had got silly in the garden, she lost her temper, they had a big row and ended up in bed. Actually, not in bed, as such. More in the hall. Which was awkward, as they have a glazed door.'

Henry Hall almost laughed. 'Clear glass?' His eyebrows rose above the frames of his glasses, a sure sign he was amused.

'That semi-frosted stuff, with the dimples, you know the one. Very popular back in the day. But it doesn't really hide much. Especially when he picked her up and …'

'Yes,' he said, 'I have the gist. So, what did you do?'

'Gave them a minute to collect themselves, told them they were that far,' she held up her thumb and finger, spaced by less than half an inch, 'from being done for gross indecency, and got the hell out of there. I don't think Mrs Bencher is going to be having much fun in her garden for a while. The boyfriend has a bit of a twinkle in his eye and is, as a matter of interest to no one, hung like a mule.'

'Jacquie!' Henry Hall was on the verge of embarrassment, but no one could have told from his expression. 'Tell the desk to filter any complaints from Mrs

Bencher through me, otherwise we'll have cars there day and night. Was that it?'

'Yes. I really only went there because I thought there might be trouble at 67, the one with the lad doing his lessons in the shed, I think I told you.'

'Oh, yes. Number 67. I remember that from the last time. Quite a sad case. Still, lightning doesn't strike twice, does it?'

'Hopefully not,' Jacquie murmured behind her mask.

'Home soon?'

She checked her watch.

'An hour.'

'Blow it. Hop off now. I'll take your calls. See you tomorrow.'

Jacquie didn't need telling twice. She needed to check that her Nelly Moser wasn't encroaching and anyway, it was time for a shout over the fence with Mrs Troubridge.

When Jacquie got home, the house was preternaturally quiet, which didn't always bode well. However, as she got up onto the landing she could hear the hum of voices from the bedroom which was a little unexpected. Peering round the door, she saw the back of her husband's head, framed by the laptop screen filled with little squares. Without turning round, he stuck his hands in the air and extended all his fingers and two thumbs. Ten. Then, using his forefinger, he mimed a Zorro slash. Z. She didn't need more. The dreaded Ten Zed Aitch, still struggling with the causes of the Second World War. She closed the door softly, to the sound of Chantal's exasperated 'whatevva'. And yet again, she shook her head, wondering why on earth anyone would want to teach, when there were so many more congenial occupations such as septic tank diver and scorpion wrangling.

Using her undoubted detective skills, she went in search of her son. Again, the murmur of voices led her and this time to the study. He too was engrossed in zooming, with the whole school competing in a Q&A. Nolan's teachers were rather more tech-savvy than Maxwell, which was not difficult. Sometimes, Jacquie thought that Bismarck could probably give him a run for his money. They had somehow fixed things so that when someone had the answer, their face popped up as an enlargement in the centre. To Jacquie's delight, currently that face was Nolan's. He was answering a history question, which seemed only right and proper and again she backed out of the room.

That left her chat with Mrs Troubridge over the fence. She dialled the number and the phone was snatched up after just one ring.

'Troubridge residence,' a voice honed on many cigarettes husked at her.

'Mrs B.,' Jacquie said, brightly. 'It's Jacquie.'

There was no reply.

'Jacquie Maxwell. From next door.'

'Hello.' From the tone, it might have been that Mrs B had never heard of her before.

'I wondered whether Mrs Troubridge was well enough to sit in the garden for a while, so we can have a natter over the hedge.'

The edge left the woman's voice. 'That's a kind thought, Mrs M.,' she said, 'but I don't think so. Not today.'

'Is she poorly, then?' Jacquie felt her heart constrict. She somehow had thought that her neighbour, though frail, might yet be immortal.

'No.' The answer came slowly. 'Not in herself. Same as always there. But … she's got a bit confused with all these rules and regulations, you know what I mean? She watches the news all the time and gets it all mixed up in her head. She doesn't like having anyone near her. Not even me, sometimes. She wanted me to wash the butter the other day, because she thought there might be germs. I've had to hide all the bleach and polish and everything because she thinks she needs to clean everything, including food.'

Mrs B rarely said so many words in a coherent whole. It showed the depth of her concern and Jacquie didn't quite know what to say. It was no good offering to go round to help, as that would undoubtedly make a difficult situation worse. And yet, to leave Mrs B to cope alone seemed so unfair somehow. So she said what everyone says when they are stuck for something to say. 'Can we help at all?'

There was a sigh. 'No, Mrs M. Not really. Unless you can make all this go away. We have deliveries of food, so we're all right for that. I have to choose things in tins or packets I can wipe. We've got a whole spare room full of loo roll. I've signed Mrs T up to Netflix, God knows what she'll think of that when it's all done and dusted, but when she's in bed, I have to have something to watch. If I had to watch the BBC and those two idiots at those blooming desks telling us we're all going to die, I think I would. Die, I mean.'

Jacquie had known Mrs B for what seemed a lifetime and she doubted she had ever heard her say as much, all added together. It dawned on her that there was a whole sub-culture out there, the looked after and the lookers after, ignored and forgotten by the lookers on. She suddenly felt the weight of the world on her shoulders. 'Mrs B., how do *you* fancy a chat in the garden?'

With what was suspiciously like a sob, Mrs B said, 'I would love it, Mrs M. But … I don't want to upset …' her voice got fainter as she put her hand over the phone, obviously answering a querulous Mrs Troubridge, '… you probably didn't hear that,' she said to the receiver, more quietly, 'but she's worried about the time I'm taking on the call. She thinks the germs can come down the line, you see, and you're not far away so … well, you see how it is. Thank you for your call, though.' And the line went dead.

With the menfolk busy and Metternich teaching Bismarck how to chase butterflies without catching one and yet not losing face, Jacquie was at something of a loose end. With Maxwell at home almost all the time, there was no need for the usual firefighting housework, whizzing round with the Shark when the bits on the carpet obscured the actual colour – which had been, as all carpets are, chosen not to show the bits – and spraying something loudly smelling in the bathroom and lunging at it with a sponge before the bubbles went. As a non-homeworker, she had no paperwork to do. The hoops that she would have had to leap through to be able to work at home had seemed to her not worth the candle. She would have had to have encryption of Pentagon proportions on her laptop, a cross-shredder and a courier booked on a twice-daily basis to pick up the results to be taken away, doubtless to be found on some distant landfill. She would have had to prove that she wasn't married to an axe-murderer or even a hacker – that would not have been hard, as everyone at the nick knew Maxwell almost as well as his own colleagues did, but still; there was a limit. And so she was at home, let off the leash by Henry Hall, and her time was her own. The question was, what to do with it?

She wandered down into the garden and there, as if placed purposely for her, was a recliner, with a cushion for her head and a small table to one side. On the table was that day's newspaper, folded neatly, a sure sign that Maxwell had not had time to read it. When he had finished with any newsprint, it looked as if it had been torn apart by pit bulls. She looked up at the house, where, if she really strained her ears, she could just hear the faint murmur of zooming voices. She looked at the recliner.

The recliner won and after trying to read the first two pages of covid statistics without falling into incoherent rage, she slept, warm and slowly relaxing in the sun. Her little snores didn't interrupt the two great statesmen of Europe as they turned their attention to bees; on a warm, late spring day, they had other fish to fry, although the fish would probably come later.

She woke with a chill in the air and a Cliff Richard song running through her head. Neither was something she relished but she could see how one would cause the other. Someone had drawn a blanket over her and the newspaper had gone. Without turning her head, she swivelled her eyes to see if she was really alone and saw a slippered foot off in the extreme right of her vision. It moved and the voice she would never tire of hearing spoke.

'Hello, sleepyhead. I didn't wake you, but perhaps we should go in now. The sun's gone round and it's not that warm.'

She snuggled the blanket under her chin. She didn't

feel like speaking in sentences yet and besides, she had to get that dratted song out of her head. 'You know that song?'

There was a pause. 'Probably.'

'Mmm.' She realised that wasn't enough. 'It's about … y'know. That bloke. Goes to sleep. Meets a girl. She disappears.'

'Cliff Richard.'

'You're a genius. What's it called?'

'Why?' He could keep this up all day.

'Well, it's in my head. I think I must have realised it had gone chilly while I was still asleep.'

'What's it worth?'

'Cruel,' she murmured, pulling the blanket higher. 'Cruel, that's what you are.'

'Pizza delivery for supper?'

'You're on.' There was something about a pizza at the door, even when delivered by a masked motorcycle rider gesticulating wordlessly from the end of the path, that could make you think things were almost normal.

'*The Day I Met Marie.*'

She smiled, nodding her head to the internal tune. She usually found that the thing with an ear worm was to sing the damned thing right through and exorcise it that way.

He watched her fondly. He could tell by the way her head wagged when she got to the bouncy refrain and when she was smooching her way through the verse. He wondered what he had done in a previous life to deserve such a woman in this. Finally, she relaxed with a sigh.

'Better now?'

'Much.' She stretched and sat up. 'I hate getting a song in my head. Some of them last for days, don't you find?'

'They don't trouble me much, to be honest. Too many voices in there telling me to do bad things.' He glanced at his watch. 'Shall I go in and order the pizza? It takes ages now they don't have their full complement of drivers.'

'Can pizza delivery drivers work from home?' she mused as he got up and walked past her up to the house, planting a kiss on her head.

'Something to think about, now your ear worm's

gone,' he said, then added something very softly.

'Sorry? What was that?' It wasn't like Maxwell to not speak clearly, so she needed to know.

'Oh, did you not hear me?' he said, not turning round. 'I said elephants have wrinkles, wrinkles, wrinkles, elephants have wrinkles, wrinkles everywhere.'

'Damn you, Peter Maxwell,' she howled, covering her ears.

'You're welcome,' he said, chuckling as he bounced up the steps into the house. 'Always a pleasure to share the worst ear worm in the world with the woman I love.'

The pizza was a success, as pizza always is, but not overwhelmingly so. Maxwell had really pushed the boat out and so, Gordon Ramsay notwithstanding, he had pineapple on his. Nolan had seafood, as it made for a better sharing experience with Metternich and Bismarck, the Austrian preferring the tuna, the German the prawns.

'Are you allowed to feed the cats at the table, Nole?' Maxwell asked, rhetorically.

There was a massed indrawing of breath. 'Cats?' an inaudible voice seemed to say. 'No cats here.'

'I just dropped a bit of tuna,' the child said, turning his innocent face up to his parents, giving them Melting Look #4 in turn.

'Try not to drop too much more,' his mother said. She knew that Maxwell, in thrall to both cats as he was, preferred them not to have Human Food, but on the other hand, things were not normal right now and so a little bit of licked-up tuna wasn't going to bring about the collapse of civilisation.

'Okay, Mums,' Nolan said, dropping a prawn.

'I think we're going to have to agree to disagree on this one,' Maxwell said. There was an odd mood in the air tonight, they could all feel it. Nolan had found that the highs of being with Plocker and then winning the quiz by a country mile could only last so long before covid ennui set in with a vengeance. Jacquie couldn't quite forget the desperation in Mrs B's voice, Mrs B who had never been fazed by anything in her life before. She knew that she and Mrs B were sisters under the skin. They were Martha's sons, who put right all the wrongs of the world, working away behind the scenes to ensure that the rest of mankind could walk happily in the sun, unaware of the chaos around them. And until now, it hadn't been too bad. But now … she looked at her two men, the loves of her life. She felt the warm weight of Metternich on her foot. She saw the familiar walls of the kitchen where she sat at least once every day … and she felt like crying.

Maxwell oversaw this like a colossus bestriding his world. He had learned earlier than most that there were things a man couldn't fix, howl to heaven though he might. His family had died on a slick, wet road back in what seemed like another age and a part of him had died with them. Then Jackie had come along, to ease the hurt, though never heal it. Then Nolan and, yes, even Bismarck. But he knew their world was rocking, along with the worlds of so many and he ached to put it right. If Jacquie was one of Martha's sons, Maxwell was one of those put on earth to make sure that their feet never faltered, while they took care of the sons of Mary. Sometimes, even Rudyard Kipling only got things half right.

After an introspective evening which even a Bugs Bunny retrospective couldn't fix, the Maxwell house was quiet before its time. Nolan was in bed and in a dreamless sleep, tired by all the running and all the boredom in approximately equal measure. Jacquie was re-reading *Day of the Triffids*. Somehow, after her brush with Mrs Bencher, it seemed the right thing to do. And it had its built in happy ending – if indeed all mankind ended up on the Isle of Wight, then the Maxwells had the drop on most of them. If they walked just a mile or two uphill from their own front door, they could actually see the damn place. Maxwell was marking. That was one thing that lockdown didn't seem to have reduced in quantity, although quality had definitely gone up. He attributed that to the fact that most of the essays had been written by furloughed parents. For example – and he tutted and wielded his pen with gusto – he had never before seen the word Weltanschauung in a year ten essay before and wrote a pithy comment in the margin. 'Mr Burns. Two things. Please make sure that Darren knows what the long words mean before peppering 'his' essay with them. And secondly, Weltanschauung has two u's and one a, not the other way around. PM'. He chuckled.

Jacquie looked up from her book, wrenched from a world turned upside down to a world turned upside down. 'Are you marking those essays on paper?'

'Uh hu. Is there any other way?'

'Aren't we supposed to stay paper free?'

'Probably.' He gave Darren Burns A+ for wheedling round his dad skills, Mr Burns C- for useless spelling and inaccurate use of Wikipedia.

'How did you even get them on paper?'

'Umm …' Maxwell turned to the next one. This one would be better; Liam's mother was a teacher, so knew how to forge an essay so that it at least looked genuine.

'Nole?'

'Of course. My IT department.'

'And to get them back?'

'Apparently,' Maxwell said, distracted, 'there's an App for that.'

Jacquie looked at him, engrossed in what he did second best. He missed the one to one so much, she could tell, but the feel of paper under his hand covered that for a while. 'If I didn't know you were quoting your son, I would be worried that aliens had taken the real Peter Maxwell and left a careful facsimile in his place.'

Without turning his head, Maxwell did a perfect zombie face and carried on marking. Jacquie carried on scaring herself witless with three legged plants lurching from all quarters of the compass. Some books could still shock and awe, even when you had read them so often the pages had come loose.

Eventually, and long before their usual bedtime, the lights were off throughout the Maxwell house and even Metternich and Bismarck were asleep on their respective cushions, the Count's, as was his right, just that tiny bit more comfortable and elevated than that of the Chancellor. Their dreams were almost identical – as they lay on their padded thrones, seafood of all kinds rained down from above, descending in luscious slo-mo into their gaping jaws. Jacquie dreamed fitfully of enormous plants, all shrieking that their correct name was Syringa Vulgaris. Maxwell dreamed of a classroom, full of adults crushed into desks made for twelve-year-olds, all shouting at once.

'Mr Maxwell? Mr Maxwell? Mr Maxwell? Can you hear me? Mr Maxwell? It's me, Marcus …'

NINE

In her life, Jacquie Maxwell had seen a lot of things for the first time but nothing she had seen had surprised her quite as much as the thing she was seeing now. In the dark of their bedroom, her husband was hunched over the laptop, lit only by the glow of the screen. He seemed to be listening intently as she woke up and she had only just focussed and realised what was going on when he spoke.

'Marcus? Are you all right? No, shush, shush, I'm here, calm down. Tell me …'

And then she heard it, the small voice coming from the laptop.

'Mr Maxwell, Mr Maxwell, they're dead. Mum and Dad. They're dead. I saw …' But the rest of the sentence was cut off in a hailstorm of tears.

Maxwell glanced up and saw that Jacquie was awake and swinging into action. He gave an imperceptible nod and she sidled out of the room to use the phone in the kitchen to call the nick and get the cars on their way out to 67 Broadgate Avenue. Ambulances too – one for the dead, one for the living. SOCO. Basically, the whole nine yards.

Back in the bedroom, Maxwell was doing his best to calm the hysterical boy. He didn't know that he had left the zoom connection open. He didn't even know that was possible. As a rule, he turned the computer off and that was it, but he remembered, thinking back, that Jacquie had come home unexpectedly while he was still teaching and somehow it had been forgotten. But in this case, thank God it had.

He had awoken from his dream to discover, as was so often the case, that the sounds continued even when his eyes were open. Except that instead of thirty strident adult voices, it was the voice of one terrified fourteen year old boy.

'Mr Maxwell? Mr Maxwell? Mr Maxwell? Can you hear me? Mr Maxwell? It's me, Marcus …'

He had crept across the room although he knew he would have to wake Jacquie before too long. Something in him hoped that this was an elaborate spoof – it wasn't even midnight, after all, and teenagers were known for keeping late hours – but he knew every intonation of a child's voice and this was not something that an average kid with no pretensions to skills in drama could manage. Marcus's face was all alone on the screen, but filling it, not confined to a little box in the corner. The light was poor and seemed to be coming from a torch. Tears still tracked his cheeks and snot gilded his upper lip. That the child was terrified was without doubt.

'What is it, Marcus?' Maxwell had whispered. He had no idea why he was whispering but it didn't seem to be an occasion for talking out loud.

When the boy saw Maxwell's face loom into view, his face showed it all. Here was someone, albeit only at the other end of a wireless connection, who could be relied upon to put things right. He had seen … his brain could hardly accept it but it had to be faced … he had seen someone in his house, creeping from his parents' room with blood on their hands. At first, he had thought he was dreaming. When he was little, he had suffered from dreams which made him whimper like a puppy and thresh about, only to have his mum or dad come into his room and soothe him back to sleep, patting his back, stroking his arms, wiping the sweaty hair from his forehead until he forgot his dream. But this … this was no dream. He could feel the carpet under his feet. He could smell the faint remembrance of Badedas from the bathroom. He could hear the dog snuffling downstairs, dreaming his own dreams of hedgehogs. And … the worst thing of all, he could hear a sound like an animal grunting from his parents' room, not the sound that every teenager dreads hearing, the sound that tells them that their parents are not old fogeys dead from the waist down after all, but the sound that speaks of tortured lungs, of brains dying, of death and the end of life as it has been.

He had stood on the landing for what seemed hours, listening, when the sound of the dog erupting in maniacal barking at an intruder woke him from his fugue. They had had a burglar once and the dog had behaved just like this, snarling, barking, flinging himself at the kitchen door. Marcus breathed again. A burglar, that was what it was. He was imagining the rest. He pushed open his parents' door.

And found he hadn't imagined it at all, except that perhaps reality was worse than his imaginings.

And now, here was Mr Maxwell, saying 'Marcus? Are you all right? No, shush, shush, I'm here, calm down. Tell me …'

And although nothing would be quite all right, not ever again, it was much better and soon there would be people to help. Marcus slumped in his chair and just said, 'Mr Maxwell, Mr Maxwell, they're dead. Mum and Dad. They're dead.'

Jacquie came back into the bedroom and gave Maxwell a thumbs up.

'Marcus,' Maxwell said gently, 'Mrs Maxwell has phoned the police and an ambulance and they'll be with you soon. Go round to the front of the house and wait for them, if you feel comfortable doing that. Wait under a street light and don't worry. They'll be there in minutes if they're not there already.' He looked at Jacquie with a question in his eyes. 'If I am allowed to be there, I will.'

She looked dubious, then nodded.

'She says I can come, so I'll be there. Don't worry.' He almost said it would be all right, though obviously that was nonsense. He settled for, 'I'll see you soon.'

'Don't go, Mr Maxwell.' The boy sounded five, not fifteen.

'I'll stay till the police arrive, Marcus, then I have to go. We have to make arrangements for our little boy to be looked after while we're both out.'

'*Don't leave him!*' Marcus was screaming. '*Don't leave him, Mr Maxwell. Something bad will happen!*'

'We won't leave him, Marcus, don't worry.' In the background, Maxwell could hear the sounds of sirens, with the whoop-whoop of an ambulance not far behind. 'I can hear the police, Marcus. Go and meet them and we'll be there soon.'

Marcus's face dopplered off into the darkness and Maxwell was left looking at the wall of the shed. He leaned back and let his head drop so he was staring unseeing at the ceiling.

'Hell of a way to wake up,' he said.

Jacquie kissed his forehead. 'Anyone else and I would assume they were talking about themselves. But it's you, so I know it's Marcus you have in mind.' She paused. 'Do you think it's real?'

His head came up and he looked at her, amazed. 'Real? Why wouldn't it be?'

'Because he's fifteen. Because he's bored.'

He nodded. 'Some of them, yes. Chantal in his class, any day of the week. She can turn a broken nail into a last rites situation. But Marcus? No. I can tell you as the poor sap who has marked his essays that he doesn't have the imagination of that lamp. I asked them to imagine what it would be like to be in the Hitler Youth and he gave a list of badges he had earned in Scouts.'

'To be fair, you do always say the Scouts are a para-military organisation.'

'Yes, there's that, but even so. I'm making the point that he can't make things up. If he says his parents are dead in their bed, then his parents are dead in their bed.' He rubbed his hands through his hair and looked madder than ever. 'What are we going to do with Nole?'

'I think what we're going to do is form an emergency childcare bubble with the Plockers.'

'Is that a thing?'

'It's not something that much is made of, because it would cause all kinds of mayhem with people claiming that the fifteen people drinking gin in their garden were all there for childcare reasons, but it is a thing, yes. I'll ring.'

'But it's …' Maxwell craned round to look at the clock. 'It's only eleven o'clock! What time did we go to bed, for heaven's sake?'

'Early. And we'd only been asleep about fifteen minutes when you heard Marcus calling. For once, I'm glad you have no idea how to sign off from Zoom.'

Maxwell did the complex shrug that said so much, used specifically for technology-related failures.

'Just don't make a habit of it.' She was holding her phone to her ear and raised a finger as the person on the other end answered. 'Did I wake you? Oh, good. It's Jacquie …' and she wandered off onto the landing, heading for the bathroom. No one multi-tasked quite like Detective Inspector Jacquie Carpenter Maxwell. While she was gone, Maxwell quickly got dressed. He had almost forgotten where most of his clothes were, having spent the recent months of his life circling between three shirts and two pairs of disreputable trousers. But to make Marcus feel at ease, or as much at ease as possible, he hauled out full school fig and soon stood there, a teacher to the tips of his toes, bow tie at a respectful angle and hair as near to neatly brushed as it could be. He was just tying his brogues when his wife came back into the room, leading a sleepy Nolan.

'I've explained we have an emergency with one of your pupils,' she said, making complex faces over the child's head, 'and so Nolan can go to stay with Plocker. I'm just going to pop a few things in a bag and also some snacks and things.' Maxwell thought privately that lockdown had changed more than the obvious. Now, when you rarely went anywhere, you had to take food and loo roll in case the delivery hadn't turned up. Strange days. 'He's staying in his jamas for now, so he can just pop into bed at the other end.' She dropped a kiss on the child's head and the boy walked across to where his father sat on the bed and snuggled onto his lap, still nine parts asleep.

'Y're all right, Dads?' he murmured.

'Fine, matey,' Maxwell promised.

'Mums all right?'

'As rain.'

'Who isn't, then?'

That was a bit of a facer. 'It's just a school thing, Nole. Nothing for you to worry about. And you get to stay with Plocker, which can't be bad, can it?'

'It's a bubble, Mums said.'

'That's what they call it. It isn't …' But why explain? Leave that pleasure for Mrs Plocker to deal with in the morning.

Maxwell thought, as he often had before, that most crime scenes when seen from a distance looked much like all the rest. It didn't matter whether it was 25 Cromwell Street or 67 Broadgate Avenue, the addition of the white tent, arc lighting and nosy neighbours made them all the same. Jacquie pointed out Mrs Bencher, unmistakeable in the growing crowd milling at the edge of the blue and white tape. She was even more startling in a crimson kimono made for a much smaller person, with extraneous bits of her wrapped in something diaphanous falling out of the front. There were two ambulances parked in front of the police cars and most of the crowd were rubbernecking to see past them. The policeman on the tape nodded Jacquie through and, after a small pause to show he disapproved, Maxwell was allowed to follow. For perhaps the first time, Maxwell was glad of the masks they were all wearing because he could mutter under his breath and actually move his lips with impunity.

In the house was a cacophony, not helped by the dog, which by now was almost demented. It could be heard flinging itself against the door and barking with a fury that not even a hedgehog could explain.

Henry Hall stood in the lobby, holding a hand to one ear. He brightened up when he saw Jacquie and even looked pleased to see Maxwell.

'Thanks for coming,' he said. 'Sorry about the dog. The RSPCA are trying to find someone to come out and get it. Apparently, and I am quoting the neighbours, it is either the usual big softie or a vicious animal not unakin to Cujo.'

Maxwell was impressed. He didn't have Henry Hall

down as a Stephen King fan. 'Has anyone asked Marcus to try and quieten him down?'

A sergeant standing at Hall's elbow tutted and rolled his eyes. 'Can you hear the damned thing? Would you let your kid go in there?'

'No,' Maxwell said, leaning in to rather less than two metres in order to be heard, 'no, not my kid. But the kid who lives here, yes, of course. The dog knows something's wrong. He's worried about his people. Let him see Marcus and he'll probably calm down.'

Henry Hall nodded. 'Good plan.' He turned to a policewoman, coming in through the front door with a thermos flask, donated by a paramedic who always liked to be ready for anything. 'How is Marcus, Fay? Would he be up to dealing with the dog?'

The woman sagged theatrically. 'Oh, can he? Please? He's really upset about it. So it would do us all a favour.' She looked at Maxwell. 'Are you his teacher?'

Maxwell nodded. Was it really that obvious?

'Can you come with me? He's done nothing but talk about you since we arrived.'

'Of course.' Maxwell touched Jacquie on the elbow and followed the policewoman into the lounge, the back end of which was shrouded in drop cloths, marking where the new conservatory was taking shape. Marcus sat in a huddle on the sofa but leapt up like a jack-in-the-box when he saw Maxwell.

The policewoman held out an arm. 'I'm sorry,' she said. 'I can't allow you to touch each other. We have to observe the six foot rule. And really, Marcus, you are old enough to wear a mask. It's under twelves who are exempt, strictly speaking.'

The child stopped, his lip trembling. He had never been much of a crier, but he had shed more tears in the last two hours than in his life before.

Maxwell dug into his jacket pocket and pulled out a mask, still in its wrapping and threw it over to the boy. 'There we are,' he said. 'That solves that. And as for six feet, officer, I am afraid that, with all due respect, I would ask that you simply go and do the other thing. If you can find me a law that says I can't hug a child who has just lost both parents, then you can take me in later. But for now,' he held out his arms and found them full of a fifteen year old who, if a day before had been offered a thousand pounds to hug Mad Max, would have turned it down flat. He looked at the aghast policewoman over the lad's head. 'If you don't want to look, I suggest you just go elsewhere. Marcus and I are going to just have a little talk but first, he's going to see to his dog.'

'Oh, Mr Maxwell,' the boy said, wiping his eyes. 'Can I? Poor Bob, he's going to be so upset. He worshipped my dad.' The tears sprang again.

'Bob?' Maxwell said, in a conversational tone. 'That's an unusual name for a dog.'

'Well,' Marcus said, thankful for something else to think about, 'his full name's Robert Plant, cos of my dad being a Led Zeppelin fan, see. But we call him Bob. Because you feel a fool shouting "Robert Plant" when you want him to come in.'

The hall had cleared a bit of police bodies as they emerged from the lounge and the dog was commensurately quieter, just leaping at the door now and then. His bark had become rather throaty and didn't sound unlike his namesake. They pushed the kitchen door open and edged inside to another storm of barking, instantly silenced as soon as the dog saw who it was who had come in.

The boy dropped to his knees and wrapped his arms around the dog's neck. In the silence that followed the barking, Maxwell could almost hear the small bones of his ear settle back into place with a relieved sigh.

The dog was no breed known to man, although according to the bloke in the pub who had sold him to Marcus's dad, he was mostly cocker spaniel. Not a cockerpoo, exactly, but something similar. Perhaps a cockermess, his mum had said. But he was a great guard dog, if noise was the main requirement. Now, he was just a boy's dog and Maxwell respected their space and looked around the kitchen.

For a room in a house which was being almost gutted by a fanatical handyman, it wasn't at all bad. There was a fine layer of dust over everything and, trained police husband that he was, Maxwell shoved his hands in his pockets. It didn't seem likely that the murderer had come this way, but just in case, he didn't want to add his fingerprints and DNA to the mix. He looked at the knife rack on the wall but it didn't help. Like knife racks in almost every house in the land, there were at least three missing. The Maxwells always chuckled when a missing knife was a big clue in a whodunnit because the only day theirs had been fully stocked was the day it went up on the wall. The filleting knife had gone missing almost at once and wasn't missed, filleting not being a large part of cooking chez Maxwell.

The draining board held what might be expected of an overnight situation in a family of three. Mugs, small plates. Heartbreakingly, there was a sandwich box on the side, with lunch made up for the next day, a day that would never come. Maxwell decided not to judge, but Marcus's dad was clearly moonlighting outside lockdown and who could blame him. Most people at this juncture couldn't see the harm in having someone down the garden building a wall or digging a pond. It would take some finding, though; he would have hardly written it all down anywhere.

The door opened behind Maxwell and Henry Hall's head peered round, his glasses reflecting the overhead strip lights which would wait forever now to be changed out for flush fitted LEDs. He looked at the pile of dog and boy on the floor and nodded approvingly. Peter Maxwell might get on your wick sometimes, but the man knew how to handle kids, there was no denying that. The next trick would be to get the dog away from the boy or vice versa.

Maxwell, using the telepathic powers which all good teachers must develop in their first year or run out screaming, touched the lad on the shoulder.

'Come on, Marcus,' he said. 'Mr Hall needs to ask you some things.'

The boy held the dog tighter and shook his head.

'No one's going to hurt you or Bob.'

Hall silently saluted Maxwell – he even knew the dog's name, for crying out loud.

'Look, why don't you both come? Mr Hall can ask you his questions in his car, perhaps?' He looked up at Hall, who nodded. What was essential now was that the house was emptied and that the SOCOs could come in. 'Then we'll find you somewhere to sleep. Hmm?' Maxwell carried on patting the boy and tried to see him as just a slightly bigger Nolan. Nolan wouldn't want to leave the Count or the Chancellor though he doubted either of them would be hanging around to be cried on like this dog was doing.

'I don't want somewhere to sleep,' the boy muttered. 'I can sleep here.'

'No,' Maxwell said and his heart broke for the child. Like teachers everywhere, his carapace was thick and resilient, but underneath, he was putty. 'No, you can't do that. We'll find you somewhere to stay until we find someone in your family. A grandma, perhaps? An auntie?'

'Haven't got none.'

Maxwell decided to let the grammatical lapse go. 'What, no one at all?'

'No.' Marcus wiped his nose on the dog's back. 'Mum doesn't have no family. She left home when she was a girl and never looked back, she says. Dad's parents died when he was …' he gulped back a sob, 'about my age, I s'pose. He doesn't … didn't talk about it much. He was in foster homes until he was old enough to leave, then in a hostel. That's where he met Mum.' He almost managed a smile. 'He said they were like the babes in the wood, looking after each other.'

Not all fairy tales have a happy ending. The words hung on the air between Hall and Maxwell as clearly as if they had been spoken.

'Foster homes aren't like they were in your dad's day,' Maxwell said. 'And it's only for a while.'

The boy sat up and the dog hutched itself sideways so it was sitting half on his lap. 'Why only for a while? You won't find anyone to have me, no matter how long you search for. And don't think that I'm going to that mad old biddy next door.'

'Mrs Bencher?' Maxwell checked.

'Yes, her. She babysat for me once or twice when I was

little and she was … well, she's mad, like I say. She's always spying on next door the other way, but she did like my mum and dad.'

'No.' Henry Hall had decided that the time out was over. 'We won't just hand you over to a passing neighbour, Marcus. There are people working on a proper solution as we speak. But we have to clear the house now. The longer we stay, the more clues we might miss.'

Marcus looked up at him, holding the dog close. 'Clues?'

'Yes. Clues to who it was who did this terrible thing.'

The boy looked around, with wide eyes. 'So there might be something in here, anything, DNA and stuff, that will find who did it?' Before he gave up his space, he needed to be sure.

'Yes. And the longer Mr Maxwell, you and me are in here, the more bits of skin, hairs, that kind of thing, float off and land.'

Marcus furrowed his brow. This had often puzzled him and this seemed as good a time as any to ask the question. 'But just having one of Mr Maxwell's hairs on the worktop can't stop you finding who did it, can it? The proper DNA is still there.'

This was a valid point and one that Maxwell had often considered himself.

'No.' Henry Hall's reply was slow and measured. 'But every single thing has to be checked and every half an.hour spent checking on a random shedding by Mr Maxwell is a half an hour not spent checking on the real killer. So, come on, Marcus. Let's get out of here, can we?'

Slowly, the boy got to his feet, clicking his fingers at Bob, who pressed himself against his leg. 'All right,' he said. 'But I'm not going to a home and I'm not going next door.'

'I understand,' Hall said, solemnly. 'I'll do my best.'

It was a solemn little group that made its way out to Hall's car. The dog, in the way that well brought up dogs do, knew that best behaviour was the only kind which was allowable today. Bob had no idea what had gone on, but he could smell blood and the other scents in the house were out of kilter, the old tobacco on one of the policemen, cat on this wiry haired bloke who Marcus seemed to trust so much. Cat was usually a reason for avoiding anyone, but there had to be exceptions, and this was one.

Henry Hall had the weight of the world on his shoulders at the best of times. At home, he had Margaret sanitising and wiping for practically 24 hours in every day. She had put polythene sheets over the doorways when he had gone home earlier that evening. Margaret, who once upon a time wouldn't even put up Christmas decorations because of pinholes in the wallpaper now had duct taped plastic to the walls and they would never be the same again. He sighed. It might not only be the wallpaper. They had been through enough over the years, but this might be the straw that broke the camel's back. He glanced down at the bowed head at his side. This was probably not something that could be put at the door of Covid – or was it? Had someone else gone batshit crazy and decided to pick off the healthy, one by bloody one?

TEN

Maxwell wasn't sure when his role would be over. As they came out of the doorway heading towards Hall's car parked in the drive, he could see his wife's head, surrounded by people in white coveralls, helmets, PPE of every extremity from a mask to a five layer Berlin Wall. She was marshalling her troops, doing what she did best, making sure no stone was left unturned. The neighbours were spread out along the police tape still, but looking quickly and doing a head count, he was pretty sure some had left. There wasn't anything interesting to see – not that that had ever stopped anyone – but the night was chilly now and social distancing just seemed to make the whole process rather odd. Mrs Bencher was still there of course. He had never met her but Jacquie's brief description, complete with arm waving had sketched her clearly enough for him to know her as well as he knew Missuses B and T. She was a strict two metres from anyone else present, though whether that was her doing or theirs was hard to tell. Another Metternich-style whole body shudder engulfed him; the thought of sending Marcus to stay with her was obviously out of the question. A sudden thought sprang into his head and he approached the edge of the crowd surrounding his wife.

A new problem immediately raised its head. How, without shouting, did you attract anyone's attention these days? Tapping anyone on the shoulder was out of the question. The last he remembered from watching the circus that was Vallance and Whitty had left him with the impression that anyone being so foolish would have their hands cut off for a first offence, a second offence therefore being unlikely. A coo-ee through a mask would be muffled and it was hard to tell from whence the noise had come. On his rare forays outside, he had noticed that no one seemed to be able to work out where people's voices were coming from and he had the same problem. So, how?

His conundrum was solved by the strange telepathy that often exists between husband and wife. Jacquie suddenly turned her head and she looked straight at him. She gestured to the anonymous white-clad person standing next to her to step aside and like a wave, they parted till she stood in front of Maxwell.

'I've had an idea for where Marcus can go,' he said.

'Sylv.' The answer came pat.

'Umm … yes. You really need to start looking inside other heads than mine,' he said, smiling at her. 'My mouth will heal up at this rate.'

'Yours? Never,' she said. 'But it didn't take much thinking. I've texted Henry – he's still with Marcus – not to contact Social Services yet. Her CRB will still be valid, Guy is bound to have one; they'll be perfect. They can even have the dog. Shall you ring her, or shall I? Henry has her number but perhaps it would come best from one of us.'

'I'll do it,' he said and nodded to the SOCOs milling around. 'You're busy. Would it be all right if I use the phone in the house? I seem …'

'To have left yours on the mantelpiece at home, yes. You'd think so, wouldn't you.' She rummaged in a pocket. 'And yet, here it is.' She handed it over and he took it reluctantly. 'I know you can use it, Max. Don't pretend otherwise. And look …' she pressed a few buttons, 'Sylv's number. It's late, but she'll understand.'

It didn't seem the time to argue about mobile phones so he took it and wandered off down the road away from the flashing lights and the socially distanced gawpers. Some miles to the south, a phone rang.

'Yes?' The voice on the phone was not enthusiastic. By now it was way past midnight and people went to bed early when they had spent all day doing next to nothing. Since leaving Leighford High in the short but draconian reign of Fiona Braymarr, Sylvia had moved nearer to Brighton, along the coast a way from Leighford. And as always happens, with even the closest friends, keeping in touch had not been as easy as everyone might think. Birthday cards and miraculously appropriate presents for Nolan turned up on cue, Christmas cards. It had been no surprise when Jacquie had shown him her Facebook page, Debunk Central. She was there for the world, but he knew that most of all, she was there for them. Or at least, he hoped so.

'Sylv? It's Max.'

'Max? What's wrong? Is Nolan all right? Jacquie?' A pause. 'You?'

Maxwell smiled behind his mask and then realised there was no need to wear it, all alone by himself, after midnight on a road which was silent and unpopulated in front of him. Behind him, not so much.

'We're all fine. You?'

'We're fine now. Guy got Covid, more or less in the first week it was in the news. Someone at work had been to Cheltenham. The office went down like ninepins.'

'But … he's all right now?' Maxwell fought down a selfish thought that this might scupper his plans for Marcus.

'He was pretty bad for a couple of weeks, but I nursed him here. I reckon that one good place to get a darned good dose of Covid is in hospital.' She chuckled. 'But don't tell anyone I said that. Not the party line. Anyway, Max, this can't be a social call, surely.'

'No, it's not.' He filled her in with a brief resumé of the last few hours. He knew it would be all right as soon as he started talking. Sylvia wouldn't leave a child in the lurch. 'So, I can't remember whether he and you would have ever crossed each other's paths. You know how it is, one year rolls pretty much into another and he's not exactly a stand-out kind of kid. But …' He realised he was almost at the end of the pavement and turned back towards the lights and hubbub.

'Consider it done,' she said. He heard another voice in the background, and a hacking cough.

'Sylv ... is Guy well enough? That cough sounds terrible.'

'Not to us, it doesn't. It's a million times less than what it was. Hang on, let me just bring him up to speed.'

The voice became muffled and Maxwell knew she had pressed the phone to her shoulder, the way she always did at school. He became almost unbearably nostalgic for the days when Sylvia would make it all better. Even this.

'Max? Yes, I've just had a chat with Guy and he's all for it. Do you have any idea when he'll be getting here? Or shall we come and get him?'

'You've got me there, Sylv. I hadn't really thought it through in that much detail. But ... Henry has your number, Jacquie tells me. Is it okay if he rings? Saves Chinese whispers.'

'Are you there? At the house? Where's Nolan?' Sylvia knew that the Maxwells would no sooner leave Nolan alone than fly, but these were strange times.

'We've pushed an envelope a bit,' Maxwell admitted. 'We have a childcare bubble with Plocker's mum. He's there.'

'And happy as a pig in shit, I imagine,' she said and sighed. 'There is so much talk about mental health and loneliness, but I wonder if anyone has little boys on their list when they are spouting the usual.'

'Knowing Nole, he'll be worrying about the Count and Bizzy as soon as he opens his eyes in the morning. He hardly woke up enough to take it in when we dropped him off, poor little bloke. But he knows Mrs Plocker ...'

'I've often wondered,' Sylvia interrupted. 'What is her name?'

Maxwell thought for a moment. 'I expect I know,' he said, 'but somehow it never comes up. Jacquie knows. Anyway, he ... oh, hang on, Sylv. Henry's finished with Marcus. I'll wave him over. Hang on.' Subconsciously mimicking Sylvia, Maxwell raised the phone to his shoulder and waved to Henry, who came over, Marcus and Bob on his heels.

'Yes, Mr Maxwell?' Henry Hall knew better than to be too familiar with a pupil, even a traumatised one, in earshot.

'I have Nurse Matthews on the line. About Marcus.'

Henry's eyebrows rose but otherwise his usual bland expression held sway. He should be used to the Team Maxwell Machine by now but somehow he never was. Maxwell held out his phone but Hall paused. Don't share phones was one of the big taboos, these days. But there were times for breaking the odd rule and this was one such. If Dominic Cummings could drive to another town to test his eyesight, Henry Hall was darned sure he could use Peter Maxwell's phone to get a child and his dog a safe place to stay. He reached out and took the phone, but as a compromise kept his mask in place.

'Nurse Matthews. Has Mr Maxwell explained …?' He swung away from Marcus and Bob, who sidled up to Maxwell. They both needed to be near someone right now.

Marcus had himself a little more in hand now, but still needed the proximity of someone who he knew was as solid as the Rock of Gibraltar, though he would have struggled to find the actual geographical location on a map. 'Is that Nurse Matthews like up at the school?'

Maxwell was pleased to have that box ticked. 'I didn't know if you would remember her,' he said.

'I never went to her. Well, she was there for the girls mainly, wasn't she? But one of the boys in my soccer team went to her when he hurt his leg.' There was a pause. 'She was really nice.'

Maxwell breathed a sigh of relief and felt the warm air puff into his eyes from behind his mask, making him blink. 'Would you like to go and stay with her?' he asked.

'What, with Nurse Matthews?' It was hard to tell what the undercurrent of the question was, but Maxwell was hoping it was enthusiasm.

'Yes. She lives near Brighton. Along the coast. At the seaside, just like here.'

Like most children who lived by the sea, Marcus hadn't been near sand in years, but understood what Maxwell was getting at and nodded. 'Has she got a dog? Because Bob doesn't like other dogs.'

'No, she says Bob would be welcome, though.'

'Or most people.' Marcus was ticking things off on his fingers. 'Hedgehogs. Loud noises. People creeping about. Balls. Bees. Cars ...'

'Let's not meet trouble halfway,' Maxwell said, hurriedly. 'I'm sure Bob will know to be on his best behaviour.' He glanced up and saw that Henry was making his way back to them, holding out Maxwell's phone to him.

'That's settled, then,' he said. 'One of our cars will take Marcus and Bob to Nurse Matthews' house in a bit. We just need to get you some clothes, Marcus, and anything else you need. Laptop? Phone?'

'My laptop's in the shed.' The boy looked at Maxwell. 'It's kind of like my office, isn't it, Mr Maxwell?'

'Indeed it is.' Maxwell thought back to the time, a day or so ago, when the only thing he worried about when he thought of Marcus was that he might be cold in his shed. 'Get that, then. Umm ... sorry, Mr Hall, does someone have to go with him?'

Hall wasn't surprised by Maxwell any more, but even so mentally doffed his cap to the man who not only understood the conceptualisation of the Felicific Calculus but also had a complete grasp of police procedure. 'Yes, in a perfect world. But this isn't a perfect world, is it?' His weariness was showing and Maxwell made a note to self to talk to Jacquie some more about her boss. He was struggling and it was painful to watch. He had gone through some things which would have floored a lesser man and yet here he was, still standing. Then along comes a virus and he was close to crumbling. Definitely another job for Sylvia. 'Mr Maxwell can take you, Marcus. Mr Maxwell, one of my men can lend you a torch.' He gestured to a uniform near the cordon. 'Usual thing, try not to touch anything you don't need to. Someone will pack you some clothes. Does Bob need anything?'

Maxwell knew that Bob would have his own bowl, bed, at least one rubber bone with one end chewed off – if

Bismarck had had to go and have a sleepover, he would need to take more than most people.

'Just his bowl and his blanket,' Marcus said. 'Oh … and if it isn't too much trouble, there's a Spongebob with no legs under the table. He'd like that, I think.'

Maxwell still awarded himself three for three – no one could have guessed the Spongebob.

'Nurse Matthews …' Henry Hall knew that that wasn't her name, but he wanted to keep to things which were familiar. 'Nurse Matthews will have an allowance to buy you anything you need,' he said to Marcus. He didn't know the woman well, but he had a sneaky feeling that, allowance or no allowance, Marcus would be getting a whole lot of things anyway, whether he needed them or not. 'But we'll try to pack you everything you need.' It was always tricky, throwing someone out of their home because it had become a crime scene. Sometimes, they had to arrest them as well, but even then it wasn't easy.

'Thank you.' Marcus suddenly looked so tired it seemed a miracle that he was still standing up. Maxwell understood that – he felt the same. Henry Hall had looked like the walking dead for weeks now and everyone was getting used to it. Even so, Maxwell wished he would go and sit down before he fell down.

'Would you like me to come with you?' Maxwell suddenly asked the boy. It didn't seem right to just send him off on his own.

Hall raised an eyebrow. If he had ever wondered, along with three quarters of the staff at the nick, why the gorgeous Jacquie Carpenter-Maxwell had married this old git, he would understand it now. He almost felt like snuggling in for a cuddle himself.

'If that's all right,' Maxwell asked Hall, suddenly aware there might be protocol. 'The police car can bring me back, can't it? Or I can get …' He paused. Were there still trains? Buses? Who knew, these days.

'The car will wait,' Hall said. 'I think that sounds like a very good plan.' He turned as a police driver pipped his horn. 'I think that's you, over there. I just saw the luggage go in the boot. Safe trip.' He didn't say to Maxwell that he would be picking his brains later, but both men knew that that particular meeting wouldn't be a walk in the park. Even socially distanced. Maxwell was not a snitch. Nor, as Nolan would have added, was he a wocket or a kwuggerbug, but that was Dr Seuss all over. He would share what he had to, but if there was anything secret told on that car ride, Hall wouldn't hear it from him. It was amazing what a lot could be said with a mere lift of an eyebrow, but somehow, all was understood and Hall waved them off knowing that somewhere in this nightmare situation, something was going almost right.

'Was that my husband I just saw riding off into the night?' Jacquie wandered over and stood an almost perfect two metres away from Hall. She wasn't particularly surprised. She just wanted to know whether she had to wait or not.

'He's taking Marcus to Nurse Matthews,' he told her.

She raised an eyebrow. 'That should work well. I always wondered why Sylv didn't have children, she was made for it.'

'She'll need all her skills,' Hall told her. 'And I hope she also likes dogs. Bob is a bit of a handful, I'm afraid.'

'I heard.' Jacquie had always considered herself a dog person, before she met Maxwell and the baleful stare of the Count. Now she wouldn't widdle on one if it were on fire.

'I wish there was a way of questioning dogs,' Hall mused. 'Without all that woo-woo nonsense with dog whisperers and their ilk. I have a feeling that dog has seen a lot that could be handy.'

'Any sign he bit anyone?' Jacquie asked.

'Don't know. They swabbed his mouth as best they could, but he was almost hysterical by that time and what with the drool and the sharp teeth … Well, let's just say that it probably wasn't CS's best work.'

'What do you think happened, guv?'

He looked at her. She didn't call him guv very often these days. It was like when your big grown up kid is sleepy and accidentally calls you Daddy. 'I don't know, Jacquie.' He shook his head. He thought he had seen it all sometimes and then a case like this came along to prove to him that he hadn't. 'I think best plan is if we all go home to bed and have another think in the morning. What do you say?'

A passing CS oik looked up, eyes wide. Hall didn't miss it.

'As you were, Simpkins,' he said. 'That wasn't an invitation. So if I hear any rumours in the canteen, I'll know where to come.'

The CS guy put his head down and scuttled off, secretly glad. He had always carried a bit of a torch for Henry Hall himself, though he would forever be too shy to say.

ELEVEN

Roger Ancaster lay just inside the bedroom door. He was on his left side, one arm extended as though it was above his head, the other thrown back slightly behind him. He was wearing pyjamas, as drenched in blood as he was. Beyond him, sprawled diagonally across the bed, was Lilian, his wife, her battered head lolling over the edge of the mattress, forming a curved pattern on the pile of the bedside rug.

Philip McIndoe was the new pathologist on the block and he'd driven through the night from his home near Arundel. He was nearly as used to disturbing phone calls in the darkness as any of Henry Hall's police people, but his on-off- girlfriend Evelyn couldn't really handle it; which was why she was 'off' at the moment. He took in the ghastly scene in front of him, his 'Murder Bag' as the old-time coppers called it, on the landing outside. Everything was lit by the torch fitted to his Perspex visor and he padded carefully on plastic feet, everybody's image of a faceless figure from the Apocalypse. He was talking into a microphone fitted around his jaw.

'Male,' he was kneeling next to Roger. 'Forties. Clothed in pyjamas. Lacerations to scalp. Contiguous.' He rolled up the dead man's right sleeve. 'Haematoma to right forearm. Defensive wounds.' He glanced up to the open door. 'He saw his attacker coming. Or perhaps just heard him if the door was closed.' A thought suddenly occurred to him and he called out, 'Anybody know who found the bodies?'

There was a muffled conversation on the stairs and a constable stuck his masked head around the door. 'Kid,' he told McIndoe. 'Their son.'

'Jesus,' the pathologist hissed. *There* was a rite of passage. Perhaps the lad had opened the door, perhaps the murderer had. It was all one. The SOCO boys and girls were beavering away in their professional silence, dabbing here and there for dabs. Thank God for Herschel, Henry, Stockley Collins and all the other pioneering greats who'd made the hard yards in the early days of fingerprinting. With a bit of luck, he'd be able to thank Alec Jeffreys, Lord of DNA, later.

In the surreal light of his own torch and the arc lights being set up by SOCO, McIndoe could count four blows to the dead man's skull. One of them lay across the forehead, almost at right angles to the others. That would be the first blow, the only one the killer had time for before he realised he had to shut the woman up before she started screaming. He did that, then turned back to the man, shattering his skull with three more blows. Just to make sure. Just for jolly.

McIndoe perched himself awkwardly on the edge of the bed. An arc of crimson blood lay on the pillows and the bedhead. She had been sitting up, staring in horror that was unfolding in front of her, between the bed and the door. The pathologist knelt down now and lifted the head. The woman's long, dark hair was thick with blood and he surmised that she had been hit twice more, as she half fell off the mattress. It was probably only the tangle of the quilt that had kept her from joining her husband on the carpet. Her nightdress was pulled up above her knees but there was no sign of sexual assault. This was what the Americans called a home invasion and it had nothing to do with sex.

'Female,' McIndoe said for the benefit of the microphone, the court and crime historians of the future. 'Early forties. No sign of defensive wounds. Nothing sexual.'

When he was satisfied that he could do no more, he called the SOCO photographer to cover all angles, the bodies, the blood spatter, the battlefield room. Then he made his way downstairs past a handful of prints, knocked off the straight and narrow by somebody running fast downstairs past them. The SOCO would be all over that like Covid. In the hall, the Superintendent of the same name was there, waiting patiently for the final brick in the wall.

Henry Hall was no stranger to crimes like this, although he had to admit, this was one of the bloodiest. He was experiencing what he always did at crime scenes, a weird stillness he couldn't explain. There was a pathologist padding down the stairs towards him, SOCO people in their pale blue overalls everywhere, cameras clicking and lights flashing. At ground level, his uniforms were all over the place, measuring distances, rummaging through kitchen, lounge, utility room, garage. They had been held up by the crazy dog and sensitivity towards the boy, but now they were well into their stride. Two of them were taking the Ancasters' car apart. Two more were destroying Roger's work van. Beyond the white tent, glowing with an eerie light that threw huge shadows into the night, the usual crowd of ghouls had collected. He could even hear them muttering – or perhaps he couldn't, but knew instinctively what they were saying.

'I just don't believe it.' It wasn't a very good Victor Meldrew, all things considered. 'Things like this don't happen around here.' 'What's going on? It's half past two in the bloody morning.' 'Ah, it's them Ancasters; I knew it.' *That* was a voice Henry Hall needed to hear again, with a tape recorder running, across a desk in an interview room. And then he *knew* the voices were real, because he heard a WPC say 'Yes, there has been an incident, but I must ask you all to keep your masks on and maintain social distancing.'

Yet, with all that, Henry Hall felt alone. It was just him, in the lobby of 67 Broadgate Avenue, standing inches from where a murderer had stood only hours before. The murderer was looking at him, grinning, saying, 'Come on then, Henry, who am I? What's it all about? Give it your best shot, there's a good copper.'

Philip McIndoe's voice shook him out of his imaginary conversations. 'As they say in all the best TV crime dramas, I'll know more when I get them on the slab.'

M. J. Trow

Hall was smiling inwardly, the only way he ever did. He remembered old coppers when he'd started out regaling him with tales of *The Sweeney*. Everyday phrases like 'We'll take the Pandas. And get on the phone. They may have firearms' became, courtesy of DI Reagan and DS Carter 'Get the motors. Get on the blower. They've got shooters'. And, of course, all of it was laced with endless, snarling 'Shut it!' accompanied by jangling music. Everything these days was led by TV sound-bites and stereotypes.

'Any guesswork at the moment?' Hall asked.

McIndoe risked the wrath of God by tilting back his visor. 'Your attacker's male, powerful. And there's a lot of anger there. He didn't hurt the child?'

'No,' Hall said, thinking of Maxwell and Marcus driving through the night. 'We've got him safe.'

McIndoe edged past the superintendent, averting his head to make up for the reduced distance in the narrow space. 'More than we can say for his parents,' he said.

Henry Hall didn't get home that night. He left a message on the answerphone for Margaret; she took sleeping pills these days, the only way either of them got any sleep, and he knew there was no way she would hear the phone. He spent the dawn hours following up on the paperwork required for a case like this. He brought DS Alan Spencer up to date because Spencer was the Press liaison officer and it would not be long before the fourth estate would be hammering on the doors of Leighford Nick, shouting obvious and predictable questions across a suitably socially-distanced space in the hope that some hapless plod would let something slip that they could work up into a story. The boys in blue were already getting it in the neck for over-zealous policing in the teeth of the pandemic; throw in a whiff of institutional racism/incompetence/fraud/how's-your-father and the journalists' day would be made. DS Spencer's back was broad – he could handle all that.

The police car purred through the night, almost alone on the coast road from Leighford to the safe haven of Sylvia and

Guy's house. Marcus was quiet, but seemed quite calm. Maxwell attributed it to the shock and knew that if anyone could look after him, that person was Sylv. Bob was not quiet. He lay across their feet in the well of the car behind the front seats and yelped and twitched as he tried to get it all sorted out in his doggy brain. It was all mixed up; the hedgehogs, the lights, the footsteps. Night after night it had got him down and he was not the dog he was. He had even heard the dread word 'vet' from time to time. But tonight … tonight was all too much. He had his Boy, so that was all right. He didn't go much on this bloke, though. He smelled of Cat and that was never a good thing. And now they were in the car, bouncing through the night. Cars meant Vet to Bob. Vet or Kennels. He hated both. He put his nose down on his paws and whimpered. How much else was going to go wrong?

'Bob's sad.'

Marcus's voice wasn't loud but it jolted Maxwell out of a light snooze he had promised himself he wouldn't take.

'Of course he is,' he said, sitting up a bit straighter. 'As are you, I would imagine.'

'I know I should be, Mr Maxwell,' the boy said. 'But I can't really take it in. It feels too much like a dream.'

Maxwell put his arm round the lad and gave him a squeeze. 'You're in shock, Marcus,' he said. 'We all are. And driving through the dark, not many cars on the road, don't know where you're going … it's bound to seem unreal.'

'It's … it's kind of you to come,' Marcus said. 'I can't think of many who would. What with the six feet and everything.'

'I don't think this is really the time for social distancing,' Maxwell observed.

'No, but … well, we're breaking the law, technically, aren't we?'

'Let's say we're a bubble,' Maxwell said. A 'my parents have been murdered' bubble. A little too niche to have been specified by Vallance and Whitty, but one he was prepared to defend in court, nonetheless.

'A bubble,' Marcus said, mulling it over. 'A bubble …'

It was only after a few minutes that Maxwell realised

the boy was asleep and risked his dignity by pulling his head down gently onto his shoulder. He put back his own head on the back of the seat and stared sightlessly into the dark interior of the car. A dream. Wouldn't that be nice …

Back at home, Maxwell couldn't sleep. Jacquie would not be back until after breakfast and with Nolan at Plocker's in the quickly assembled bubble, he was at a loose end. He fed the statesmen of Europe, then headed up the stairs to the War Office.

As soon as he got up there, he forgot that it was just an attic above the castle that was 36 Columbine, but this was an inner sanctum like no other. There was a phone, for emergencies, but otherwise no links with the outside world. On a huge table in the centre, lit by the light of the sky, sat 421 of the 673 riders of Lord Cardigan's Light Brigade, all plastic, all 54 millimetre, all painted in the accurate uniforms they had worn on that fateful day in October 1854 when they had ridden to glory. Maxwell was in the middle of working on Number 422, Captain Arthur Tremayne of the 13th Light Dragoons. The man had married twice and was later Conservative MP for Truro but Maxwell's politics was a broad church and he didn't hold it against him. The man's horse, which Maxwell was painting a handsome bay, was shot in the Charge, but the great modeller had all his plastic warriors lined up just before the action; no blood yet.

He looked at Tremayne, lying on his back, unhorsed, his hair and overalls still unpainted and he just didn't feel like modelling today. He preferred working in daylight, not the artificial glare of his modeller's lamp and the day was too young to provide enough light. Instead, and just for a laugh that Maxwell desperately needed, he began to space out his models for social distancing, imagining the ratio distance of the now obligatory six feet. He found his mind wandering to the dialogue of Balaclava that he knew so well and how it would sound today.

At the head of the Brigade, Lord Cardigan himself, mounted on Ronald, gave Trumpeter Brittan the order, 'The Light Brigade will advance, Trumpeter. Take that stupid mask off or we won't hear a note.'

What utter madness had descended on the world in the year of somebody's Lord 2020. And how much worse was it at 67, Broadgate Avenue.

'How goes it, heart?' Leighford's absent Head of Sixth Form had abandoned the War Office and was waiting, welcoming cup of tea in hand, as his good lady DI came in through the door.

'Given that I've been knee deep in somebody else's blood for four hours, just peachy thanks.' She took a deep draught of tea, made just how she liked it, strong enough to make a builder blench. 'But how about you – you must be shattered.'

Maxwell shrugged. 'To be honest, I slept most of the way there and all of the way back.'

'How's Sylv?'

'I hardly saw her. She was in full PPE and was really only interested in Marcus, as it should be. She blew me a kiss, or I think she did. Her Perspex mask misted up for a second. Guy was in bed – he's still not that well, no matter what they are saying – and your chap was beginning to get a bit twitchy because he seemed to think I was predisposed to break rules for some reason.'

'Gosh,' Jacquie muttered into her mug.

'So, that was my exciting journey in a nutshell. But we'll hear more, I'm sure, when the dust settles a bit.'

'Have we heard from Nole?'

'Not specifically *from*, no. Of, perhaps we could say. Mrs P left a message last night. The boys were both in bed, asleep with big smiles on their faces. She's up for keeping him as long as we need. I don't know, really … shall we leave him there a day or two? He'll want to come home by then because he'll miss the cats.'

'Or us?' Jacquie sounded a little wistful. Being involved in the murder of two parents of an only child will do that to a person.

'Possibly. But mainly the cats, I would imagine. But bubble or no bubble, we can't keep chopping and changing.

So what do you say? Let the boys have some quality time?'

'I suppose that might be for the best.' She put down her empty mug and stretched. 'I need a shower.' But she didn't move. Somehow her legs weren't as keen to have a shower as her head was.

'No leads, I suppose?' Maxwell sat down next to her. Long ago, before they were married and she was just plain old WPC Jacquie Carpenter, he had started asking her questions like that. She had tied herself in knots, trying to keep him out. The man was brilliant, with a mind like Occam's razor, but he was not of the police persuasion and had not taken the oath. She was torn between telling him everything (her natural instinct, especially as he could be so insightful) and nothing (her sworn duty). It had been a difficult tightrope but now she had fallen off it so often she had lost count. And anyway, this one was different; Mad Max was in it, via Marcus, almost before Mrs Mad Max.

'Early days, Max,' she smiled. 'Early days.'

'Hobnob?' He proffered the packet.

'I couldn't,' she sighed. 'But I wouldn't say no to a full English.'

'That's my girl,' and he instantly turned into Mary Berry but mercifully without the jeans pulled up to the armpits and the free range false teeth, clattering frying pans and marshalling sausages into obedience.

'This new bloke seems to be on the ball,' she said, 'the pathologist, McIndoe.'

'One of the sillier North British surnames, I've always thought,' he said. 'Mushrooms?'

She looked at him sideways. 'Does the Pope shit in the woods?'

Just one of life's unanswered and rhetorical questions.

'What's his take on it all?'

'Well, I haven't seen his report yet. He'll be doing the post mortems this afternoon, given a suitable headwind. Henry's setting up an Incident Room as we speak. Do you know, and this is said for information rather than proof that the world has gone mad, before he could take the bodies to the morgue, he had to check them for Covid.'

'And if they were positive?'

'They would go down on the statistics as a Covid death and McIndoe wouldn't be allowed to do a PM.'

Maxwell carried on turning the sausages as if everything were normal. But his wife was right, the world had indeed gone mad.

'Is Henry all right?' He changed the subject. He checked the sell-by date on the eggs; it was not something that he really cared about, but he knew that Jacquie cared, so he checked. 'I thought he looked bloody awful last night.'

'A double homicide will do that to a man,' she said. But you're right; he does.'

'This may be kettles calling pots a darkish hue,' Maxwell was wrestling with the freshly-cut rashers of bacon made impossible to separate by unscrupulous butchers intent on selling you even more, 'but he can't be long for retirement, can he?'

'He can't,' she nodded, 'but I think all retirement is on hold for the duration and anyway, it would give him more time with Margaret and I'm not at all sure he could cope with that.'

'He really needs to talk to Sylv. And I suppose he will, now, what with Marcus living there.'

'Margaret has really gone doolally,' Jacquie said, 'so I hope he does. She's deranged, on anybody's compass.'

'There but for the grace of Boris Johnson go we all.'

'Amen, husband. Amen.'

TWELVE

The thin blue line had never been thinner. The government had promised 20,000 more coppers on the beat but there was no sign of them yet. And anybody under 35 already on the force had no idea what a beat was anyway. So the ranks were decidedly thin that Friday morning as the Incident Room team assembled. There were, as ever, more computers than people and the coffee machine was red hot with overuse.

'Alan.' Henry Hall may not have had any sleep, but he was in charge nevertheless. 'How did it go with the press?'

'Buggers haven't got out much recently, guv,' Spencer said.

'Wanking from home,' somebody murmured to general guffaws but Hall let it go.

'They were pretty hungry for info.'

'Of which you gave them …?'

Spencer mimed a zip across his lips. 'Zilch,' he said. '*The Advertiser* weren't happy. Neither was the *Express*.'

'Television?'

'BBC bloke didn't show. ITV didn't send Peston, so that was good news in itself. I gave them the usual platitudes, holding exercise, information gathering, any number of public with any information, et cetera, et cetera.'

'Right, Tom.' Hall's gaze fell upon a chunky detective slumped against a wall. His mask hid his perennially sulky mouth but he looked sulky all the same. 'I want you to coordinate house to house. Everybody along Broadgate Avenue. Hardly anybody's at work at the moment so that should give us more eyes than usual. Who's on background?'

'That's me, guv.'

'Alison. What have we got?'

In a less misogynistic world, no one would have noticed DS Alison McGuire. As it was, this was a room full of largely male coppers; all eyes swivelled to her breasts.

'The deceased was a jobbing builder,' she swept on regardless, fully aware of her colleagues' prurient interest, 'and, as you'd expect of late, work has dropped off. That's why he was renovating his own place.'

'Busman's holiday,' somebody grunted.

'I'm running down his recent jobs as we speak. See if anybody had a grudge, not happy with his work, that sort of thing. By all accounts, he was a popular bloke, hard worker.'

'Mother Bloody Theresa,' somebody grated.

'Cathcart!' Hall exploded.

'Yes, guv,' the policeman of that name sat bolt upright in his chair as if it was Old Sparky.

'So far we have had from that fertile brain of yours – and I quote – "wanking from home", "busman's holiday" and "Mother Bloody Theresa". Do you have any other quips you'd like to share with us?'

'Er … no, guv.'

'Delighted to hear it, because you're on surveillance. Outside 67 Broadgate Avenue, graveyard shift. Got it?'

'Got it, guv.' Cathcart's face had just fallen through the floor.

'Jacquie, I want you to talk to the boy, Marcus. See what he remembers.'

'Yes, guv.' Jacquie knew full well why she'd been given this one. Hall hadn't exactly said 'and take your hubby' but he might as well have done. 'I'm going to have a chat with the immediate neighbour, Mrs … er … Bencher. That's one you can cross off your list, Tom.'

'Thanks, guv.' That only left another hundred and three houses.

As they broke up to their respective tasks, Jacquie took

Alison McGuire aside. 'Don't overlook the wife in all this, Alison.'

'The wife, Inspector?'

'She looks like an afterthought, doesn't she? In the wrong bed at the wrong time, but it may be more complicated than that. Do we know what she does?'

'Hubby's books by the look of it. Helps out at a charity shop in the High Street every Wednesday. Or at least, she did before they closed it.'

'All right,' Jacquie smiled. 'Keep up the good work. Oh, and Alison …'

'Yes, Inspector?'

'I know some of the lads around here are a bit near the knuckle, sometimes. Don't let the bastards grind you down.'

'I won't, Inspector,' the girl laughed. 'Thank you.'

When Jacquie had gone, Alison spun on her heel and looked PC Cathcart straight in the tie knot. 'You look at my tits like that again, Cathcart, and I'll cave your fucking face in, get it?'

'Er … got it.' It was not Cathcart's day.

'Got it, what?'

'Got it, Detective Sergeant.'

'You got *that* right,' she said.

'I've already spoken to you people,' was Amelia Bencher's response to Henry Hall's warrant card, held up politely at her front door. 'It's bad enough with that blasted tent and all this fluttery tape. I have to say to you … er … Chief Inspector,' she was peering closer at the card, 'it does somewhat lower the tone of the neighbourhood.'

'I'm very sorry about that, Mrs Bencher,' he said, 'and please, do not take this the wrong way when I say I'd very much rather not be here myself. But two people are dead. It's my job to find out why.'

She hesitated for a moment, then relented and let him in. The chief inspector was large, square and deceptively bland. He appeared to have no eyes behind those rimless spectacles and, quite probably, no heart under that tweed jacket. As for the token woman with him, all trousers and no mouth, she was clearly there just to tick boxes.

Once they were all in the living room, Hall checked the view from the patio doors. There was a solid fence between the Benchers and the Ancasters, the outer curtain wall as Maxwell might have put it, that defends an Englishman's home. Hall could see the garden clearly and noted the boards resting against the rear wall of the house, together with bags of cement stacked neatly alongside. There was the shed where the Ancaster's boy did his homework. He had seen it all before, of course, but that was at night and in a very different circumstances, when butchered bodies inevitably took centre stage.

'Have you lived here long?' Hall asked.

'Years,' she told him, sitting primly on the sofa, watching the gel make notes.

'Did you know the Ancasters well?'

'No, not really. We're not that sort of neighbourhood. I did notice Charles eyeing her up from time to time.'

'Charles?' Hall interrupted.

'My husband.'

'Ah, yes.' Hall had read Jacquie's report. 'He's away at the moment, I understand.'

'I suspect he's away for good,' she bridled. 'And I do mean *good*. When you marry a man, Chief Inspector, you don't expect him to be ogling everything in a skirt. I mean – and I know you won't take offence – most men are beasts, but you hope, nay, you pray, that yours won't be. All that love and cherish tosh in front of the vicar doesn't add up to much, does it?'

'Indeed.' Hall sensed that the conversation was getting away from him. 'So, the Ancasters …?'

'He was a builder. You see his van all over Leighford. Or you did, before this Covid nonsense started.'

'He was working on his own house, I believe.'

'He was, yes. Well, you have to feel sorry, don't you? Small businesses like his are very much in the firing line, whatever the Chancellor says he is going to do about it. I suppose, too, he'd have all the materials he needed in-house, so to speak. I've no idea what they were having done.'

'Have you ever been round? Morning coffee, that sort of thing.'

'No. They'd only been here six years or so. Before that, the place was rented out.' She shuddered. 'All human life was there then. I remember an old boy and his two sisters, bachelor and spinsters to a man. From the West Country, if memory serves. Are you getting this?' Amelia Bencher suddenly snapped at Hall's DC. 'Not going too fast for you, am I?'

The DC smiled. 'No, no,' she smiled. 'I'm fine.'

Amelia snorted. She appreciated that they had to have women in police forces, although personally she would have liked Hall and his DC to swap places; that would put the smug git in his place.

'Who owned the house during this rental period?' Hall asked.

'Lord, now you've asked me.' Amelia leaned back on the sofa. 'That would be the Leadbetters. Or their estate, at least. But you know about all that.'

'I do?' This had come as a surprise to Hall; what was to know?

Amelia straightened, then leaned forward. 'How long have you been a policeman?' she asked.

Hall managed to stop himself from saying 'forever' and settled for the truth. 'I joined Thames Valley out of school,' he told her. There was no need to say when that was. It was none of her business, and certainly none of his DC's, who was looking a little avid.

Amelia Bencher bridled a tad. 'Ah, so you're not local?'

'No, not really.'

'Well, then, check your records. It's not *that* long ago; you've probably got some crusty old cobwebbed sergeant in the bowels of your station who'd remember the case. It was the year of the Great Storm, 1987. That idiot weatherman Michael Fish pooh-poohed a viewer's warning and told us there was no cause for concern. Buffoon!'

'And … the case?'

'What? Oh, yes, the Leadbetters. Well, they were

murdered, Chief Inspector, out on the Dam if memory serves. Beaten to death.'

Hall and his DC exchanged glances. He had been a young copper in uniform, miles away in a different force. She hadn't even been born.

'It was never solved, of course,' Amelia said, as though that were par for the course with police enquiries. 'But everybody knew who did it.'

'They did?'

'Of course. Today, we'd have to call them Roma, because they're virtually a protected species. Back then, they were gypoes or pikeys. They'd been hanging around the area for weeks, cadging, stealing, the usual thing. And of course, they'd moved on by the time the bodies were found. So you see, I've been here before. Charles and I were married in the March. The Leadbetters met their end in July.'

'You were interviewed?'

'We were. I seem to remember the investigating officer had a young gel with him, too. Come to think of it, Charles was gushingly attentive even then. I was too green and doe-eyed, if that isn't a metaphor too far, to notice. Ah, the naivety of it all …' She pulled herself together. 'I was, as it happened, interviewed several times, due to the fact that I have lived in this road almost my whole life. My parents had No 12 and I was brought up there. Charles and I moved in here so we could be near if darling Mummy and Daddy needed us as they got older. As it happens, it was not to be.'

'Oh?' Hall knew in his gut it would have no bearing, but it seemed unkind not to ask.

'No. Darling Daddy would insist on driving though we begged him not to and he drove off the car park up on the Dam. Mistook the gears, he often did that. Dead on impact, poor dears.'

Hall remembered that. A courting couple down below had been lucky to survive and rumour had it the chap had never been able to unzip his fly in the open air ever after. 'I do recall … very sad. Thank you, Mrs Bencher. I think that's all …'

She held up an imperious finger. 'Now, while you're

here. The Lemons.'

'The …?' Hall sighed. Not another mad old biddy who thought the police had jurisdiction over shortages at the supermarket.

'Those ghastly people next door the other way. Well, *she's* a Lemon. He's something else. They're *partners*, such an appalling term. Not that there's any sanctity in marriage, of course, these days.' She suddenly turned on the DC. 'Are you getting all this down? If it's no use to the investigation, then it's a life lesson, young lady. A life lesson!'

There were stories about Joe Metcalfe. There were always stories about old coppers, ranging from 'Ah, they don't make 'em like that these days; proper copper was old Joe, a policeman's policeman' to 'Thank God that old bastard Metcalfe's gone' to, still further, 'He's dead, surely.'

But Joe Metcalfe wasn't dead. He wasn't yet 86 and despite the dodgy hip (which he hadn't got in the line of duty, even though he said he had) was pretty sprightly. He was a widower now and his kids had long ago flown the coop. His house stood on a hill overlooking Tottingleigh and he could see Leighford and the Bay stretching away to the west. On a clear day, if he had been able to balance on his garden fence, he could even have seen his old nick.

And in front of him today as he opened the door stood someone from that very place, who introduced himself as DCI Henry Hall. Metcalfe had never made *Chief* Inspector and that still rankled after all these years, but it was hardly Henry Hall's fault and Metcalfe made them both a cup of tea. It wasn't strictly legal, but Henry Hall reckoned that on official business, a few lines were drawn to be blurred a little. He was a little concerned at Joe Metcalfe's age – didn't he class as vulnerable? Should he be shielding? This was a whole new page in the book on etiquette, policemen for the use of. Was it ageist to even ask? Metcalfe was wearing a Perspex mask, which Hall knew was about as much use as a chocolate teapot on its own, but what with Margaret waking him every two hours for a new spray down with Dettol and the yellow footprints painted on every horizontal surface wherever he went, Henry Hall was more than ready for a bit of laissez faire.

'Yes, I remember the Leadbetter case,' the old man said, once they were sitting at his kitchen table. He had pushed the visor back so he could reach his cup and now it stuck out like a bizarre duck's bill from his forehead. Hall chose to take this as a sign he didn't consider himself in the vulnerable category. 'I remember it because it was my last one. Whatever your last case is going to be, Mr Hall, you'll remember it too.'

'I'm sure I will,' Hall said, 'and that's Henry, by the way.'

'Joe,' the old man fired back.

'So, what happened?'

'Well,' Metcalfe leaned back in his chair, 'a double murder like that was pretty unusual. Most of our time at Leighford was sorting out Mods and Rockers – God, that makes me sound like a dinosaur, doesn't it?'

'It'll be the same for me with Extinction Rebellion,' Hall prophesied.

'Arseholes,' Metcalfe rumbled. 'Only the clothes were different. And the violence, of course.' He ducked his head to blow on his tea and his visor steamed up. 'I couldn't really get a handle on the Leadbetters. Ordinary couple; nobody had a bad word to say about them. He was some sort of accountant. She ran a bookshop in the town. It's gone now, of course. Nobody reads any more, do they? It's all tablets and all that nonsense. Anyway, it was next to Lloyd's Bank – oh, that's gone too, hasn't it? We didn't get very far to be honest with his business. He was pretty senior and even when I'd kicked the usual client confidentiality bit in the bollocks, his colleagues didn't have a bad word to say about him. I was looking for potential enemies, of course.'

'And you didn't find any.' Hall had often been down this road.

'Not a sausage. So we tried her.'

'Any joy?'

'Well,' Metcalfe was enjoying this. 'There was some talk of a bit on the side, some bloke who spent a *lot* of time browsing the erotic fiction.'

'Did that lead anywhere?'

'We got a name. Parker, was it? Potter? Something like that. Fell over himself to help, but he didn't seem particularly cut up about Mrs Leadbetter.'

'What about MO? They were found on the Dam, I understand.'

Metcalfe frowned. 'Have you read the file, Henry?' he asked.

'Not yet.'

'Don't tell me; it's all computerised somewhere at HQ. Am I right?'

'I presume so.' It would have seemed strange to Henry Hall if it wasn't computerised and he realised what a lot had happened since 1987. 'I just haven't got round to following it up yet. Thought I'd do better at the horse's mouth – no offence.'

'None taken,' Metcalfe chuckled. 'They're one reason I got out when I did.'

'What are?' Hall was beginning to realise that Joe Metcalfe's meanderings needed a bit of watching.

'Computers. Oh, yes, I know. They speed things up. You can cross refer. But this was the early days. Do you know, it took me up to seven minutes to fire the bloody things up?'

'What a coincidence,' Hall said, smiling behind his mask, which he diligently replaced after every sip of tea.

'I knew it!' Metcalfe slapped his good leg. 'Thirty plus years later and we're not further forrard. Give me the old shoe boxes, every time. Type it up by all means, then put it in a box clearly labelled and you can't go wrong. Most of my last weeks consisted of me staring at a green screen that told me I had just completed an illegal manoeuvre. I might as well have sat there playing Pacman!'

'And the Leadbetters?'

'Bludgeoned. I don't remember the exact date, but we're talking high summer. A dog walker found them, in shrubbery on the edge of the Dam. By the time my team and I got there, it was well and truly dark. It's all in my report.

And Jim Astley was the pathologist – did a pretty good job, as I recall.'

'Blunt instrument?'

'The same,' Metcalfe nodded. 'Probably a pein hammer. Although we never found it. He died first. Blows to the head. Can't remember how many. More than necessary, at any rate.'

'Nothing sexual,' Hall asked. 'Clothes disarranged?'

Metcalfe shook his head and his plastic bill swayed madly this way and that. He put his hand up to steady it and sighed. 'Load of bollocks, all this, isn't it? My son says I should be shielding and wearing … what is it he calls it? … full PDQ? Anyway, this is as far as I'm going. He checks up on me every day on some kind of screen thing they've set up, but I don't know … I can't be doing with it.' He rubbed his eyes and Hall, trained and honed by Margaret, could hardly bear to watch. 'Where was I?'

'Clothing. Disarranged.'

'No. Nothing like that. But I do remember the attack was frenzied. The killer went completely overboard and he'd have been covered in blood. He killed them in the house.'

'What?'

'Astley was sure about that – and I reckoned Jim Astley.'

Henry Hall did too; he had worked with the man before his retirement on cases too many to recall, but now he had joined the other Great Pathologists in the sky lab. 'What was Jim's reasoning?'

'A lot of blood on the wounds and clothing and not much on the ground. Oh, we had footprints galore and bike tracks, but surprisingly little blood.'

'That was because it was all at the house, 67 Broadgate Avenue.'

'You'd think so, wouldn't you? But chummy had gone to great lengths to clean up there, too. Everything had been wiped clean, knobs, furniture, windows. He'd done a pretty good job, too, but you can't kid a SOCO team.'

'Indeed not. Tell me, Joe, had the place been turned over?'

'No. Oh, it was a break-in, fair enough. Glass all over the hall floor, but no sign of upheaval other than in the bedroom. As I say, it was as clean as the killer could make it, the bed remade, pillows plumped. He must have washed the sheets in the washing machine. Astley reckoned the time of death about eight o'clock, give or take.'

'High summer,' Hall said. 'So still daylight.'

'Very much so. I reckoned the killer stayed in the house until dark, with the bedding on quick spin and dry, then bundled the bodies into a vehicle. There were no black bags in the kitchen, so I guess he used them to wrap 'em up.'

'Why the break-in if it was still daylight?' Hall wondered aloud.

'Beats me,' Metcalfe shrugged. 'Except for the obvious, that the door was locked. I assumed the Leadbetters didn't know their killer or he'd just have knocked on the door or rung the bell, wouldn't he?'

'You'd think so,' Hall agreed. 'But why transport the bodies at all? Why not leave them where they were?'

'Good question. And that was one we argued about day and night. We're not talking about a deranged blitzer here, some dysfunctional Herbert who has a sudden compulsion to kill. This one was pre-planned and, as it turned out, well executed – excuse the pun.'

'Thank you, Joe.' Hall extended a hand. 'You've been very helpful.'

'My pleasure,' Metcalfe said. 'But you haven't told me why you're interested in a case that's so cold.'

Hall looked at his man, the steady blue eyes, the determined glare not dimmed by his Perspex visor, now back in position. 'Because it's not a cold case, Joe,' he said. 'It's red hot. There's been another one.'

Peter Maxwell had not clapped eyes on Sylvia Matthews, except under half a ton of PPE, for what seemed like years. Back in the day, at Leighford High when he was pushing ninety and she was a slip of a thing, some people took them for an item. For Maxwell, Sylv was a whiff of common sense and sensitivity in the ever-more-deranged parallel universe of education. For Sylv, Peter Maxwell had been, before she met Guy, the love of her life.

Maxwell and Jacquie had been to her new house once or twice, but never in an official capacity. It seemed strange to be pulling up on the drive with a bag containing a tape recorder and an official notebook, but these were strange times so everyone was ready for everything. Especially, needless to say, Sylvia. On the glass door of the porch, there was a neatly printed notes, which said, 'We're round the back. There is sanitiser to your left' – they looked and sure enough, on a small table, was a pump containing alcohol wash – 'and masks to your right in case you don't have one.' Maxwell and Jacquie both automatically patted their pockets; Maxwell wondered how long that habit would remain WATIO – when all this is over. He suspected for a long, long time.

They followed the path around the side of the house and saw a scene before them so typically Sylvia that they both burst out laughing together. On a long cedar table under the shade of a laburnum tree, sat Sylvia and Marcus, one at each end. In the middle was a skateboard, with a piece of thick string attached through eyelets screwed into the top. By pulling on it, they could share anything they needed to, in this particular instance, Marcus's maths homework and a bottle of Diet Coke in an ice bucket. They both looked up as they heard the footsteps on the gravel.

'Mr Maxwell!' Marcus half stood before he remembered that there was a distance rule which wasn't even slightly stretched in this house. Although he was living there, he was strictly six feet apart until any possible incubation period was over. Sylvia might have a heart as big as the great outdoors, but that didn't mean she wasn't a stickler for protocol.

Sylvia stood too and walked across towards them and stopped at a position so precisely judged that it might as well have been measured. Above her mask, her eyes were tear-filled. 'Oh, Max ... Jacquie ... I have missed you both. Are you well? What about Nolan? The Count? Bizzy? Come and sit down ... we've got chairs over here. Marcus measured them out, didn't you, love?'

Jacquie smiled under her mask and looked at Maxwell. They had known that Marcus would be safe with Sylvia; they had forgotten about the love bit.

'Yes, Mr Maxwell, Mrs Maxwell. I allowed for the wind direction as well, as an added precaution. We've been doing all that as part of my maths. It's good to be practical.' He wasn't the shocked child he had been when Maxwell had brought him here two nights before, in a jumble of lights and sorrow, but he was still not quite right, anyone could see. He was just too … good. He had never been a problem at school, but the spark had gone.

'Where's Bob?' Maxwell asked. He knew he always thought more of people who asked after Metternich and Bismarck and his intuition was spot on.

Marcus laughed and had to pull his mask back on straight. 'Bob is loving it here. Guy made him a bed in the utility and he just can't get enough of it. He can see the garden and go out if he wants, but mainly he likes the quiet.' He laughed again. 'No hedgehogs.'

Sylvia smiled. 'I used to think that was a disadvantage, but after hearing how Bob reacts to them, I'm glad we don't have them. He's a good dog, quiet as a mouse.'

Maxwell raised an eyebrow. Good might be the word – he had, after all, not seen Bob at his best – but quiet? Perhaps that was in the ear of the beholder.

Marcus had measured the chairs in the shade of another tree in the opposite corner of the garden. There were three and Jacquie sent up a small thank you to the gods of sensitivity that Sylvia had yet again got it just right. 'You can stay if you want, Sylv,' she said, aware that she was inviting someone to sit down in their own garden.

'No, no, I'll be just over here. My blog is keeping me busy – I'm glad I started it, but it has grown into a bit of a monster. People are so confused by the data, the rules … I'm having about a message every thirty seconds.'

Maxwell was glad. He had thought perhaps that the pinging on the edge of hearing was a sign that his ears were going.

'So, I'll get on with that. Can I get you anything?'

'Just some water, if that's okay,' Jacquie said.

'And some biscuits.' Marcus had not wasted time in making himself at home.

'Coming up.' And Sylvia turned for the house. 'Oh,' she said, 'sorry. There's Guy waving at you. He's upstairs, look. Middle window.'

'Is he still ill?' Maxwell couldn't help but worry that they had put too much on the couple.

'A bit weak still, but he's WFH.'

'Pardon?' Maxwell was a little startled. Sylv had never usually resorted to bad language, even in extremis. Perhaps retirement did that to a person.

'WFH. Working From Home.' Jacquie hurriedly told him.

'Oh. WF*H*! I misheard. Soz, Sylv.'

She went on her way into the kitchen, shaking her head. If Maxwell lived to be a hundred – and she seriously hoped he did – he would never change. She gathered the fresh bottles of water, newly-dishwashed glasses and an unopened pack of KitKat and put them on a tray. She took it out to the garden and put them down on the table, waving Marcus to take it to the little interview room beneath the cherry. Then she sat back down at her laptop and started on the messages. So many people. So much distress. And just a crumbling wall of sanity between them and the abyss. She felt a twinge of jealousy when she thought of the plague doctors back in the day. Nothing between them and oblivion but a beaked mask and a handful of lavender soaked in wine vinegar. Perhaps ignorance truly was bliss. She clicked on the first message and was soon miles away.

At first, the three under the cherry just sat, Marcus with his eyes downcast, the adults ready for anything. They both knew that, even with Sylv in the mix, healing was not possible in less than 48 hours. It was probably not possible in a lifetime. So they waited. Eventually, the boy lifted his head.

'Mr Maxwell, Mrs Maxwell … have they … have they … made my mum and dad more comfy?'

For a moment, the Maxwells were horrified. Surely, he knew they were dead? Then Jacquie realised. She had felt the same about her grandmother, who had died in a fall and had been found at the foot of the stairs. She hadn't seen her crumpled body, but her mother had and she knew how it haunted her, that she had lain there all night, with nothing to cover her, no one to straighten her bent limbs.

'Yes, Marcus,' she said, gently. She wanted to hug him and cursed the stupid rules that prevented it. If she had been in her own garden, she would have said sod Whitty and Vallance and SAGE and the rest, but this wasn't her garden so she stayed the right side of the law, the wrong side of humanity. 'They are in the …' she baulked at 'morgue' '… police station, but properly looked after. We need to do that, to make sure that we catch who did this.'

There was another silence. She had said so few words, but there was so much meaning in them.

'Have you found any clues?' The boy's eyes were bright as he looked from one to the other.

'They are doing interviews,' Maxwell told him. 'The neighbours. Passers-by. Some people have got CCTV. They're looking at that. DNA.' Maxwell suspected that Marcus knew more about police procedure than he did. *CSI* trumped *Midsomer Murders* any day of the week when you wanted to know the actual nitty gritty.

'We need to talk to you, now, though, Marcus,' Jacquie said. 'Do you mind if we tape this?' She took a little gizmo out of her bag and when Marcus shook his head, she clicked a switch and leaned over to put it on the table. 'Interview with Marcus Ancaster,' she began. While she was adding the date, time, location, Maxwell looked around him. Sylvia and Guy's garden was like an oasis in a sea of madness. It was much bigger than the one they had had in Leighford, but looked like less trouble. That one had been a square of grass which seemed to sprout daisies and dandelions literally as you looked at it, some parched looking shrubs did their best to hide the bins and against the hedge at the back, there was an apple tree which only ever seemed to have fruit on the branches which overhung the lane. This one had been landscaped until its pips squeaked, every bush in exactly the right place, ground cover covering only the ground it was intended to and not another millimetre. He looked round at Sylvia, who caught his eye and rolled hers.

He got up and approached as near as he dared, while the interminable introduction to the interview droned on behind him.

She smiled at his confusion over the fact that she had suddenly become Gertrude Jekyll. 'It was the previous owners,' she said quietly, so as to not appear on the tape. 'Old couple who needed to downsize. He still comes twice a week – we make sure we're inside, though he don't old with these here new laws, apparently.' She laughed. 'Love him, we'd be lost without him, but his approach to the job is a bit … draconian. I said I fancied having a water feature and he nearly decapitated me with his spade. That was back in the days when he could have got near enough, of course. He knows he's moved out, but he doesn't, if you see what I mean. But it suits us, because Guy has brown thumbs. He's been known to kill a plastic holly wreath.' She nodded. 'I think they're ready for you now.' She blew a kiss through her mask. 'Poor boy.'

Maxwell could only nod as he turned back and took his seat.

'For the benefit of the tape, Mr Peter Maxwell has joined us as an Appropriate Adult,' Jacquie said. 'Now, Marcus, let's just chat about the other day, before this dreadful thing happened.' She was trying to avoid any buzzwords which would upset the boy, though as she walked him through the day, it would become impossible. 'Let's start around lunchtime, shall we?'

The boy nodded and hung his head. 'Can I take this mask off, Mrs Maxwell? Only, I can't breathe very well.'

'Of course,' Jacquie said. She turned her head. 'Is that acceptable to you, Mrs Matthews?'

Sylvia nodded. There was only so much bollocks a person could take, legislationwise. And who was going to tell, anyway?

Marcus peeled the mask away and took a deep breath.

'Oh, that's better. We had our lunch in the garden, me and Mum. Dad was picking up some bits from B&Q. I don't know what, I'm afraid. I'm not good with my hands.' A tear welled up in the corner of his right eye and rolled down his cheek. 'But I helped him sometimes, with painting and stuff. Holding the ladder. That kind of thing.' He wound his fingers together and looked down at his hands as if seeing them for the first time.

'Did anyone come to the door while you were having lunch?' Jacquie asked.

'No. People don't, any more, do they? Mrs Bencher was outside, but she was watching her next door in the other direction. She doesn't like them because they're not married, Mum says … said.'

Jacquie smiled ruefully. The list of who and what Mrs Bencher didn't like was longer than that, she knew.

'We were having a giggle, because she thought she was hiding, but she's a bit … big for that, so her bum stuck out. Then someone called hello to her from the footpath and she went in.'

'Do you know who that was?' Maxwell asked. He wasn't strictly sure whether he could ask questions, but he was sure the Mem, in official mode, would tell him if not.

'No, just a dog walker. There's a lot along that path. Drive Bob mad, they do, some of them. He doesn't mind some others, depends on the size of the dog, really.' He smiled and another tear crept out of his eye. 'Bob doesn't really like to tangle with anything bigger than him. He's a wuss, on the quiet.'

'Is Bob a good guard dog?' Jacquie asked.

'Not really.' Marcus didn't want to be disloyal, but this was his mum and dad they were talking about. Saving Bob's blushes was not what all this was about in the end. 'Sometimes he'd bark his head off because a hedgehog was outside but Dad always … said' – he was already getting into the swing of the past tense, something which Maxwell found unutterably sad – 'that he would probably lick a burglar to death, if he was in that mood.'

'So, you had lunch. Then what happened?'

'I had some Zooms. You, Mr Maxwell, and biology. That was tricky, because we're supposed to be dissecting a frog, but that isn't something you can get down Tesco. Mum said that.' The boy smiled. 'I do miss them, Mr Maxwell.' His voice rose almost to a howl, choked off. 'I … sometimes they annoyed me, you know. Mum would call me Marky in front of my friends. There's this bloke … I don't know, an actor or something, used to be in a band called Marky Mark. She thought it was funny, I suppose. I used to get cross and she stopped.' The tears fell now, good and proper. Jacquie poured him a glass of water which, being Sylvia, was chilled Pellegrino. She and Maxwell waited while he gathered himself together. They could tell that he would give the world to have her call him Marky one more time.

'Do you want to have a break, Marcus?' Maxwell asked. He had dealt with so many emergencies and disasters in his years at the chalk face, but what could prepare anyone for this?

'No, I want to go on. It might be that I know something. I've seen it on the telly, where somebody knows something and … well, let's carry on.' He sniffed and wiped his hand across his face, smudging the tears.

'After lessons, then what?' Jacquie was making notes as well as the recording. Although she wasn't as phobic as Maxwell about tech, it had been known to fail.

'I helped Mum in the garden for a bit. It's a bit overgrown at the bottom, near the gate to the lane. We haven't had the time before to work on it, really. Mum and Dad were always working before lockdown. So we went at it with a pair of shears and piled the stuff up for a bonfire. Then Mrs Bencher came out and said that we couldn't have a bonfire, because of the smell and also the hedgehogs. They hide in the bonfires and get burned.' He smiled. 'Mum said she didn't give a tinker's cuss about the hedgehogs, she just didn't want the smoke. Dad came down then and said he would dance round it, bollock naked and give the old trout a treat.' He looked anxiously from one Maxwell to another. 'He wouldn't have, though. I think most people in the road are a bit scared of Mrs Bencher. I know I am.'

Jacquie nodded. She didn't mind being included in that list. She looked at Maxwell. 'Big woman. Behind the cordon.'

Maxwell cast his mind back and remembered a looming shape with an attitude that could be seen for miles. 'Gotchya,' he said, then, to Marcus, 'Scary lady.'

'She probably means well, Mum always said.'

Jacquie noticed with interest how the boy now talked about his parents almost more than was necessary, like someone picking a scab. He would find a happy medium one day, but today was not that day.

'And after that?'

'Tea, some telly, showers, bed. Same every night.'

'What time did you go to bed?'

'Same time as Mum and Dad. We've done that since lockdown, with no school or work the next day it didn't seem to matter about having an early night,' he said. 'So about ten, half past.'

The atmosphere changed gear a little. After this, it was not going to be such smooth going. Jacquie's voice was gentle as she asked her next question.

'Why did you wake up, Marcus?'

He tipped his head back and looked up at the canopy of leaves, squinting against the sun. At the table, Sylvia stopped typing and listened. The whole world seemed to hold its breath; even the robin which had been shouting its joy to the air was suddenly silent.

His voice was low when he began to speak, held in check by willpower alone. 'I don't know how long I had been asleep, not long. I think perhaps Bob had woken me but he wasn't barking when I woke up. I didn't … it wasn't like *hearing* something, something loud. It was more as if there *had* been something loud, but now it has stopped. Like when thunder wakes you up, something like that.'

Jacquie looked down. She knew what that sound had probably been, the sound of something heavy knocking the life out of Roger Ancaster. She hoped Marcus wouldn't realise the same thing, or at least, not yet.

'My bedroom is along the landing from Mum and

Dad's, because it's the biggest and they were going to turn it into a sort of bedsit when I got older.' He coughed, but it was in lieu of a sob. With a supreme effort, he recovered and went on. 'After a minute or two, I heard the stairs creak, so I thought it was Mum or Dad going downstairs. So I thought perhaps it had been Bob woke me up and they were going down to check. So I waited a minute or two, but they didn't come back. There was …' he closed his eyes and waited, fighting nausea. 'There was a smell. It smelled like … poo.' He looked up at Jacquie and reached out his hands to her. 'It was poo, Mrs Maxwell.'

Jacquie knew that evacuating the bowel was usually the last action of a person dying, whether in bed or on the carpet in their own blood. She hated a world where a teenage boy also knew that. To hell with regulations. In a moment, she was up on her feet and was beside Marcus. He was standing too and was in her arms, sobbing as if he would never stop. Jacquie held him, hugging him for all the little boys in the world who wanted their mothers, today and for all time.

'It's all right, Marcus,' Maxwell heard her say. 'It's all right. That's all for today. That's all for today.'

And Peter Maxwell found that, to his surprise, masks did actually serve a purpose. They mopped up tears.

THIRTEEN

'Well, that's quite bizarre.' Maxwell was peering at the world though his glass of Southern Comfort. Sometimes it was the only way to look at it.

'What is?' Jacquie was curled up in the armchair, the Maxwell family centre for cuddling kids, cats, the relevant toy de jour.

'The house. 67 Broadgate Avenue. What are the odds of *two* sets of owners being murder victims?'

'Don't you believe in haunted houses, Mr Maxwell?' she asked. 'You should; we met in one. Or very nearly.'

'Indeed,' Maxwell smiled. The Red House had been a long time ago, before Nolan, before the wedding, when that nice Mr Forster was passing his 1870 Education Act. One of Maxwell's Own, his sixth form, had died in that house and Jacquie had been the new woman policeman on the block.

Since they had left Sylvia's, Jacquie had gone back to the nick to report to Henry. She'd heard his information from Metcalfe and had gone straight to records to check it out – not that she used that kind of cross-Atlantic talk in front of Maxwell; it would only upset him.

'All I knew about the place was the relatively recent stuff. Before the Ancasters. There was a trio of ancient siblings, earlier, but between them and the Ancasters, the place was something of a squat. Cannabis alley. Children's Services. Complaints from dog walkers.'

'Dog walkers?' Maxwell cut in. 'Why, pray?'

'One of the arseholes who rented the place had a thing against dogs apparently. If he saw any on the path at the back or on the road, he'd throw stuff at them.'

'So the ancient biddies and the Ancasters must have restored the karma.'

'Until now, yes. You know the de Feo story?'

Maxwell clicked his tongue. 'And here was I thinking you were a shrewd, astute, no nonsense detective,' he smiled.

'I am,' she said, just a little affronted.

'Not if you believe the de Feo story,' he said. 'The whole thing was made up by a film company to promote *The Amityville Horror*, which, by the way, was nowhere as good as the book …'

'But de Feo was real, surely?'

'Oh, he was. A particularly nasty mass murderer, but the *house* was completely innocent. It was just bricks ands sticks, Jacquie, like No 67. The evil that men do can't soak itself into the fabric of a building. Not only is that not a law of physics, it's a load of bollocks, if I may use the technical term.'

'So we're looking at a coincidence?' He knew perfectly well that she was dipping a toe into murky waters, just to test him out.

He chuckled. 'Don't get me started on that. There's no such thing.'

'I'm glad you said that.'

'What's Henry's take on it all?'

She rolled her eyes. 'You know Henry. He put the 'com' into noncommittal. Still, it opens up a whole line of enquiry.'

'Cold cases, eh?' He topped up her drink.

'They're not like they are on the telly, that's for sure. You end up hitting brick walls left, right and centre. People who know exactly where they were and what they said yesterday have no clue twenty, thirty years later; and why should they? I don't know how you do it.'

'What, remember my own name, do you mean?'

'Teach history. It's all cold cases for you, isn't it?'

'It is,' he nodded, topping up his own glass. 'Marcus

was great today, though, wasn't he?'

'He was,' she nodded, picturing for a moment her own brave boy, returned from his Plocker bubble and sleeping the sleep of the just gone down, sandwiched between two cats just above their heads. 'But, unfortunately, nothing he said takes us any further forward. Do you fancy a bit of reconstruction?'

'I'm game,' Maxwell said and cleared the coffee table between them.

'What's this?' She held up a volume which had been lying on the floor next to her chair.

'It's a book, dear heart.' He was starting to have concerns about her already.

She looked at him through narrow eyes. 'Specifically.'

'Specifically, it's *The World We Have Lost.* Peter Lazlett.'

'Any good?'

'Brilliant,' Maxwell said. 'It's a reprint, of course. It was on my reading list for Jesus eternity ago.'

'Right.' Jacquie put the book centre table. '*The World We Have Lost* is No 67. Pass the poker, will you?'

He did.

'This is the Avenue, along the front. Here,' she added other books to each side of the Lazlett, 'are Nos 65 and 69. Along the back,' she grabbed Nolan's foam rapier that he had left carelessly about, 'the footpath that's the dog walkers' heaven.'

'All right.' He was with her so far.

'You're a bent out of shape bastard ...'

'Thank you, heart. I was beginning to think you hadn't noticed,' he said.

'Just for the purposes of role play,' she said, looking down at the peaceful suburban scene on the table top. 'For whatever reason, you've got it in for the Ancasters.'

'I'm not just your common or garden burglar, then?' Maxwell checked. You couldn't be too careful.

'You may be, but you didn't take anything.'

'Because I was interrupted by the Ancasters waking up, and the kid.'

'True. But there's the damage to the front door. Not the work of a pro, that's for sure. A pro would have gone round the back. On average, a back door is less well-protected than the front.'

'All right, so I'm an amateur thief, with or without a striped tee shirt, a mask, not the new sort, the old sort,' he mimed the Lone Ranger, 'and a bag marked "Swag". I've broken in. Now,' he was looking down at the cover of Lazlett, 'the great British question – what about the curious incident of the dog in the night time?'

'Ah, yes,' she nodded. 'Silent Bob.'

'That dates you,' he laughed. 'Comedies of yesteryear.'

'I'm older than I look,' she said.

'From what I remember, he didn't stop yapping or worse the whole time I was there, so he wasn't drugged.'

'So he knew the intruder,' she reasoned.

'Right. Whatever woke the Ancasters up, it probably wasn't Bob. According to Marcus, he often went crazy at the hedgehogs, so they would have probably just turned over and gone back to sleep anyway. Then, afterwards. Why not kill Marcus? If the intruder knew Bob, he knew the family. He knew the boy would be in the house. If this has nothing to do with a robbery gone wrong, why leave the boy alive? That's not how home invasions work, is it? Or should that be, do they?'

Jacquie shrugged. 'They're so rare in this neck of the woods, I have to say I don't know. From what I've read, *everybody* is at risk in that situation.'

'So, Chummy has a soft spot.'

'Or it's a grievance thing.' She was thinking aloud, 'Mr or Mrs Ancaster – or both – had pissed him off and this was payback time. Marcus wasn't even collateral damage.'

'Even so,' Maxwell said. 'He took a chance – sorry, *I* took a chance leaving him alive. What if he'd seen me?'

Jacquie sighed. It was late and tomorrow was another lockdown day. 'Yes,' she said. 'This case is full of "what ifs", isn't it?'

The next morning, Jacquie was at her desk, bright eyed if not very bushy tailed. Talking the case over had not achieved much as far as catching anyone went, but seeing things laid out, even using books and swords, had clarified things in her head. She looked through her open door across the corridor and could see that Henry Hall was beginning to visibly flag.

'Chief Inspector!' When shouting across two rooms and a corridor it was best to keep it formal. There was a discernible time lag before Hall lifted his head.

'Yes, Detective Inspector?' Even the light banter sounded weary.

'Could we meet in our doorways?'

'Could I sit here and you meet in my doorway?' The blank lenses gave nothing away but if there had ever been a man too long without sleep, here he sat.

'Of course.' Jacquie checked her mask and crossed the corridor, doing a hurried lookrightlookleftlookrightagain before crossing, to avoid unseemly contact with a rushing colleague. She peered in and saw at once that she was going to have to do everything in her power to make this man go home. She broke protocol by going in and shutting the door. She pulled a chair over and sat, tight against the wall and looked at him severely.

'Henry,' she said, using much the same tone she often used to Nolan. 'Go home. Go to bed. Don't wake up until your eyes open, no setting an alarm. Tell Margaret … tell Margaret you …' At that point, she realised there was nothing he could tell Margaret that wouldn't send her into a flat spin. Tell her he felt ill, she would completely flip out and either spray him with Dettol and make his sleep in the garage, or drive him to A&E, neither of which would be helpful. Even telling her he was tired would have the same effect. Then, inspiration struck.

'Guv, listen to me. I know you are having problems at home and I can't help you with that. Have you spoken to Sylv?'

Hall nodded. 'Margaret follows her blog. They've messaged.'

'And?'

'And Margaret knows that everything that Sylv says is common sense, that she shouldn't be like she is but … she is like she is. I'll be fine.' The eyes he raised to his Number Two were bloodshot and desperate.

'You know the family suite upstairs, the one we use for emergencies?'

Again, a lacklustre nod.

'Well, by definition, it's empty. Go up there. Draw the curtains. Lock the door. Go. To. Sleep.'

Hope dawned in the desperate eyes. 'I … couldn't. The first days of any murder investigation are vital.'

'Indeed they are. And they need to be led by someone who isn't ready to play the lead in *Night of the Living Dead*. If you have anything I need to know, tell me now. And then bugger off and go to sleep, for the love of God.'

'That would be nice. I am quite tired.'

As a contender for the understatement of the year, that was a surefire winner. His waste bin was overflowing with cups from the vending machine all of which, Jacquie suspected, had contained espresso. Happily, the cheapo coffee they used had about as much caffeine as a banana, so there was no health risk. Jacquie fished in her pocket and threw across the protein bar she had been saving for later. It landed neatly on his desk and she gave herself a secret high five. Usually anything she threw went anywhere but where it was aimed. Nolan would have been so proud.

'What's this?' Nolan would have been proud of Henry's wrinkled nose as well.

'It's not broccoli or anything, Henry. It's just a protein bar. Eat it. It will stop hunger waking you up. Now, quick, before you fall unconscious across your desk, is there anything I should know?'

'Hmm … actually, this isn't that bad … not much. Donald rang to say the pm reports are done in note form so you could go and get those. You know how Donald likes a visit from you. He's also collated the forensic stuff; I hope he never gets a real girlfriend because we'll be in the soup then. I had a look through the records of the Leadbetter thing again. It's the thing with the sons that bother me, the fact that they were left alone. Turns out, the Leadbetter boy was at a PGL week at the time. Everyone knew, apparently; several lads from the road went together. So it may have been planned to coincide.' He screwed up the wrapper and lobbed it into his bin. Even half asleep he was better at throwing than any Maxwell. 'So that may be something, may be not. To tell the truth, I can hardly tell.'

He levered himself to his feet and stretched.

'Are you sure you don't mind me catching some shuteye?'

'Absolutely.' Jacquie backed off into the corner so he could leave and stay six feet away. When would this stop being automatic, she wondered? Would it ever? 'Sleep tight. Switch your phone off. Or better still leave it here. Margaret will ring me if she can't get you.'

Henry turned and looked at her. 'She does that?'

'Oh, yes.' Jacquie raised an eyebrow. 'She'll be all right, Henry. Don't worry. You should see the lengths Mrs Troubridge has gone to. Mrs B has to wear binliners and has explicit instructions to spray everyone with bleach.'

'Good God! Does she?'

'Binliners, yes. Bleach, fortunately no.'

'But Mrs Troubridge is … how old? A million, something like that?'

'Henry. You're making jokes. Go and sleep.'

He stood there like a tired child. All he needed was a threadbare teddy and the picture would have been perfect.

'Wake me in an hour,' he said, sternly. There was credibility at stake here.

'Might do. Nightie night.' And, shooing him off, she went to get her coat. Donald awaited and she would need to keep things official. Give Donald an inch and he would inevitably take a mile. Before she left, she pressed the button for the front desk.

'Genghis?'

'Yup.'

'DCI Hall and I are out. Can you put all calls through to my mobile, including personal ones, please? But not if they are about loo roll. I've had about as many nosey neighbours as I can take.'

'Will do.' And the phone went down, with the totally unnecessary violence with which Genghis did everything.

She patted her pockets. Spare mask? Gloves? Phone? Check. Right – Donald, ho.

Jacquie hadn't been near the hospital since lockdown began, though like everyone else, she had watched the news. She was glad she could go round the back and park in the designated spaces outside the morgue, because the front looked like something out of the Seventh Circle of Hell. Traffic cones and signs seemed to have come there to breed because she had never seen so many. Arrows sent traffic in what looked like an endless loop. No entry signs seemed to be in the majority, with others admonishing people that they shouldn't be there anyway. A line of ambulances snaked out of the A&E canopy where usually there was one or, if there was a traffic accident, two. People – it was impossible to guess their sex – in layer after layer of PPE stood in the middle of it all, gesticulating at anyone foolish enough to venture near. A sign on the front door in letters so huge she could read them as she drove past read 'Strictly No Visitors'.

Round the back, it looked a little more like it usually did. Donald's car was unmistakeable. As a diehard *Supernatural* fan, he had tried his best to make his Renault Clio look as much like Dean Winchester's Impala as he could, but simply adding a silver stripe along the side and a new grille had not made it look that authentic, except to Donald, who loved it like a child. The other car in the spaces was a Ford C-Max, with *Frozen* sun shades on the rear windows. From this, Jacquie assumed that Philip McIndoe was the father of girls, though these days, who could be sure?

She tapped on the door as instructed by the hand written sign taped to the glass. After a moment, Donald's ghostly shape loomed up and he said, 'Yes? We're not accepting face to face callers. Please email your request.'

'Donald,' Jacquie said, trying not to sound exasperated. 'It's Jacquie. Apparently, you rang …'

The door was flung open to reveal Donald in all his glory. Lockdown had slowed him down for a day or so until he had found a way around it. He obeyed all the rules, but on his own terms. So his hospital-provided personal protection garments were adorned with as many fan badges as he could fit on them without actually tearing the fabric. Under the Perspex mask, his fabric mask was a print of his nose, mouth and chin, which Jacquie had seen advertised everywhere online but had hoped no one would actually buy. His gloves were standard issue but across his forehead, he wore a bandana. He nodded his approval to Jacquie's Wonder Woman mask and stepped aside.

'Have you lost a touch of weight, Donald?' Jacquie wouldn't usually make personal remarks, especially to Donald, but he really did look trimmer.

'How lovely of you to notice!' Donald was delighted. 'I know people talk about lockdown weight but, well, you know me, bit of a nibbler.'

Donald indeed had horrified Jacquie more than once by standing only inches from a corpse while eating a Macdonald's Whopper and slurping on a giant Pepsi, so nibbler wasn't quite the word, but it would do.

'Well, of course all that's gone by the board with these new regs.' He swept a hand from head to toe to show her what he meant, 'so I'm not eating in the day. It's dropping off me, to tell the truth. I'll have to go shopping soon, virtual, of course – my clothes don't fit me.'

'It's nice that there's an upside,' Jacquie said. 'DCI Hall said you have a report …'

The door into the lobby from the post mortem room swung open and Philip McIndoe edged through, using his hip to hold the door. His general stance on hygiene would have knocked those of Donald and Jim Astley into a cocked hat at the best of times, but now he was on a different plane.

'DI Maxwell?'

'*Carpenter*-Maxwell,' Donald said. He was always quick to remind everyone that Jacquie didn't have to be linked to the old geezer, as Donald always called her husband in the privacy of his head.

'Maxwell is fine, but do call me Jacquie.'

Donald fumed but his mask kept smiling.

'Philip. I've seen you around, of course. Welcome to our humble abode.'

'Donald tells us you have an interim report.'

'There isn't much to say about the actual cause of death that I couldn't tell you all at the scene. Blunt force, I would imagine a single blow to incapacitate, then deal with the wife, back to finish off the husband. Brutal, vicious but only enough to do the job, allowing for the fact that he couldn't stop to tell between blows. As to weapon, I'd speculate a ball pein hammer.' For a detective of any experience, or an afficionado of true crime, a weapon like that conjured up memories of Peter Sutcliffe, the Yorkshire Ripper, who used one of those by way of bloody introduction to any number of women.

'Were the bodies moved, do you think?'

McIndoe furrowed his brow, or what could be seen of it. 'I don't think so. Why?'

'No reason. Just thinking of a cold case. Anyway, Donald said you had the forensics here as well. That's new.'

'Just a matter of logistics, really,' McIndoe said. 'The head lab is more than the designated distance away and although we're exempt, we have the word from on high that we have to be seen to be doing our best. So they send everything here and we collate it. We're not supposed to print out, either, so I'll send it as an attachment, if that suits.'

'Absolutely.' Despite her husband's views, Jacquie had been hoping for a paperless office for years.

'But long story short, no fingerprints except those belonging to the deceased and their son. Or at least, we assume it's him; no one wants to fingerprint the poor kid. How is he, do we know? Shoved into the system, I expect.'

'No, actually. He's staying with some friends of ours.' Seeing his face, she explained. 'She was a school nurse, lovely woman. My husband and I saw him yesterday and he seems to be doing as well as can be expected.'

McIndoe looked askance. What the hell had he landed in here? A lab assistant as mad as a box of frogs and a DI who seemed to be able to do nothing without hubby holding her hand.

Jacquie was learning to read faces just by the position of one visible eyebrow. 'He is a teacher. He was there as

Appropriate Adult.'

'I see.'

But she doubted he did. One thing she didn't doubt was that Donald would have trashed Maxwell to McIndoe before she got out of the car park.

'The forensics. Anything interesting?'

Donald felt he had been silent for long enough. 'Dog hair.'

'Not surprising, really. They do have a dog.'

'How many?'

'Just the one.'

'There you are, then. It may be a clue. There were hairs from at least two dogs in the house. In other times, I would say they could be from a guest, but not at the moment, obviously. The house was very clean, the lab boys say. Like many people working from home, Mrs Ancaster had obviously become a bit of a cleaning junkie. She had Mrs Hinched the place till its pips squeaked.' Donald was more of a Cillit Bang person, but could see the charm of watching a stacked blonde hoover, so he knew all her hacks. 'They got loads of bicarb and white vinegar, all the usual suspects. So the dog hairs, they think, were recent additions, possibly from when they were walking the dog, but also could be from the killer.'

'Can you tell what dog?' Jacquie wasn't as up as she might have been on dog DNA, should there even be such a thing.

'There isn't a dog DNA register, if that's what you mean,' McIndoe said.

That solved that question, then.

'But you can make a guess, of course, from colour, length, texture etc. That's how we knew that these hairs – from the landing, by the way – were not from the family dog.'

'So …? Long, short, black, tan?'

'Yes.'

'Yes, what?' Jacquie was confused. Cat hairs she knew about. They were everywhere and clung to your clothes like glue. But dog hair was more of a grey area.

'There were some long ones, suggesting something like

a spaniel. Others were short, but that might be from a trim. The lab have reached out …'

Jacquie shuddered on Maxwell's behalf at the dreaded phrase.

'… to some groomers, but most of them are furloughed. I think Donald might have done something on Facebook, haven't you, Donald?'

'Facebook?' Donald's eyes rolled in disbelief. How *old* was this guy? 'Instagram, yes.'

'No names, no pack drill, of course. But he just asked if anyone had a dog with long and short hair, cream with a touch of tan. Best we've had so far is a rough coated Jack Russell.'

'But we don't know if it was from the killer?'

'Not for sure. It might literally have blown into the garden and come in on someone's shoes. If someone was grooming their dog, you know, outside …'

'I've only got cats,' Jacquie said, with a silent apology to the Count and the Chancellor, who owned her, rather than the other way round, 'and I've seen that. When we brush them outside, the little mats of hair off the brush often blow away.'

'Well then, there you are. My girls are both allergic, so we just have newts.' McIndoe didn't give many insights to his homelife and this was perhaps a share too far. 'Not affectionate, as pets go, but little trouble. Anyway,' he budged the door into the lab open with his hip; this conversation was over, to all intents and purposes, 'I must get on. Donald.'

The big lab assistant looked at Jacquie with puppy dog eyes which were at odds with his still rather substantial frame, but she just smiled as broadly as she could so he could tell despite the mask.

'Thank you both,' she said. 'Very helpful.' So, that was simple enough. Just swab every dog owner who had or had been near to a dog with long and short hairs of almost every colour dogs came in short of purple and that would be it. An arrest by nightfall. She sighed. Who'd be a detective?

FOURTEEN

Tim Cathcart wasn't a vindictive man – well, all right, he was, but he didn't hold grudges for as long as some. Here he was, nights after the Ancaster murders, sitting in an unmarked car along Broadgate Avenue. He'd seen both the *Stakeout* films back in the day and in terms of boredom, they didn't come close. They didn't touch the endless cloying monotony of it. Especially, they didn't question the point of it all. What were the bloody CID thinking? All that crap about killers returning to the scene of the crime went out with Arthur Conan Doyle and it had never been a proven fact.

Cathcart shouldn't have left the car, but his left buttock was numb as buggery already and he'd only just come on duty. He got out, trying to make his leg work and wandered along the path next to next door's hedge. The smell of privet was nauseating, close up and personal like this as the leaves gave off the lingering heat of the day, but it was activity beyond it that held his attention. The outside lights were on at Number 65 to take the edge off the encroaching dusk and that vicious old biddy Bencher was kneeling over a bed of potentillas, dead-heading ruthlessly and weeding where soil dared show in the mass of groundcover. Cathcart hadn't been privy to any of the CID reports in circulation; the graveyard gig meant that he spent his days in bed, blissfully unaware of the Covid regulation hell that normal people had to go through. He didn't know that the Bencher woman had been abandoned by her husband and that she barely had a good word to say about anybody, except, perhaps, the Ancasters.

He peered through the privet. The old girl wasn't as old as all that and still cut quite a figure in her jeans and sweater. Cathcart wasn't a film buff like Peter Maxwell. Had he been, Amelia Bencher would have vaguely reminded him of Ava Gardner before the bags got in the way. The letters MILF crept unbidden into his mind but he dismissed them – what would his Mary say? Mrs Bencher was humming to herself, having, apparently, lost all sense of time. she was throwing weeds into a bucket, the hum accentuated by every thrust of her trowel, every clip of her secateurs. Cathcart checked his watch. Only another nine hours, thirty seven minutes to go.

Back in the car, he checked the radio. Usual banal bollocks along with the static. Bit of an argy-bargy at the Cock-a-Hoop on the seafront, which was serving drinks to take away only. A couple of the regulars had tried to barge in and sit in their usual seats and it had taken four uniforms to dislodge them. Some octogenarians could be unusually strong, or so it seemed. Report of a break-in at Fortescue's, the jewellers in Albemarle Street. Most of that would keep until the morning, but Cathcart would give his eye teeth about now for some action.

Back at the nick, he knew, the desk man would be sifting through the hate-crime register which had about as much relevance to actual police work as Enid Blyton's incomparable *Noddy Goes To The Toilet*. And with that thought in mind, Tim Cathcart switched off the radio and drifted into the Land of Nod …

… From which he was awakened with a jerk. He sat bolt upright, his bum numb again, and looked around. Broadgate Avenue was silent as always. He checked his watch; nearly half past one. Bugger. He'd slept through two of his checks. Now he'd have to forge the odd entry on his log, back-dating a few mythical cars passing. He could probably work in a few canoodlers on their way home from a bit of bubble-bursting, jotting down an appropriate time but not any number plates

– that would be totally unfair as well as being the grand opening of a can of worms.

He was suddenly aware of the outside lights still on at Number 65. That stupid old trout, the one with the still-reasonable tits, must have forgotten to turn them off. Shit! His leg was really giving him gyp now and he had to go walkabout. He had a cast-iron bladder so that was never a problem, but cramp, that was something else. He stood outside the murder house, all darkness and mystery. The gentlemen of the press had been besieging it for days, but once the press conferences had come and gone and sleepy Leighford sunk back into its slumbers, their numbers dwindled. There was nothing so ludicrous as socially-distanced paparazzi – scruffy cameramen behind the pale blue masks, longing for a fag or a pint or both, all of them dreaming of that life-changing moment when the photo op of the century came their way. Perhaps Elvis would come rolling out of No 67 or the Loch Ness monster or …

Cathcart was back at the privet hedge, the night air appreciably cooler than it had been when he was there last. Shit! No, that wasn't possible; Amelia Bencher was still there, kneeling on the edge of the lawn facing her flower beds. Cathcart checked his watch again – one thirty four. Who the hell gardened at that time of night? And there was something else. Mrs Bencher wasn't humming now. There was no sound of clipping and trowelling. In fact, she wasn't moving at all.

When Henry Hall had given Cathcart this gig, he had insisted on plain clothes. No swat vest, no cuffs, no radio. What Cathcart refused to relinquish however was his truncheon. The damn thing didn't fit well in his pocket and almost certainly contributed to his cramps, but even in sleazy Leighford, he wasn't leaving that behind. There was a murderer on the loose when all was said and done. Cathcart flicked the club out, just in case. There was no way through the hedge, so he backtracked to the road and dashed up the driveway. There was a wooden door to the left of the house and he shoulder-barged it open. The lights hurt his eyes, flood-lighting the garden with its neat flowerbeds and trimmed lawn. A little fountain tinkled in the centre, the light catching the water beads like a shower of liquid stars.

'Mrs Bencher.' Cathcart's voice shattered the stillness of the night, intruding on tranquillity. Nothing. The policeman tightened his grip on his truncheon, checking the hedges, the house, the garage front and the shed. He could see nothing out of the ordinary, certainly, no sinister shadow lurking, ready to pounce.

'Mrs Bencher?' He touched the woman's right shoulder. For a moment, she knelt there, immobile. Then she toppled sideways, in slow motion like a calving glacier, and he could see that she had been resting her chin on a long-handled dibber thrust into the soil. In the glare of the lights, Cathcart could see the drying blood clinging to the woman's hair, soaking into her jumper. Her mouth was slightly open, her eyelids drooped, frozen in that second that someone had killed her.

Alf Rogers didn't get out that much, especially now that this new disease was tearing its way through the country. His family, or his bubble as they stupidly called themselves, said he had dementia, but that couldn't be right. He was as sharp as a tack. It was them what had dementia, if anyone should ask, though they didn't, not as he could remember, anyway. That morning, though, as he opened his living room curtains, he found himself more confused than ever. For days now, he'd watched the comings and goings at No 67 opposite – the ambulances, the police cars, those blokes in their science fiction suits and an army of pressmen strung all the way along the pavement.

Then, he'd watched as they took it all away – the tent, the white and blue tape. 'There's been a murder, Dad,' his Milly had told him, 'or more precisely, two – them at No 67. The Ancasters.'

'The Ancasters?' he'd repeated in his thin, reedy voice. 'Who'd want to kill them?'

'That's what the police are trying to find out, Alf,' Edgar had told him. Edgar had less patience with the old git than his wife. Ever since her father had moved in with them years ago, Edgar had warned it would never work out. And he'd missed a golden opportunity; there'd be no chance of a care home for the old bastard now – they were all no-go areas. When Edgar was feeling particularly bloody, he'd smile to himself at the prospect of driving past old Alf's care home every Sunday, waving to him through protective layers of glass. If only! Instead of which, the mad old duffer was right here, in Edgar's castle, getting under his feet and leaving his dentures in inappropriate places.

But the old duffer wasn't wrong, not this time. Oh, he sometimes was, he conceded that. Thinking that nice Mrs May was still prime minister, looking for his pipe in the microwave, that sort of thing. But this was different. The tent. The tape. The police cars. They were all back again. Except that this time, they were outside No 65.

Outside No 65, PC Tim Cathcart looked like shit. Not only had he been up all the previous night – well, part of the previous night – he'd found a body. The body of a woman who had been murdered on his watch. He'd called it in, of course, on his car radio, and waited for all hell to be let loose, with blaring sirens, flashing lights and the whole cacophony of armed response. It was routine in these days of growing gun violence. At least two officers attending any crime scene were armed to the teeth. He thanked his lucky stars that he hadn't already faked his log – that would have taken some explaining.

Cathcart had spoken to Jacquie Carpenter Maxwell who had been rousted out of bed along Columbine at a little after three. By half past, she was there, dressed to kill, as it were, without so much as a slug of coffee inside her. By contrast, Henry Hall was wide awake and bushy-tailed – his nap in the family room had made a new man of him and as a bonus, Margaret had been recommended a sleep app by Sylvia Matthews and it appeared that Matthew McConaughey could put a woman to sleep in thirty seconds, something which Hall would have doubted had he not seen it for himself.

'Coincidences, Jacquie,' Hall was saying as he followed her into the house. The ambulance had come and gone, so had Philip McIndoe, muttering about people not having the good grace to be murdered during working hours.

'Different MO, though,' Jacquie said. SOCO had already been over the house with their various gizmos and declared the kitchen a clear area, so that was where Henry and his DI sat, on Amelia Bencher's excruciating stools. Jacquie was not short as women policemen went, but she couldn't reach the floor and even that silly little rung between the stool's legs was at the wrong height for her.

They had both seen the dead woman's corpse in situ, but now was the time for some initial conclusions to be drawn. 'What did you see?' he asked her. Long ago, Henry Hall had discovered the hard way that two people had seen one thing and remembered it totally differently. The suspect was short, at least six foot one. He had sandy coloured hair that turned out to be dark. Oh, and he had a dodgy left eye, sort of on the wonk. Come to think of it, he could have been a woman.

'We know who she was,' Jacquie started from basics. 'Amelia Bencher, aged sixty or thereabouts, probably between husbands, if what she says is true about the Opium addict in Scunthorpe.'

Hall's eyes nearly fell out of his head. 'Opium?' he said, aghast.

'You had to be there, I suppose,' Jacquie said. 'We'll have to trace him, the husband.'

'Of course,' Hall nodded. 'I think when all this pandemic nonsense is over we'll find an awful lot of how's your father coming to light; one night stands turning into a couple of months, that sort of thing. Cause of death?'

'McIndoe was cagey, like pathologists always are,' she said, 'but it looks like a pruning knife, the kind you'd use on fairly stout branches, delivered from behind. One clean cut, McIndoe thought.'

'And then she was posed?' Hall moved the conversation on.

'Yes, but in an unusual way.'

'I suppose weeding your way into the hereafter is a bit unusual,' Hall offered.

'Well, because the victim is female, we have to assume a sexual dimension.'

Hall nodded.

'But there was no sign of anything untoward. Clothes weren't disarranged. No obvious signs of violence except for her head wound.'

'So he … and I'm sticking with that for the moment … comes up from behind, hits her with the pruning knife, then adjusts her body into a kneeling position and balances her on her chin on the handle of a dibber.'

'To hold her up, yes. The question is, why.'

This had been bothering Hall since he arrived. 'To buy time,' he said.

'Come again.'

'The woman was gardening. If you look along the lawn's edge from the house, the grass is flattened where she'd been kneeling. Had one of those padded kneeler jobbies. Cathcart says he had seen her weeding.'

'She was working her way along.' Jacquie wasn't a great gardener, but even she weeded sometimes.

'That's right. Whoever killed her wanted people to think she was still alive and still weeding.'

'In the middle of the night?'

'Aha, but it wasn't supposed to be the middle of the night, was it? As far as the killer knew, it would be well and truly day before anyone noticed Amelia. Anybody passing, coming up the drive with a delivery, for instance, would see a woman with her back to the road, kneeling, gardening. It's not as if these days anyone is going to call round unexpectedly with a "coo-eee, it's only me". Delivery men don't engage, they just dump the parcel, take a quick picture and run.'

'Anything from SOCO yet?'

Hall looked from left to right. 'Miracles take a little longer, Jacquie,' he said, 'you know that. Between you and me, the house is a waste of time. The encounter, whatever form it took, took place in the garden. If it had been in the house, there'd be signs, blood at the very least. I haven't seen any.'

'Nor I,' she nodded. 'Can we get back to coincidences, guv?' she asked.

'I suppose we have to,' Hall said. 'Three murders in adjacent properties over a four day period.'

'If somebody's got it in for *all* the residents of Broadgate Avenue, you'd think he'd start at one end. Even so, we've got more differences than similarities.'

'One body rather than two, obviously.' Hall began the list.

'Different MO. Weapon of choice this time is a pruning knife, not a blunt object.'

'Attack from behind, not the front.'

'Murder outside, not inside.'

'Body posed, rather than merely abandoned.'

'Which could be, in the case of the Ancasters, because of the untimely arrival of Marcus. Perhaps the killer had planned to do something elaborate but the boy put the mockers on that.'

'Murder weapon,' it was Hall's turn, 'was simply something that came to hand – and was left behind – rather than something he brought to next door with him.'

'Which leaves us,' Jacquie took up the theme, 'with a home invader who becomes a garden invader and an organised, careful killer who becomes a disorganised chaotic killer four days later.'

'Or?' Hall was prompting her.

'Or we're talking about two different killers entirely,' she said.

'Which brings us back,' he nodded, 'as vicious circles will, to coincidences.'

The dawn was well and truly breaking as the policeman from the Lincolnshire force pressed the doorbell of the rather elegant house in Frodingham, the suburb of Scunthorpe where Charles Bencher was sitting out his lockdown. He had told his wife the address but she preferred to say he was in Scunthorpe, a word rather more given to venom when said out loud than Frodingham, which simply sounded rather pleasant, which it was.

The policeman stood back and scanned the front of the house. Four bedrooms, unless he missed his guess, couple of bathrooms. Nice. If you had to spend lockdown away from home, there were certainly worse places. His brother-in-law, for example, was stuck in a Travelodge on the M4 and that was no walk in the park, for sure. But this … nice. Very nice.

He was awakened from his reverie by the sound of a window being thrown back in the bedroom just above his head.

'Yes?'

The policeman narrowed his eyes against the growing light. 'Mr Bencher?'

'Who's asking?'

'I am, sir. Police Constable Adrian Fetching. We have been asked to visit you, sir, rather than call.'

'I am Charles Bencher, yes. Why are you visiting? Is it my bloody wife again, accusing me of breaking lockdown?'

'I'd rather not discuss this by shouting up at a window, sir, if you don't mind. Could you please come downstairs?' PC Fetching was not a happy copper these days. When those three dimwits on the telly had announced this lockdown, he had been on the verge of taking his sergeant's exams and then, the world would have been his lobster. Now, instead of using his brain a bit more – and, despite outward appearances, PC Fetching did have a brain – he was walking round his patch at the regulation two and a half miles an hour, stopping old ladies from feeding the pigeons and checking any groups of two to make sure they were a household. It was starting to get on his wick. Plus, he had a cold he didn't seem able to shift – with his luck, it would be sodding Covid.

'I was in bed.' Bencher was truculent and with good reason. He had moved in with alacrity when Amanda had made the offer, only to discover that when domesticity struck, so did she – from being an animal in the back of his company Range Rover, she had become positively stingy in her super-king bed. However, that morning, something in the air had kicked in and he had woken to find some rather pleasant bits of her pressed against some rather enthusiastic bits of him.

So, no, he really didn't want to go downstairs. 'And she's always kicking up a fuss, bloody woman. I'm tired of it.'

'Please come downstairs, sir.' Fetching pressed the doorbell again and the Westminster chimes rang through the house, on and on, getting tangled up and sounding like music from hell.

'All right, all right. Take your finger off the bell, for God's sake. I'm coming down.'

Fetching stood back so that he would be at least the statutory distance when the door finally opened. He heard feet thumping down the stairs and a muffled oath as Bencher stood on a discarded dog chew on the mat. Finally, with much bolt-drawing and chain rattling, the door was flung open and Bencher stood there, pyjamas hastily flung on and hair tousled. Fetching had heard stories about the merry widow Amanda Grier and his first thought was that she could probably have done better. However, in lockdown, all cats were grey.

'Mr Bencher?'

'For God's sake, man. We've established that. Yes.'

'Do you have any form of identification?'

'I'm in my pyjamas, man. Of course not. Do you want to see my interesting birthmark in the shape of the island of Corsica? No? I thought not. Spit it out and let me get back to bed, please. You'll wake my landlady otherwise.'

'Landlady? I see, sir. That would be Mrs Grier, would it?'

'Yes. Nice old soul. Now, what is it?'

'Is your wife Mrs Amelia Bencher, sir?'

'Yes.' Bencher rolled his eyes. So it was her, stirring it as usual.

'I'm afraid to tell you, sir, that your wife was found dead in the early hours of this morning.'

Bencher stepped back and went visibly paler. 'Sorry … say what?'

'Your wife, Mrs Amelia Bencher, was found dead in the garden this morning, in the early hours.'

'My God. What was it? A heart attack or something? Poor old Amelia. I mean … she could be a pain in the arse but … I can't believe it. She always seemed as strong as a horse.'

'I'm afraid I can't go into details, sir. The local police will be in touch later today. Is the number we have on file the correct one for you?' The PC rattled off a string of numbers so quickly that Bencher had to request a repeat.

'Yes, that's it. I … I'm sorry, officer. I must have seemed very uncaring before. But …'

'I understand, sir.' Fetching put his notebook back in his pocket. '*Nil nisi bonum*, sir.' Goddamn it, the man thought to himself. That bloody sergeant's exam would have been a walk in the park. Out loud he added, as per the sensitivity training they had all had in preparation for lockdown duties, 'I'm sorry for your loss, sir. Can I help you with anything?'

'Umm … no, no, thank you. I'll … I'll just …' Bencher stood in the doorway as if he couldn't remember how to walk away.

'I expect you'll need to tell your landlady, sir,' Fetching said, stifling a grin behind his mask. 'I won't keep you.' And with a respectful touch of his cap's brim, he walked down the drive to where his partner sat behind the wheel of his patrol car. He looked back and saw Bencher had finally closed the door.

'How'd it go, Ade?' his partner asked.

'He's gone to tell his landlady.' Fetching managed to keep his voice from wobbling, but only just.

'Landlady? Amanda 'Get it out and don't spare the horses' Grier? Oh, that's a good one. That *is* a good one. Next stop?'

Fetching pulled out his notebook. 'High Street. Apparently, the bakery is letting people enter the shop, in defiance of regulations.'

'Right.' The driver let in the clutch and moved out into the non-existent traffic. 'It's early. They'll probably still have doughnuts.' He chuckled. 'Landlady! He'd better move out soon or he'll be there forever. Remember that last one? Oh, my Lord.'

'I dunno. This one might be a bit long in the tooth for her. But a murder, eh? Some coppers get all the luck.'

FIFTEEN

It was nothing like a normal morning, Chez Maxwell, but it was almost what had started to seem like normal. Mums had disappeared – nothing new there, since Nolan was a baby he had been used to her random comings and goings – but happily, Dads was in situ and this got Nolan out of what might have become a deep, dark hole. His parents were agreed, he was an amazing child with many talents and many more to be mined when the time was right, but one thing that needed work was his tendency to only tell any news to one person. It didn't need to be an important person in his life, anyone currently with a pulse would do. It was in this fashion that his mother only found out about his solo in the Carol concert by chatting with the school dinner lady and that his father found out about his prize for reading (aged four) by getting into conversation with Plocker – not an easy job at the best of times as Plocker was not much of a natterer. As he got older, Nolan knew he had this failing, but knowing it and doing something about it were two very different things.

'Dads?'

'Yes, mate.' Maxwell sometimes wished he kept a diary, so he could have kept a tally of how many times the day had begun like this.

'You know about school.'

'In principle.' Maxwell ladled Marmite on his toast. With the Mem elsewhere, it seemed silly not to.

'And you know about Zoom.'

'Oddly enough, I do.' Leighford nick was still agog that it was a Maxwell Zoom call that had alerted everyone to the Ancasters' murder.

'Have you got any today?'

Maxwell glanced at the planner on the wall. 'It looks like that's a nope, mate. I've got some tutorials with Year Thirteen, but I'll get the schedule from the office later. And they're on the phone. Why do you ask? Need the laptop?'

'I do, sort of.' Nolan dropped a gobbet of butter down to the waiting cats and tried to look innocent.

'Stop trying to clog the cats' arteries,' Maxwell said, without looking up. 'And tell me what you're planning.' Practically since the two Maxwell men had first looked into each other's eyes, they could read minds. It was pointless to deny.

'*I'm* not planning anything.' The child was outraged. 'It's school. They did the planning.'

'Of what?'

'Take a Parent To School Day. Only on Zoom, of course.'

'Of course. And when is this day of days? More milk?'

Nolan risked certain death. 'I'm good, thanks. I mean,' he adjusted his statement in light of the baleful gleam in his parent's eye, 'I've had enough for now.'

'So, when is it?'

Nolan looked everywhere but at his father. 'Today?'

'Are you not sure?'

'Yes, I am. Today.'

'When?'

'What time is it now?'

'Five to nine.'

Nolan looked down at his hands and did some furious maths. 'In twenty minutes.'

'On Zoom.'

'Yes.'

Maxwell gave a longing look at the remaining toast and the pot of Marmite, gleaming blackly in the morning sun. He pushed himself away from the table. 'Okay. Go and brush your hair. Are you supposed to be in uniform?'

Nolan looked stricken. 'Yes. It's for the website.'

'There's a clean one in the top left hand drawer in your bedroom.' Maxwell was becoming something of a domestic goddess in lockdown. 'I'll see you in the garden in ten. Let's knock 'em dead, shall we? What do you want me to say? I don't want to embarrass you.'

'You know that thing you do sometimes when I can't sleep. The stories about the kings and queens in order?'

Maxwell looked at his son. 'Yes.'

'That.' And with his best showstopper yet, Nolan was out of the door and up the stairs as if the hounds of hell were after him.

Ten minutes later, they were sitting at the table in the garden, looking as though butter wouldn't melt in their mouths.

And that was why they didn't hear the ambulance.

Henry Hall was still feeling hot to trot when he and his DI got back to the Nick. He breezed into his office and sat down at his desk, fingers interlaced and ready for action. Jacquie had got her second wind, but even so, stood in the doorway, leaning against the jamb for much needed support.

'This sleep lark,' Henry said, 'it's a good idea, isn't it?'

'You should try to make it into a habit,' Jacquie said. 'It's done you the world of good.'

'You, on the other hand,' he said to her, 'do look rather knackered. Please don't go and complain about sexism, will you? I mean it with the best intentions.'

'I don't think there is a tiredism department,' she said. 'I wouldn't mind a nice deskbound morning, though, if there's anything I can do from there.'

'Look, tell you what,' Hall said, leaning back. 'Why don't you try a bit of working from home? If it applies to every other government department, I don't see why you shouldn't have a crack at it. Just today, mind – but it doesn't bother me and you'll feel the benefit.'

Jacquie's eyes widened. 'That would be great, guv, but … what if there's an emergency?'

'You only live down the road. If someone else is killed in Broadgate Avenue, heaven forbid, then I'll let you know, I promise. Look, take the list of numbers we need to call – Mr Bencher hasn't been spoken to yet, although I understand the local plod in Scunthorpe have visited – and do that. Send the reports in encrypted and then take the rest of the day. We'll be fine. Apart from cross questioning joggers and moving on people having a sip of tea on park benches, there seems little to do.'

'But … the murder …'

'Make the calls. Wait. Tomorrow will be just the same, whatever you do.'

Jacquie didn't need telling twice. Twirling her keys, having grabbed the list of numbers, she was heading home in a twinkling.

Alison McGuire didn't get out much, any more than anybody else. Her role in the case had kept her in the nick since Day One, but now someone, probably Jacquie, her unofficial mentor, had taken pity on her and let her out.

Even with the mask, fresh air felt good, even if she was standing feet from the murder site. The edge of the lawn and the flower bed was double taped and there was a blue and white cordon around the whole garden, front and back. The paparazzi had come back, like flies around shit but most of them were at the front, where SOCO people and plainclothes men and women came and went. There were only three cameramen on the path at the back, chatting quietly as well as they could, given that they were six feet apart. She wondered whether anyone would still be able to master the art of muttering when all this was over or whether it would become a rare skill, like spinning or skinning rabbits.

Alison had engaged with the photographers briefly when they arrived and had then done her best to ignore them. By late morning, she'd have killed for a cup of tea and Amelia Bencher's kitchen with every amenity known to man beckoned from beyond the cordon.

'What's all this, then?'

The screech of rubber on gravel had made her spin

round first and now she stood facing a cyclist, gleaming in pointless plastic helmet and shimmering in lycra. The paps moved away slightly.

'This is a crime scene, sir,' Alison told him.

'No shit, Sherlock. Yeah, I remember reading about that in the *Advertiser*. I thought you'd have moved it all on by now.'

'This is another one,' one of the cameramen said. 'First one was next door.'

'Bugger me.' It wasn't so much an invitation as an expression of astonishment. 'So, what are you doing about it, then?'

'My job, sir.' Alison could feel her knuckles whitening, but this sort of question came with her sort of job.

'Look,' the cyclist said. 'I live around here. I've got a wife and kids. We've got a right to be protected.'

'And I've got a right not to be run over by a lycra lout.'

All eyes turned. No one had heard him arrive, but he stood there now, like an ox in the furrow, his golden Labrador at his heels.

'You what?' The cyclist was clearly scowling behind his mask.

'The last time I looked,' the man said, 'this is a public *foot*path. It is not intended for some pushy bastard who wouldn't know a rule of the road from the hole between his ears.'

'Did you hear that?' The cyclist's voice rose to a crescendo. 'Can he talk to me like that?'

'I'm afraid he can, sir,' Alison told him. 'Because in essence, he is right. This *is* a footpath.'

'Well, excuse me for breathing,' the cyclist said.

'Yes,' the dog-walker said. 'You breathing is a tad unfortunate.'

'Would you mind dismounting, sir?' Alison asked, 'and wheeling your bike the rest of the way?'

'Fuck off!' the cyclist snapped and pedalled off in a hail of gravel.

Alison spoke into the radio on her shoulder. 'Cyclist, Geoff, rounding the corner in two. If you've got that book handy, you might throw it at him. Tyres, brakes, gears, the usual.'

Geoff squawked an 'I'd be delighted' by return and the dog-walker nodded appreciatively.

'Well done, officer,' he said. 'Bad business this, eh?' He was nodding towards the house.

'Indeed,' Alison said. 'Do you walk this way regularly?'

'Quite often,' the man said. 'Paul Mitchell. Oh …' he had instinctively held out his hand but withdrew it.

'I'll settle for an elbow,' she smiled and the paparazzi looked at each other.

Alison and Paul, thrown together by a chance meeting at a murder scene duly bumped their forearms together. 'Did you know Mrs Bencher, who lived here?'

'Vaguely, yes. When you say "lived", do I assume …?'

Alison hesitated. To get information back, you had to give some out. The trick was knowing how much. 'I'm afraid Mrs Bencher is dead, yes.'

'Murdered?' one of the paparazzi asked, fiddling with his camera.

'Yes,' Alison told him.

'Like the Ancasters, eh?' another cameraman chipped in.

'Not exactly, sir,' she said. 'Mr Mitchell, were you here yesterday?'

'I was,' he said. 'Working from home now, of course. Don't tell that buffoon who just left, but I normally cycle to work. Phaedo's never had so much exercise.'

The dog wagged his tail endearingly at the sound of his name.

'What time was this?' Alison asked.

'Oh, later than this. Must have been … late afternoon, I suppose.'

'Did you see Mrs Bencher as you passed?'

'I did, actually; she was in the garden, having a rest on her recliner. I waved, but there was no response.'

'Can I ask where you live, sir?' Alison was pushing envelopes, but nothing ventured, nothing gained.

'Are you allowed to do that?' one of the paparazzi

asked.

'No, no,' Mitchell laughed. 'It's quite all right. I live at 16 Anderson, round the corner and back a bit. Near the Arndale Centre.'

Alison knew it. 'You say you knew Mrs Bencher vaguely. In what way?'

There was a snigger from one of the paparazzi. 'Better get your lawyer present, mate, the way this is going.'

'Which way *is* this going, officer?' Mitchell asked.

'Just routine, sir, I assure you,' Alison said. 'Mrs Bencher?'

'I'm a freelance accountant. I did some work for Mr Bencher, Amelia's husband, a while back. I only met her once. She seemed a little frosty, shall we say?' He tugged gently on Phaedo's lead. The dog was getting bored and next thing he would be peeing up this nice woman's leg, always a way to make a conversation go downhill.

'We may need to talk to you again, sir,' Alison said. 'You may be one of the last people to see Mrs Bencher alive. You and Phaedo.'

'No problem,' Mitchell said and walked on. He hadn't gone far, just around the curve in the footpath in fact, when the paparazzo who had been at his elbow for the last few minutes was there again.

'Look, mate,' he leaned in as far as social distancing would allow. 'I don't want to alarm you at all, but I've been around coppers for years. All very cutesy, cutesy, pretty little woman PC and all, but you see what she's done, don't you?'

'Er …'

'Linked you with a murdered woman. And her husband. *And* she knows where you live. You know those bastards are obsessed with the two Ms and an incongruous O, don't you?'

'Umm?'

The pap held up his fingers. 'Means, Motive, Opportunity. When she clocks off duty here, she'll be round the nick chewing you over with CID. Expect a visit, any day now.'

'Yes, well, thank you … er … I won't be reading any

of this in the local rag, will I?'

'The *Advertiser*? Don't make me laugh. I don't work for them. They change editors pretty well every week. I couldn't handle that. No, freelance, me. I can control things that way. I don't really do change.'

'Thank you.' The dog walker watched the man go back to the little gaggle outside the back gate of the late Amelia Bencher's house. 'I think.'

Letting herself in to the house, Jacquie still couldn't really believe her luck. A beautiful day in the neighbourhood, not a cloud in the sky. There were hardly any flights because no one could go anywhere and no one wanted strangers anyway, so the skies were not just blue, they were quiet. The slight hum of traffic which could occasionally be heard from the A27 to the north was now so little it might just as well have not existed. Even the raised voices from the enforced lockdown couple across the road seemed to have abated. Rumour had it he had gone back to his wife, but no one knew for sure. Inside the house all was just as peaceful. A peep round Nolan's door showed him deep into an interactive geography lesson, diligently tracing an outline of France on screen with a pencil – she hoped it was an actual Apple pencil rather than a pencil, then stopped herself; this was the boy, not the man of the house, so there was no need to worry. A muttering from the sitting room and a glance at the planner in the kitchen confirmed that Maxwell was busy talking some Year Thirteen down off a ledge. So, all was well, in Maxwell-land, if not elsewhere.

Mobile and coffee in hand, she wandered down into the garden and sat at a shady corner of the table. Metternich and Bismarck immediately arrived from nowhere, one jumping up on the table to nudge her under the chin, the other sitting on her feet. She smiled as she dug her fingers into Metternich's thick pelt. They had become a team in record time; if they were even just a little bit bigger, nothing smaller than a horse would still be alive in a five mile radius. As it was, they confined themselves to the smaller rodentia.

She took a sip of coffee and got out her list. On top was

the mobile number of Charles Bencher. She had had a text from PC Fetching to say that he had been informed of his loss. There was no detail and Jacquie decided that this could mean either that he was prostrate or couldn't give a fart. She suspected the latter but decided to keep an open mind. She touched the numbers and put the phone on speaker. Judging from the silence all around, there was no one to hear.

The phone rang twice before it was answered and she could tell from the outset that the grieving widower was in a terrific snit. 'Yes?'

'Mr Charles Bencher? This is Detective Inspector Carpenter-Maxwell here, of the Leighford Police.'

'Is it, indeed? You took your time.'

'I do beg your pardon, sir. Our usual practice of course is to do these things in person, but as you are so far away and as travelling is to be kept to a minimum, we have to do it second hand, as it were.'

'That moronic bobby knocked me up at something stupid o'clock. And it's nearly midday now. So what's been happening in between that you couldn't ring?'

Jacquie had felt sorry for the amorphous Mr Bencher before, but now simply couldn't help thinking that they had clearly deserved each other. 'I thought perhaps you might need some time to assimilate …'

'Assimilate? Are you mental? I can understand being told my wife has carked at dawn without too much need to consider.'

'Perhaps I misspoke. To grieve, then. To come to terms.'

'Met my wife, have you?'

'I did meet Mrs Bencher, yes.' Jacquie almost knew what was coming next and although the man sounded like an unmitigated git, she did see his point.

'Well, then don't be hypocritical. We were separated all but the shouting and if it wasn't for this bloody stupid lockdown I would have moved out lock, stock and barrel and would have been suing her for my share of the house.'

Jacquie heard a laugh in the background and the phone went dead for a moment. What was happening under the cover of the mute button, she could only guess.

'My landlady has just pointed out that that is no longer an issue.' He was back and just as belligerent as before. 'I have pointed out that that was a very tasteless remark, but her point is well made. Was the house … damaged at all?'

'Damaged?'

'Yes. I'm assuming that it was a robbery gone wrong, like the one next door. You'd hardly credit the cheek of it, would you, trying again more or less in the same spot. Still, burglars aren't the brightest apples in the barrel, are they?'

'This wasn't a burglary, Mr Bencher. Your wife was killed in the garden.'

'In … in the garden? We've got nothing of value in the garden.'

'I think, Mr Bencher, that you need to stop thinking of this as a burglary. Your wife was killed with a garden implement and, as far as we can tell at this point in the enquiry, this was a targeted attack. No other homes in the road have been so targeted, so we will need to know the names of any friends …'

'There aren't any.'

'Family …'

'Just me.'

'Or anyone who may have had a grudge against your wife.'

This time, the laugh in the background went unnoticed by Charles Bencher. There was a long pause before he answered. 'She was a pain in the arse in many ways, Detective Inspector, but … at heart, Amelia was a good enough sort. She was nosy, critical, she found it impossible to believe she wasn't always in the right but … well, that's loads of people, isn't it? I could name a dozen worse than her who haven't been killed.'

'So … no one, then.'

'Is … was she still going on about next door? Not the dead ones, the other ones?'

'She had made a recent complaint, yes.' Jacquie was cagey. There were those at the nick who were beginning to think along those lines but the couple in question didn't know when enough was enough when it came to having sex against an uncurtained window – Alf had told Edgar time and again about it, but it had just been put down to his dementia making him go a bit funny – but they didn't seem to have an aggressive bone in their usually conjoined bodies. 'We followed it up and took no further action.'

'That's you lot all over, though, isn't it?' Bencher snarled down the phone. 'No further action when you've got a couple of nymphomaniac serial killers on the rampage but you'll hound a perfectly respectable member of the public for drinking a cup of tea on a park bench. I read the papers.' His voice was becoming shrill. 'I know what's going on. You lock us all up and then …'

Jacquie could hear soothing noises in the background, against the increasingly disjointed shouts from Charles Bencher. After a moment, a woman's voice came over the phone.

'I'm terribly sorry, Detective Inspector. Can you call back? I'm afraid Charles has been taken ill and I'll have to get him to rest for a bit.'

'Oh. Oh, all right, then.' Jacquie could only imagine the mayhem at the other end, with Bencher flinging himself about with no one to take an actual jab at. 'I hope he feels better soon. For the record, may I have your name, please?' Was it her imagination, or was there just a whiff on Opium on the air?

'Of course. I'm Amanda Grier. I'm Mr Bencher's …' there was a pause. 'Mr Bencher's fiancé. Perhaps in an hour, if that's okay? He'll be a bit better by then.'

And the connection was cut, leaving Jacquie looking at a blank screen, reflecting the sky above. She shrugged and sent Henry a very quick text, to the effect that Mr Bencher was currently half cut and probably permanently aggressive, also that he was already engaged to his 'landlady'. Drink had clearly been taken so she wasn't speaking out of turn – hopefully, in an hour, a couple of pints of black coffee would have done their work. She pressed a button and spoke to her phone. 'Alexa, set a reminder for one hour from now.'

'What's the reminder for?' the pleasant woman's voice

asked.

'Callback.'

'What's the reminder for?'

'For the love of … Callback.' Jacquie enunciated a little more clearly.

'Okay. I've set a reminder for one hour.'

Jacquie chugged her cooling coffee and, closing her eyes turned her face up to the sun. It was so peaceful. In this dystopian world they were in, why did anyone bother to murder anyone else? It seemed so much more unnecessary even than usual. She practiced some yogic breathing for a moment or two and then, she heard the sobbing.

Sixteen

Jacquie's head came up with a jerk, breathing forgotten. She jumped up and was five paces towards the house when she realised that that was not where the sobs were coming from; they were coming from over the fence, on Mrs Troubridge's side. She hauled a garden chair across to the fence, balancing it precariously on the uneven baked earth which in almost any other garden would have been a flowerbed, and looked over. Mrs B., divested of her binliners and multiple masks, was sitting on the edge of a reclining seat, bolt upright, a cigarette in one hand, a handkerchief in another. The sobs racked her, making the chair shake.

'Mrs B.? Mrs B.? Is everything all right?'

The woman took a huge drag of the cigarette and seemed to hold the smoke in forever before blowing it out, shaking her head as she did so.

'Not really, Mrs M., to tell the truth. No, it isn't.'

Jacquie could see where she was coming from. Locked up 24/7 with Mrs Troubridge would take a toll out of anyone, even someone as tough as Mrs B. She didn't want to say anything else, for fear of putting her foot in it, so she made herself as comfortable as possible on the fence and waited.

Eventually, the cigarette smoked clear down to the filter, Mrs B. spoke. 'It's Jessica. I'm surprised Mr M. didn't tell you.'

'What? Tell me what? He's doing calls to his pupils right now but … what's happened?'

Mrs B. got up and walked nearer, but still keeping her distance. Even without Mrs Troubridge to measure, it had become second nature to her, as it had to almost the entire world. 'I had to call the amb'lance. She had been coughing all night, then this morning, she couldn't catch her breath properly. She was confused. Well, more confused. So, I called that number, that 119, is it? I'm that mithered …'

Seeing Mrs B. so unfocussed was like watching a film about dinosaurs. You know that it had to exist at one time, but seeing it here and now just seemed so wrong.

'Anyway, there was a kid on the other end, sounded about twelve. I told him about Jessica and he said why wasn't she in a home? Bleedin' cheek. Anyway, I got his supervisor in the end, snotty little shit, I wasn't having that. But … they sent the amb'lance anyway and they measured her oxygen and it was down in her boots.'

She blew her nose and waited a moment, kicking at a daisy with the toe of her indoor shoe, another sign that Mrs Troubridge was not in residence. She would have never gone outside in her indoor shoes otherwise. The world was indeed turned upside down.

'So I said, can't you give her some, surely, that ain't hard, a whiff of oxygen. But they said …' She took a deep breath and closed her eyes. 'They said, she needed to go in. She'll be assessed and then … they'll see.'

'Well, that's good,' Jacquie said, encouragingly, though everything she had read and heard suggested the opposite. 'She needs proper assessment, Mrs B. She's in the right place.'

'No! No, she's not. *Here* is the right place. Where she understands where she is and can control things. You don't know how bad it's got, not really. You're the best neighbours we could wish for, but you don't see her all the time. When she wakes up in the night and thinks I'm her mother. Or worse, her husband.' Despite herself, the woman grinned. 'I suppose we can only be grateful that Mrs T didn't really do much in the matrimonial department.'

'I've heard that,' Jacquie said, smiling back.

'She's only eaten out of tins since all this began, and I have to soak them in bleach first. At least, she thinks I do, but I don't, of course. I just put some on a piece of kitchen roll so she can smell it. She's skin and bone. She …' she trumpeted into her handkerchief again, 'She *is* in the right place, I know. But she'll be scared tonight when I'm not there.'

In normal times, Jacquie would have gone round and hugged the woman, so steeped in grief and worry. As it was, she could just empathise over a fence. 'She'll be back before you know it,' she said. 'Are you allowed to visit?'

'No.' The word sounded immeasurably bleak. 'No visitors.'

'But surely … you're her carer. Surely that makes it different?'

'No exceptions. No visitors.' The woman gave herself a shake. 'I need to tidy up indoors. She wouldn't let me do a lot of things in case it stirred up viruses in the dust. So a darned good clearout, that's what I'm going to do. For when she's better.'

'That's the spirit,' Jacquie said. 'For when she comes home.'

'Yes. For when she comes home.'

Walking a country mile it would have been unlikely that anyone would meet two women less alike than the two that faced each other over six feet of Sussex garden that day. But they both had exactly the same thought in their head – not when, but a very, very big if.

Inside the house, Jacquie was very glad to hear Maxwell still on the phone and Nolan still busy with his geography. She needed a minute to get used to the idea of Mrs Troubridge being in hospital and Mrs B, in pieces, two ideas that took a lot of getting used to. When she had first come to Columbine, Mrs Troubridge had seemed as old as God but she had always bounced back, no matter how hard she fell – sometimes quite literally. But this – this was felling strong young men with muscles on their muscles, without a single underlying condition, as the papers had begun to say almost as if 'underlying condition' was a condition in its own right. So, how would a little old lady, with more underlying conditions than you could shake a stick at, expect to beat it? She gave herself a shake and an admonition not to meet trouble halfway. She stood at the sink, slowly washing her mug and was still there when Maxwell came in, looking for lunch.

'Hello, heart. Didn't hear you come in? Are you all right?'

She turned to face him, meaning to say that yes, everything was just fine, but there was a problem with that. Every time she opened her mouth, all that came out was a pointless little squeak. And then the tears began and it all tumbled out in a rush, everything from horrible women who shouldn't be dead even so and little old ladies and Mrs B. Being Maxwell, he sorted the wheat from the chaff and had wiped her eyes and started on a pan of scrambled eggs before she could wink. By the time Nolan arrived for lunch, she looked presentable and was able to wade in when he made his usual complaint.

'Not scrambled eggs *again*?'

'You like scrambled eggs, Nole. Don't be ungrateful. What would you be having today if you were at school?'

'Poo pie.'

'Well, there you are, then. Even Dads' scrambled eggs are better than that, surely?'

'Thank you for that, heart. I always thought that you liked my scrambled eggs?' There was something in the air that was just aching for a row, but Maxwell was almost as good a diplomat as the cats and deflected it before he said something he would regret. 'Look, they're not on the heat yet. Let's put them aside for now and everyone say what they want for lunch.'

'KFC!'

'Not going to happen, buddy. Sorry. Try again.' Maxwell made a mental note to get Mrs B. to help him with a Tesco delivery, then remembered that she might not even be there to ask. Slots were like hens' teeth but she seemed to almost smell it when new ones came online.

'Mums, what would you like?' The little hand slipped into hers and the big brown eyes nearly finished her off, but she settled for planting a kiss on his head and saying, 'I fancy pizza, if that suits everyone. There's one in the freezer, I saw it this morning.'

'Pizza!' Nolan started the pizza dance around the kitchen and soon the kitchen smelled like downtown Naples, but without the drains.

When the last slice was eaten and Nolan had taken himself off to Facetime Plocker, Maxwell sat opposite his wife and took her hands across the table. 'She'll be all right,' he said.

'I doubt it, somehow,' she said. 'We have to be practical. It's Mrs B. I worry about. She doesn't want to leave here, I know that.'

'Does she have to?'

'It's not as if she has a proper arrangement. She just sort of … stayed.'

'And there's no reason why she shouldn't, is there? From what I know of them, the family have probably hardly noticed she's gone. And there isn't anyone here to make her leave. As far as I can tell, Mrs Troubridge is the last of the line. Someone needs to look after the house.'

'That's true. Perhaps one of us could pop round and let her know. She's feeling a bit vulnerable, as you might imagine.'

'I'll go. Are you going to be here for a bit?' Something suddenly dawned on him. 'Why are you home, in any case? Don't tell me you've solved it already?'

'Hmm?'

'The case. Solved it. Whatever it was that dragged you out of bed at some unearthly hour this morning.'

What with one thing and another, she hadn't even had a minute to tell him about Amelia Bencher. 'Sorry, I meant to …' Before she could go on, her phone rang with an unassigned number but one she recognised all the same. 'Oh, bugger,' she said. 'I should have called back … hold on, stay there, I've got to take this.' She picked up the phone and pressed the green button. 'Mr Bencher. Yes, sorry, there's been an emergency … Yes, I do appreciate that you too have an … They've what?' She looked up at Maxwell and pulled a rueful face. 'I didn't know. I'm sorry, no one … Well, yes, we do communicate, but …' Even Maxwell, at a distance, heard the crash as Charles Bencher's phone was flung across the room.

'He seems a bit testy,' he said, after a moment.

'He has every right to,' she said. 'He's being brought back to Leighford, to help the police with their enquiries.'

'Into what?'

'Sorry, I forgot you didn't know. Long story cut short, Mrs Bencher, of 65 Broadgate Avenue, was killed in her garden sometime overnight. I daresay McIndoe will be able to pin it down. Her husband is claiming to have spent the night with his landlady, now his fiancée, but obviously, Henry doesn't believe it. So he is bringing him back here, for questioning.'

'Where was he?' Maxwell had probably been told, but had forgotten.

'Scunthorpe.' She caught the look in his eye. 'Don't. I don't know who put that in Scunthorpe, so we'll take that as read, shall we?' She still smiled though. If she didn't, she would start crying again.

'Blimey. That's far enough away, surely, as alibis go.'

'Yes, it's …' She pressed a button on her phone. 'Alexa, how far is Scunthorpe from Leighford?'

After the usual pause, the pleasant tones came back with an answer. 'Scunthorpe is four thousand seven hundred and thirty nine point three two miles from Leighford Ohio.'

The Maxwells looked at each other. Perhaps it was time to admit the bloody woman was a liability. She tried again.

'Alexa, how far is Scunthorpe from Leighford, West Sussex, by road?'

Maxwell put his thumbs up. Adding the 'by road' was a touch of genius.

'Scunthorpe is two hundred and thirty nine point six two miles from Leighford, West Sussex.' The tones were as mellifluous when giving gibberish results as when the answer was correct. Maxwell said this was Alexa's superpower and would one day mean she would rule the world.

'I just don't see how it's possible, then, do you?' Jacquie said, doing a quick calculation in her head.

'I don't think we can rule it out, though, can we?' Maxwell said. He hadn't driven for decades, ever since the night when his first family had died on a wet road. He often dreamed of that night, but had trained himself to be a fairly calm passenger, at least, but driving was no longer something he could do. But he could do maths in his head, at least at the level needed to calculate journeys. 'He could have set off at any time to come down to do the murder, so time isn't an issue at that end. After he did it, he could have skedaddled back up north, and been back in what, about four hours? No traffic, that's a given. And I doubt he'd want to stop for coffee and a bun. So, death timed at midnight, say, he could be in bed by four or a bit after.'

'A policeman called on him in person to tell him she was dead. He was in bed, or said he was.'

'It's not hard to fling on some pyjamas. Or to fling your clothes off. He doesn't need to have put bum to mattress.' Maxwell looked at her. She was looking a lot brighter with a puzzle to solve. 'And I have to say, that on my albeit second hand acquaintance with the man via the gaps around your phone, he doesn't sound a very nice man.'

'That's true. He is a total piece of work. But … I just don't see him as the murderer in this one. Why would he … I'm an idiot.'

'I wouldn't say that, exactly, heart.'

Jacquie was too engrossed in her thoughts to take offence. 'He knew about the Ancasters. He mentioned them this morning. So …'

'He just took the opportunity and went down and knocked off his old lady.'

'It is a thought. A bit of a reach but … yes, it might just explain it. I had wondered …'

'Use your words, Detective Inspector Carpenter Maxwell. You're rambling.'

She jumped up and grabbed her jacket from the back

of her chair. 'I'll be back late, perhaps,' she said. 'Oh … do you want to pop round to see Mrs B. before I go?'

'No, no. You go. I'll text her.'

'Really?'

'I can text. I know things. Or … can you text her? I don't know where my phone is.'

'Yes, you do. Nolan has it. Okay. Hang on.' She hammered on her phone using her thumbs in a way that still had Maxwell in awe. 'Okay, I've said we'll be in touch, and that we would love it if she would stay, so the house isn't empty. She'll go for that.'

'Perfect. But … what had you wondered?'

'Different weapons. It wasn't in the paper, you see, so he wouldn't know. I'll let you know when I'm on my way back.' And with a kiss on the top of his head, she was gone.

On the way to the nick, Jacquie took the opportunity to marshal her thoughts. She didn't think that Charles Bencher had killed his wife. He was unpleasant, argumentative, unfaithful, dishonest – but that, to paraphrase Rod Steiger in one of the Maxwells' favourite films, *No Way To Treat a Lady*, didn't necessarily make him a bad person. But it would probably be a bit of a salutary lesson to be hauled down south in a police car, away from the perfumed embrace of his 'landlady', oops, sorry, fiancée. There would be a goodish wait at the nick until he arrived and her day off had been thrown to the sharks, but she was amazed how much fresher she felt, just being at home with other things to worry about for a change. A pang went through her as she thought of Mrs Troubridge, alone and probably very scared in the hospital, surrounded by strange figures in extreme PPE. Then she smiled – if she knew her Mrs Troubridge, she would be very impressed that they had donned all that stuff just for her. The universe, as everyone knew, was Troubridge-shaped.

Her neighbour was still in her mind as she pulled into the car park. How many times, she wondered, had she had to drive round and round and end up parking up some residential street because the car park was too full, designated spaces notwithstanding. And now, there were ten cars, top whack, Genghis's old battered Ford, Henry's very anonymous Rover she recognised, but the others, scattered about as though cars too had to socially distance, were usually too packed in to have any individuality. She really needed to know whose car it was that had the pink fluffy dice hanging from the rear view mirror – she so wanted it to be Tim Cathcart's, then she remembered he was on nights, so was hopefully at home, sleeping the sleep of the terminally knackered shift worker.

She swiped herself in. 'Afternoon, Genghis,' she said and he looked at her with lacklustre eyes. He could have sworn she was gone for the day and a synapse fired in his head and made him jump. Surely, it wasn't tomorrow already, was it? Time was beginning to all merge together. Without his darts on a Monday, dominoes on a Tuesday, Miriam's Zumba on a Wednesday, the kids' Taekwondo on a Thursday and the pub quiz on a Friday, he didn't know where he was from one day to another. If it wasn't for his allotment, he would go completely batshit. All this went through his mind, but he settled for a grunt. It didn't do to let the guard down; these plainclothes buggers thought they owned the place as it was.

Up on the CID floor, it was as if her couple of hours furlough had never happened. Everything was still deserted, but for Henry Hall, moving paper around at his desk. She leaned in his doorway without speaking and eventually, sensing the change in the light, he looked up.

'Hello,' he said, mildly. 'What are you doing here?'

'I'll have to shoot you now,' she said, automatically. 'But in fact, the short answer is that I have heard from Mr Bencher, who apparently is packing a small bag as we speak prior to being brought down to Leighford for questioning under caution.'

'Ah. I didn't think you would be speaking to him before I let you know.' It was hard to tell, but Henry did look a little shamefaced.

'Our initial conversation was interrupted by him having what I suppose will become a funny turn when he makes his complaint about his treatment. When I rang him back, he was even more prone to screaming incoherently than he had been before. Why, I have to ask, is he suddenly in the frame? And why isn't all this taking place over Zoom?'

'He's in the frame – insofar as he is in the frame – because his prints were found on the pruning knife.'

'Hardly a surprise, is it, that? He did live there until very recently.'

'Point taken. But the odd thing is that there was barely a print of his to be found in the house. In fact, there were no prints in the house except Mrs Bencher's. And a few of yours, I take it from your initial interview.'

'Yes, we sat in the lounge. But … no others at all? That's rather sad, isn't it?'

'I would imagine there are lots of houses like that at the moment. People with time on their hands, cleaning to fill the long days, no visitors. But I think that Amelia Bencher probably just wanted to expunge Mr Bencher from her life. All his clothes were in black bags in the garage, labelled things like 'C's old tat', C's disgusting underpants' and similar bitter remarks.'

'Having spoken to the man, she does have a point. She was well rid … if only for a while.'

'My point is, though, that she had been so thorough in getting rid of him, that a perfect set of prints were a bit of a red flag. I'm sorry I didn't let you know but I was hoping that you were having a rest.'

'I was … well, it was a bit emotional, really. Mrs Troubridge has been taken in to hospital.'

'Oh, I am sorry.' Henry had met Jacquie's neighbour from time to time and quite liked the crazy old bat. She was certainly a lot better as a neighbour than the family with four screaming kids next door to him, particularly since the arrival of the twelve foot diameter trampoline. 'Do we know …?' The etiquette of well-wishing had changed over the last few months. A good outcome from a hospital stay was no longer a given and when someone was as old as Jessica Troubridge, well – who knew?

'Not yet. No one is allowed visitors, of course. But Mrs B. will be calling later, I think. She'll keep us updated.'

'Mrs B. as in …?'

'Up at the school, yes. She's a bit ubiquitous, but we're glad she's there. She's been full time carer next door since this all started and it's only down to her that the ambulance hasn't been before. We're just crossing our fingers, but …'

'I know, yes, poor old soul.' Henry made a note to self – do not share this bit of information with Margaret when I get home.

'So, anyway, what with one thing and another, I didn't ring Mr Bencher back on the dot and when I did ring, he was … cross.'

'So, we're not going to have exactly a friendly chat, then?'

'I would think no. Does he have a solicitor here?'

'He's getting in touch with the family solicitor. Mrs Bencher's family seem to have been in Leighford since Adam was in the militia and so they have all that, like royalty.'

'Right. But why not Zoom? It could be hard to explain, if he makes a thing of it.'

'We could do with someone on the spot who knows the house. We might be missing something. And getting him down here seemed the simplest way.'

'Yes, I do see that,' Jacquie conceded. 'When is he due?'

'Not for some while. Why not go home again? I'll give you a ring when he's here.'

'No, I'm fine. I just needed a break.'

Hall stood up. 'Why don't we go for a walk?'

'A do what now?' Jacquie was so surprised she went into home-speak. 'Do we go for walks?'

'No. Perhaps we should.'

She pushed herself upright from the door jamb and hitched her handbag into position. 'Why not? Where shall we go?'

'The seafront, shall we? Blow the cobwebs away. See how many stupid idiots are trying to get away with pretending they all live within five miles and need sand to do their essential exercise.'

'That's true … let's not. How about the park?'

'Or the path behind Broadgate Avenue?'

'I thought you'd never say it. Separate cars, I suppose.'

He sighed. 'Yes. Better be seen to be obeying the rules.' Margaret would be proud of him. Perhaps the Dettol spray would be less vigorous tonight, if he could convince her he hadn't been hobnobbing with anyone that day. 'Margaret seems to think I spend all day going out licking strangers just to bring in the maximum viral load.' He shrugged on his jacket. 'If I thought I could get away with it, I would kill Whitty and Vallance.'

Jacquie laughed. 'Max spends his time working out the best methods. At the moment, his favourite is nailing Whitty's feet to the floor at the bottom of a high building and then pushing Vallance off the top. He's even calculated wind shear.'

'A man after my own heart.' Hall had never thought he would live to say that, but these days, he spoke as he found. After all, if Margaret was to be believed, there might not be a tomorrow.

'And mine,' Jacquie agreed. 'I've just thought – how if we go up on the Dam? That path behind Broadgate Avenue is a bit narrow for a walk. One of us would always be talking over their shoulder.'

'We can pretend it's work. We can check on where Mr Bencher's in-laws drove off the car park and …'

'Pardon?'

'Didn't I tell you? Well, it's quite a story. Come on, last one to the Dam's a cissy.'

With that, Jacquie followed her boss out and Genghis watched them go with narrowed eyes. This wasn't a rumour he had heard before, but it was certainly one which would take sharing. The next time they were allowed to share a table with a colleague in the canteen, he would start it on its merry way.

SEVENTEEN

The blow out on the Dam did them both the world of good, and Jacquie and Henry Hall were feeling relaxed and ready for anything when the call from the front desk came up to say that the squad car bearing Charles Bencher was just drawing up. His solicitor had been there for upwards of an hour, squirming on the impossibly hard seats in reception, made no more comfortable by the yellow striped tape across two out of three chairs and the legend 'Do Not Use. Hands, Face, Space'. The labels had to be replaced almost daily, due to disfigurement from sundry graffiti, but the general message was clear. At first, the solicitor, a dried up little creature who could have been the poster boy for 'family solicitor' in any drama on the big or small screen, had tried to catch up on emails, but quickly found that there was no WiFi, not even 3G, which would have done at a pinch. He asked at the desk whether there was a password so he could use the nick system, to be given a dusty answer by Genghis, who was preparing to go off duty. So he contented himself with playing solitaire, but found that that was a game that quickly palled and was reduced to staring into space.

The door swinging back woke him from his daydream, in which he was watching a film of his life being made, with George Clooney in the title role. He looked up and saw the choleric face of Charles Bencher outlined against the evening sky. He stood up and extended his hand, then withdrew it.

He had never liked the man anyway, so it was nice to have an excuse not to shake hands.

'Charles.' It was a statement, rather than a greeting.

'Maurice.' If anything, Bencher's greeting was even less warm. Behind them, the police driver from Lincolnshire was finalising the paperwork before he headed back for another long drive, at least this time not accompanied by Bencher who, as he swore to his colleagues the next day, had not stopped bitching from the minute the left to the second they arrived in Leighford. Which, to add insult to injury, looked like a dead and alive hole if ever he had seen one.

The desk man, paperwork stowed, buzzed the intercom and Henry appeared at the inner doorway, gesturing the men through. The usual interview room was not ideal for four people all socially distancing, so the currently unused staff room was pulled into service instead. This was also not perfect, but at least they could be the statutory distance apart without one of them having to be in the corridor outside. With everyone stowed, with unopened bottles of water from the fridge in front of them, Henry began the proceedings.

'First of all, Mr Bencher, may I thank you very much for coming in this evening. I know it can't have been an easy journey. I am very sorry for your loss.' He had almost forgotten the mantra, but managed to squeeze it in just in time. 'For the benefit of the tape, present today are Detective Inspector Jacquie Carpenter Maxwell, Mr Charles Bencher, his solicitor, Mr Maurice Bennett and myself, Detective Chief Inspector Henry Hall. Mr Bencher, you are not under arrest, but I would like to caution you …'

Jacquie sent a silent apology to her absent husband for the 'myself'. But he liked Henry, so would probably have forgiven him anyway.

'Yes, yes, I know all about that. You can skip the caution.'

The solicitor immediately leaned forward and waved a hand to attract Bencher's attention. Really, this was all so difficult and it wasn't what he was used to – conveyancing was his stock in trade, with the odd bit of probate. *Crime* was just so unpleasant. 'Ermm …' His voice was reedy and weedy, to match his appearance. 'Charles, I really must advise.'

'Just shut the fuck up, Maurice. You've seen crime dramas on the telly, I assume. Have you ever seen a solicitor speak on one of those?' Without waiting for an answer, he went on. 'No, you have not. So take a leaf out of their book and just shut up. Make notes if it makes you feel any better, but really, this is all nonsense and you objecting all the time just gives it credence it doesn't deserve. So, Detective Chief Inspector, just get on with it. Sooner we're done, sooner I can get back home.' He looked around at their faces. 'What?'

'Home, meaning …?'

'Scunthorpe, of course. My landlady gets nervous on her own.'

'Your landlady or your fiancée?' Jacquie couldn't help being a little mischievous.

'My what?' It didn't seem possible that Bencher could go a darker shade of purple, but he did.

'The lady I spoke to, she introduced herself as your fiancée. I'm sure that's what she said.' Jacquie smiled sweetly behind her mask.

'She … she misspoke. Anyhow, I need to get back. I don't expect that copper will wait for long.'

'I'm afraid the squad car from Lincolnshire has had to return, Mr Bencher,' Hall said. 'But I am sure we can sort something out in the fullness of time.'

Bencher turned to his solicitor. 'Maurice. What's the score with Amelia's car?'

The solicitor shrugged. 'No idea. It's at the house, I assume, Detective Chief Inspector?'

'I believe so,' Hall said. 'It was checked by SOCO but had nothing germane to say. Why do you ask, Mr Bencher?'

'Well, I can go home in that.'

Hall made a note. 'I will have to check on the Covid regulations, sir,' he said. 'But, meanwhile, we have some questions to ask you. Would you like to begin, Detective Inspector Carpenter Maxwell?'

Henry Hall was dragging this all out as much as he

could. Like Jacquie, he didn't really see Charles Bencher as a murderer, but he was just so horrible, something deep inside, buried well beneath Hall's professional carapace, just wanted to let him have it, right between the eyes.

'Thank you, Detective Chief Inspector. Could you tell me, Mr Bencher, where you were yesterday?'

'What part of yesterday?'

'From getting up, shall we say? I know working from home can make the days merge a bit, so do your best.'

'Amanda, that's my landlady, usually wakes me up with a cup of tea at around eight.'

No one missed the slight pause before the cup of tea, but they watched him in silence as he recounted his day.

'She has kindly assigned me the dining room as an office, so from about nine until lunch, I caught up with emails and made some calls.'

'Have you brought your laptop with you, sir?' Jacquie asked.

'Of course I haven't. I wasn't really given much time.'

'We can check with your server and your mobile service provider, if we have to, sir. And after lunch?'

'More of the same. Then I had a bit of golfing practice in the back garden and then we had supper and went to bed. The next thing was that idiot copper knocking me up this morning.' His eyes bulged. 'This morning? Bloody hell, how is that even possible? It seems like a lifetime ago.' He suddenly slumped back in his chair. 'And my wife's dead.'

Jacquie had a sudden stab of pity for the man. He looked momentarily poleaxed.

'She wasn't a bad old stick, you know. Not really. Just a bit … entitled, I think the word is these days. Few years older than me, but that didn't seem to matter back when we got married. But then,' he looked down at his hands for a moment, 'then she sort of … well, she didn't age very well. Didn't,' he mimed general face care with a sweep of his hand, 'didn't do the maintenance, if you know what I mean?' He looked up and met Jacquie's eye. 'You'll have to excuse what I say, Detective Inspector. It's not a comment about women in general, just my wife in particular.'

Jacquie nodded. If he wasn't careful, he'd have her liking him. But then it dawned on her – this is what this man did. With his careful grooming and his blandly handsome face, when he wasn't going purple with rage, he could be considered quite attractive by a certain type. The certain type who still slathered the Opium on every morning and popped down to the local Spa for a spot of Botox every once in a while. But that woman was not, was *definitely* not Amelia Bencher.

'I used to ask her, wouldn't she like a quick visit to a Spa. Just as a treat, you know. My treat. But she always pooh-poohed it. She said she was happy as nature had intended and so should I be. Well, I tried. I really did. Every now and then, she didn't have a headache and I … tried. But …' he blushed and looked desperately around.

Hall came to his rescue. 'We don't need this kind of detail, Mr Bencher,' he said. 'But it would be better all round if you dropped the landlady thing. Just tell us the truth.'

'We're not engaged.' He spat out the repudiation in his old style. 'I'll have to have a word with her when I get back ho … back to Scunthorpe. Amanda's nice enough but … well, lockdown and everything. It was …'

'Expedient,' the solicitor said.

Bencher glared at him. 'I suppose that's as good a word as any,' he said.

'No, it's more than that.' Bennett's thin voice held the room. 'Amelia rang me at the beginning of next week, to begin divorce proceedings. I don't really deal with that kind of thing myself.' Somehow, his voice managed to suggest that the whole idea was just too outré for his sensibilities. 'We do have a partner who does, though, and he had begun the preliminaries when …'

'When someone hacked my wife's head open,' Bencher completed the sentence.

'Yes.' The solicitor looked down in confusion. 'When Mrs Bencher passed away, yes.'

'Passed away?' Bencher rolled his eyes. 'Good Lord.'

'So, Mr Bencher.' Hall decided to call the meeting to order. 'You worked, ate, went to bed.'

'In a nutshell, yes.'

'And your …' Hall looked down to check, 'Mrs Grier can corroborate that, can she?'

'She took the dog out a couple of times. Yapping little shit won't go anywhere with me, just plants its paws foursquare and unless I drag him, we can't even get to the end of the drive.'

'What breed is the dog, Mr Bencher?' Jacquie was remembering the comments from McIndoe.

'Breed? God, I don't know. Is horrible a breed? Umm … one of those mixed jobs? Labradoodle? No, they're too big. I don't know, something. It would have been called a mongrel, back in the day. Heinz Fifty-Seven.'

'But apart from that, you were together?' Henry wanted to be sure.

'Well, yes, more or less. You know, usual thing, I was in the house. Amelia was in the garden.'

'Amelia?' The police heads came up, scenting a clue.

'What?'

'You said "Amelia was in the garden",' Maurice Bennett said gently, extending a hand that couldn't reach for a pat.

'Did I? She did love her garden.' And suddenly, unaffectedly, Charles Bencher, lothario, roue and potential murderer, burst into uncontrollable tears.

Maxwell had waited up, as he tried to do whenever he could. The day had been a bit of an up and down sort of affair, starting with an ad hoc whistle through the kings and queens of England, via Mrs Troubridge being taken into hospital and now ending as so many days did these days, with the two eldest in the house sitting in the garden after dark, the citronella candle more or less failing to keep the mosquitoes at bay, the rustling in the bushes only now and then terminated with an offended squeak, the last utterance of a Metternich-caught vole.

'And then,' Jacquie was saying, 'he burst into tears.'

'He sounds the kind of chap who wouldn't baulk at a few crocodile tears,' Maxwell said, sipping his Southern

Comfort. He had considered making a jug of Pimms, but it seemed altogether too celebratory for a day with not that much to celebrate to its name.

'I would have said that, but no. I've seen enough fakers to know and this was the real McCoy. He had to have the first aider in the end. Couldn't breathe, the whole nine yards.'

'Panic attack.' Sylv had kept a stash of brown bags in her desk drawer against just such an eventuality. And not just for the kids, either.

'Henry and I talked it through and we agreed, it did seem genuine.'

'Just because he is sorry doesn't mean he didn't do it.'

'Whose side are you on? I thought we agreed it was unlikely that he was the perp.' Jacquie liked descending to TV cop speak when they were alone.

'No, he isn't. It just doesn't seem feasible that he could drive all that way without being stopped. People are being stopped for driving ten miles to a better supermarket than the one that's local. All that way, what did Alexa say? Two hundred and thirty odd miles? He wouldn't stand a cat in hell's chance.' He turned his head to the shrubbery. 'Sorry, lads. No offence.'

'No, you're right. He's staying in the family room tonight and then he's going round to look round the house tomorrow. Then, Henry has relented and is letting one of our drivers take him back. Amelia hadn't signed it, but she had made a new will cutting him out of everything but common property. And, how's this – he's not on the deeds to the house. Her parents lent them the deposit back in the day, on the understanding that he wasn't a co-owner.'

'Ouch. That's actually rather horrible.'

'Yes, it is. He knew, but I think he thought it was water under the bridge. Anyhow, because she hadn't signed it, their mirror wills stand officially, but Maurice Bennett, the solicitor … what are you doing?'

Maxwell had hunched over and was looking like something which had been basking on a rock for millennia. 'I'm doing Maurice Bennett. He's the brief for the local education body and pops in to school sometimes.'

Jacquie laughed, but quietly. She didn't want to wake Nolan, whose window glowed above her head with the faint light of his dinosaur lamp, nor did she want to upset Mrs B., still resident in what she couldn't help but consider a house already in mourning. 'That is actually very good. Where was I?'

'Mirror wills. No signature. Officially …'

'Yep, okay. I'm there. Officially, the original will stands, but apparently, Maurice Bennett – don't do it again, thank you – is going to contest, as he doesn't think that represents his client's wishes.'

'Blimey. Old Maurice. I never would have thought the old man had so much blood in him.'

'There was no love lost, for sure. So, that's where we left it. Charles Bencher kipping in the nick, checking the house tomorrow and then going back to Scunthorpe – and again, don't do it again, thank you – when convenient. Which will probably be late afternoon.'

Maxwell extended a hand. 'Come on, Mrs M. Time for bed, I'm thinking. You've been up for best part of twenty hours and it's time you closed those eyes.'

She reached out and grabbed the hand. 'That sounds like a plan.' She didn't let go and she didn't get up, so he waited for what was coming next. 'You'll never hate me, Max, will you?' she asked, her voice just a whisper. 'Even if I let myself go.'

He hauled her to her feet and put his mouth to her ear. 'My love, I will never hate you. And if you let yourself go, I never will, so don't you ever worry about that.'

EIGHTEEN

S o, there he was, back on the graveyard shift again. If anyone had said to Tim Cathcart, back in the day, how would you like a job working nights, he'd have run a mile, seeing what years of that had done to his dad, falling asleep over his breakfast or dropping his ciggie onto his lap as he dozed in his chair.

Now, of course, Cathcart had two houses to watch. He didn't really see why he was still watching 65; the husband – and the smart money was on the fact that the bastard did it but Hall let him off – had checked it from stem to stern that day and there was nothing amiss. And Cathcart had been inside and he couldn't but agree – you could have eaten your dinner off not just the floor but any horizontal surface you cared to name. And surely, he had said to DCI Hall when he was trying to weasel his way out of the gig, now everyone was dead, the murderer was hardly likely to come back. But it had been no good, so here he was.

He glanced across the road to what, arithmetically and postally, came between – Number 66, two thirds of the address of the Beast. Like all the other houses along Broadgate Avenue, it was dark and silent, largely because it was a quarter past two in the morning.

Shit! There it was again, that bloody cramp. He was becoming a martyr to Voltarol and that stuff you sprayed on and also some cockamamie herbal crap that Mary had bought on Amazon. It tasted like the bottom of a pond but she swore by it, so he swallowed it to keep her happy. He took a chance again and got out of the car. The night air was surprisingly warm and the wind from the sea didn't reach this far inland unless it was blowing an absolute hoolie. He heard a dog barking somewhere in the distance, then falling silent, suddenly, as if someone had given it a kick.

Cathcart found himself on the path of Number 65 from where he'd seen the kneeling body of Amelia Bencher two nights before. There were no outside lights on now, just the black bulk of the house and the lawn faintly illuminated by the street light down the road. He reached the end of the path with the privet to his right and the wall of 65 to his left. The wooden gate ahead of him swung open to his touch and he was in the Ancaster's back garden. There was a wheelbarrow upturned in one corner and the bags of cement had all the hallmarks of a builders' yard. He even felt the gritty remnants of cement mixing under his shoes and took in that undefinable smell of plaster and buckets.

Cathcart was no slouch when it came to DIY. Mary was secretly proud of him, coming, as she did, from a family that could not knock a nail in straight. At their home in Tottingleigh, he'd redone the kitchen and was on the bathroom now, after endless arguments over the taps and the shower connection. There were times, and tonight was one of them, when Tim Cathcart thought he'd jack all this in, hang up his helmet and truncheon and set himself up as a jobbing builder, ex-policeman and van, as it were.

Then he noticed that the shed door was open. He'd never been part of a SOCO team, but he knew perfectly well that rule number one was to shut the bloody door behind you. He peered inside, switching on his torch to check the corners. This wasn't part of his brief, of course, but he couldn't resist the odd rummage. He was surprised how neat it all was, Roger Ancaster's tools neatly lined up along the wall, their handles gleaming as if they'd been polished. Somebody had told him that the lad, Marcus, used this place as a sort of study-cum-classroom, with a computer set up and the whole lot. But there was no sign of that. The shed looked as if it were brand new, as did everything in it.

Idly, Cathcart found himself fingering the tools. Some of these went back a few years; along with the power drills and yards of cable, there were adzes and bradawls, granny's teeth and spoke-shaves he hadn't seen since he used to stay with his granddad back in the day. He'd forgotten about spoke-shaves and he lifted the gadget down from its shelf. He glanced behind him. No one about, clearly, and some ridiculous impulse made him try it out. He placed his torch on the table, angled to throw light on the folding chair against the wall. He slid this outwards, running his hand over the curved wood at the top. There was no vice here so he gripped the chair between his thighs and started to slide the blade of the spoke-shave over the wood. He smiled. There was that familiar scrape as the wood shavings peeled away. There was the dust flying like myriad tiny insects in the torch's glare. There was the smell of virgin teak filling the whole shed. And soon, he was away with the mindless fairies of DIY which had captivated wood carvers for centuries.

So he didn't hear the padding of careful feet on the path. He didn't hear the gate swing open again. He saw no probing torch because there was no torch. He barely felt the slight breeze as the door opened wider and he certainly didn't see the pein hammer hurtling through the air to crush through his skull and into his brain. The torch flew wide, clattering to the floor. The spoke shave fell alongside it, the chair crashing with his body as they both went down.

And there was only one person who heard and saw what followed, the sickening thud as another two blows rained down on him and the last breath left his body. And only one person heard the words, 'You couldn't leave it alone, could you?'

Edgar Morrison joined his father-in-law at the window and looked out at Numbers 65 and 67. There were no tents now, just some tape across the front door but even that had a slightly unkempt look about it, like bunting left out in the rain too long after the happy event it was there to celebrate. What was there, though, was a car parked plumb across his drive. Bloody cheek. He turned and called for his wife.

'Milly! Milly? How long has this bloody car been there? Across the drive, no less. No consideration, some people.'

The woman went to the window and peered out. 'What does it matter, Edgar?' she asked. It had been bad enough living with these two before lockdown but being with them all the time was truly doing her head in. If it wasn't one, it was the other. 'You're not going anywhere, are you?'

'That's not the point, though, is it? I *might* be going somewhere. And what if the old bu … what if your dad should need emergency medical treatment? How could the ambulance get to him?'

'Amberlance? *Amberlance*? What amberlance? I don't need an amberlance. Mill! Mill! What amberlance?'

'Oh, for the love of God, Edgar,' she snapped. 'Now look what you've done. It will take all day to …'

'Amberlance, Millie.' Alf had degenerated into a high-pitched whine. He had almost forgotten what had scared him, he just knew he had to keep his daughter's attention then everything would be all right.

Edgar Morrison stepped away from the chaos and went out of the front door, down to the end of the drive where the offending car was parked. He peered in through the driver's window and saw that the passenger footwell was full of coffee cups, Coke cans, crisp bags and sandwich wrappers. Some people lived like pigs, there was no doubt about it. He jotted down the number on his hand using the biro which was always in his shirt pocket, working from home or no working from home. On legs stiff with irritation, he marched back up to the house and went in, not neglecting to slam the door. From the lounge to his left he could hear Alf still whining, sounding not unlike the vehicle he feared so much, so he went through into the kitchen and picked up the phone.

'Emergency. What service do you require?'

'Police.'

'Could you tell me something about your emergency, sir? Are you in immediate risk of personal injury?'

'No. There's a car parked across my drive.'

'And is this causing you immediate risk of personal danger, sir?'

'No. But my father-in-law lives with us and is very elderly and frail. We might need an ambulance at any moment.'

'So you want ambulance, sir?'

'No. But if we did, it couldn't get in.'

'Do you mean the road is blocked, sir?'

'No. Not the road. My drive. I ...' Edgar Morrison decided that a little stretching of the truth wouldn't hurt. 'I need to get to work.'

'Are you a key worker, sir?'

'Er ... yes.'

'For my records, sir, may I ask what discipline you work in?'

This was getting in a bit deep and Edgar didn't really want a fine. Telling the truth – that he was a quantity surveyor currently on furlough – wouldn't get him far and he had a horrible feeling that lying about key worker status might well have a statutory custodial sentence attached. Watching those mad buggers every night on the telly, it was probably totally likely. He decided on discretion as the better part of valour.

'Oh ... look. It's being moved now. Sorry to have bothered you. Goodbye.'

Edgar was glad he had used Millie's mobile. She would have to fend off the Sage goons as best she could. He sat at the table and drummed his fingers for a moment, looking with distaste across at where his father-in-law habitually sat. The table top was besmottered with gravy, porridge, over-dunked digestives – he closed his eyes. Why couldn't the mad old sod just *die*. Everyone else seemed to be, after all.

He had a thought. He'd ring the nick at Leighford. See what they had to say. After all, this was almost a crime scene, so they should be interested. He dialled 118118 – Millie would be livid when she saw the charge, but it would be water under the bridge by then. He'd blame Alf – he had rung a chiropractor in Bogota not long ago, claiming he was trying to ring his sister, who incidentally had been dead since 1998.

So he was on safe enough ground there.

He chose to be put through and was soon on the phone to a civilian receptionist, working from home.

'Leighford police. How may I help you?'

'There's a car parked across my drive.'

'May I have your name, please, sir?'

He sighed. 'Edgar Morrison.'

'Could you spell that for me, sir?'

'E. D…'

'Echo Golf … yes, sir?'

'No. Echo … umm Delta Golf … umm …'

'I'll come back to that, sir. Address?'

''66, Broadgate Avenue. That's B for Bravo …'

'No, sir, that's fine. I know Broadgate Avenue. I'm putting you through to CID. Please hold.'

CID! Now, that was more like it.

'Leighford Police. Detective Sergeant Alison McGuire speaking. How can I help?'

'I've been put through. My name is Edgar Morrison and I live at 66 Broadgate Avenue.'

Alison McGuire stood up, instinctively ready for action as she heard the dread address. Everyone in the room, spread out as they were, looked at her, waiting.

Keeping her voice level, she asked, 'What seems to be the trouble, Mr Morrison?'

'There's a car parked across my drive.'

She sagged but didn't sit down. It was probably nothing, but even so. 'Do you have the registration mark, sir?'

'Yes.' Edgar turned his hand and read it out, having to squint at the last digit because his hand had been sweating holding the phone.

'Could you tell me the make, sir?'

'I'm no good with cars, I'm afraid,' he said. 'It's blue. Green. A bluey-green. A Toyota, perhaps? A Kia? One of those.'

Alison decided not to panic. That it was Tim Cathcart's car was beyond doubt. He had probably just dropped off, but if so, why wasn't he in the car?

'I'd like you to stay in the house, sir. Someone will be

along shortly. Thank you for your call.'

She hung up and faced the room. 'It's Cathcart's car. It's still parked in Broadgate Avenue.'

'That's crazy,' someone said. 'He should have knocked off hours ago and you know Cathcart. He's on his toes before the time if possible, not after. Who's on duty for days?'

'Just someone passing, checking from the road.' She glanced up at the clock. 'Probably not done the first sweep yet.'

'Check with the guv'nor,' someone called from the corner of the room. 'Get him to put a call out, nearest unit to check Broadgate Avenue. Even if it's only to wake the lazy bugger up.'

But everyone had that crawling feeling in their stomachs, and it had nothing to do with the canteen hash browns this time, they all knew.

Peter Maxwell was also receiving a phone call, but less stomach-churning than Alison McGuire's. He was sitting at his desk, thinking how odd it was that when there was nowhere to go at any specific time, everyone seemed to be ready for the off at an almost unseemly hour. There was a bird with a megaphone which sat on their bedroom windowsill and started practising just as dawn was breaking and that more or less put the kibosh on further sleep. When school was in the offing, he would turn over with the duvet over his head and mutter imprecations on all bird life, but now he had nowhere to go, he would lie there listening to nature doing its stuff and then get up and start the day.

Typing wasn't a skill that came naturally to him, but he was, nevertheless, writing a worksheet for the putative incoming Year Sevens. As a rule, in normal times, this would be the week that the seemingly tiny children from the feeder junior schools would start coming in for taster days. He had always wondered what happened to the fresh faced little dears over the summer holiday, because they always arrived for full time incarceration looking as thuggish and disillusioned as all the rest. He usually gave them a tour de force of some kind, with them all assembled in the hall. The way he saw it, the only way to grab their attention and make them his for life was to give them blood, guts and gore – so Jack the Ripper it was!

He had come to a bit where he needed to embed an image, or so he had heard it called. He needed Nole or Mrs B., though probably leaving the latter alone right now was a good idea. She had called an update over the fence to Jacquie earlier that morning, while they were both engaged in hanging out laundry. He smiled to himself as he remembered the scene. Before lockdown, laundry was something that just seemed to happen Chez Maxwell. One of Jacquie's indulgences was to put it all outside in a hamper on a Tuesday and received a perfectly ironed stack of clothes in the same on Friday. A ruinous amount of money changed hands in the interim, but it was worth it for the crisp shirts and razor sharp creases in the trousers. But the hamper had gone the way of all good things and Jacquie was actually enjoying the hanging out and fetching in of clean clothes, if not the ironing. He hadn't heard the details as he watched from an upstairs window, but the short version was that Mrs Troubridge was on oxygen but not in an induced coma. She was on a high dependency ward, but not ICU. And for the moment, they decided that that was good news.

He had pushed his chair back to go in search of his in-house IT guru when the phone rang.

'War Office Annexe,' he said.

'Peter Maxwell, I believe that working from home is suiting you down to the ground.'

'Sylv, hello, dear heart. How lovely to hear from you. How's Marcus?'

'Very well, really. We're not discussing …' there was a pause as she checked behind her, 'things, unless he wants to. Sometimes, in the evening, he will tell us a few odds and ends, but it seems that he and his parents lived a very quiet life, very self-contained, if you know what I mean. Just happy to be together. He had friends round for sleepovers when they were actually a thing. Mum went to Pilates when she could be bothered. Just the usual.'

'He is coming to the lessons, still. Mine at least.'

'That's been great. He's still with all his friends, as far as that goes. His schedule is much the same. He and Guy get on really well. They're playing I Saw It First at the moment and Guy is getting thoroughly whipped, I am glad to say. He's had it his own way for far too long.'

'I Saw It First?'

'Max!' Sylvia was horrified. 'You mean you don't have I Saw It First? That's it – I'm sending one for Nolan as soon as I get off this phone. He'll love it. It will drive you bananas.'

'Nole is a lot younger than Marcus, don't forget.'

'Doesn't matter. He'll still beat you into a cocked hat. There – did you hear that?'

And Maxwell had indeed heard a distant cheer.

'He's done it again. Guy doesn't stand a chance. But enough of my husband's failings. I've rung with a favour, for Marcus.'

'Anything I can do, of course.'

'The police have been really great – I've had long chats with Henry's wife, by the way. Poor thing, she's really letting this get to her; isn't she?'

'Jacquie has said, yes.' Maxwell didn't know Margaret Hall very well, but could tell how much Jacquie was worrying about Henry. 'I know Henry will be grateful for any help.'

'She had got things out of proportion. She's following my blog and I think it's helping.'

Maxwell chuckled. 'Sorry, Sylv, but I am just so proud of myself for knowing what you are talking about when you say "blog". I'm quite the IT expert these days.'

Sylvia snorted. 'No, you're not, Max. I know you still rely on Nolan and Mrs B. Oh – presumably not Mrs B. these days.'

'She's next door, as it happens. But she's got a lot on her plate – Mrs Troubridge is in hospital.'

'Oh, Max, I am sorry. Poor old soul. Is she …?'

Maxwell was not surprised that even Sylvia was stuck for words when asking if his neighbour was at death's door. There really needed to be some kind of new vocabulary to cope with all this. 'Just on oxygen at the moment,' he said.

'Well, that's something,' Sylvia said and there was a

pause. 'Anyway, Marcus's favour. He wants some things from the house, but wants you to get them. As I say, the police have been very good, keeping in touch and everything, but he doesn't want them ferreting about, to quote him. So, if you could … well, it doesn't have to be you, he wouldn't know, but if Jacquie could …'

Peter Maxwell felt strongly about lots of things – split infinitives, not ending a sentence with a preposition, the pronunciation of Kabul – but mostly he felt that you shouldn't lie to kids when you promised them something. And so if Marcus asked him to do something and he said yes, then he would do it himself. 'I'll do it. I'm sure there'll be no problems with that.'

'As long as you're sure. I'll …' she chuckled, 'I'll send an email, shall I, with the list of things?'

Maxwell cleared his throat and adopted a mock formal tone. 'I would like you to know, Madam, that I am perfectly able to open emails.'

'With attachments?'

'If required.' He sounded less certain.

'Well, don't worry, you dinosaur. I'll just write the list in the body of the email, then you won't have to click on any scary boxes. Get Nole to help you print it out.'

'Print it out, woman? Wash out your mouth! I'll write it out the old fashioned way, with a pen and paper.'

'That's my Max. You do that.' There was a silence. 'Max … I really miss you.'

'I miss you, too. It's been too long.'

'I was all right when I knew I could pop round whenever I wanted. It's being told I can't that gets to me.'

'It gets to us all, Sylv. Keep your chin up. Keep blogging.'

'I will, Max. Keep safe. Please.'

'I will, don't worry. Hands. Face. Space.'

She chuckled. 'You're obeying the rules. Wonders will never cease.'

'No, indeed. Don't forget to send that email, now. How are we going to get the stuff to him?'

'Perhaps Jacquie could arrange something? Or Henry

… isn't it mad that just sending a few things over for a child who has gone through all this should be like a military operation?'

'A military operation? If only. We are lions led by donkeys, Sylv, that's the trouble. But we'll sort something out, never fear. Love to Guy and Marcus. And to you, of course.'

'Yes. Love to everyone. Oh, must go – sounds like Guy might be cheating. Bye.'

And she was gone.

Maxwell put the phone down slowly, reflecting that at least one person in all this madness had gained something.

He looked at his worksheet and then at the clock. Time for elevenses, despite being just shy of quarter past ten. He carefully saved the document – none of this new-fangled ctrl s for him, he did it properly with more key strokes and mouse work than many people used for a whole novel – and then went in search of his son. A ton of hobnobs and a glass of milk and he might get the kid to divulge all he knew about embedding images – it was that or staking him out over an anthill and that had been banned by his mother as unnecessarily cruel to ants.

'Nole?' he called, as he went down the landing. 'Nole? Fancy a snack?'

NINETEEN

Jacquie Carpenter-Maxwell stood in the shed of the dead. Cathcart's body had gone now and the SOCO team had vanished like ghosts in the morning. She knew they would have put everything back exactly as it was when they arrived and that there would be crisp photographs to prove it. She had a sense of déjà vu, in a way, over this. Same old, same old. But there was nothing monotonous about murder. She could never say, as many could, just another day at the office.

Three murders in one house; well, technically, two in the house and one outside it, not to mention the slaughter beyond the hedge. But that one was different. Different weapon. Different angle of attack. But could there be two killers wandering a sleepy seaside town at a time when nobody was supposed to be wandering at all?

Jacquie had been to all the courses. She'd read all the articles in the journals. Hell, she'd even read some of the books, the ones intended for a prurient public. She knew about Oedipus complexes; the triad of warning signs in small children; she understood triggers and compulsions without number. And she knew that beyond all that was the basic fact that no psychologist or psychiatrist could fathom; those pesky little motives for murder – 'he looked at me funny' and 'I fancied his trainers'.

But somehow, this was different. She didn't know how long Marcus had been using the shed as his study; perhaps only since lockdown started, perhaps longer. She'd have to ask him. But there was no sign of him. No laptop, obviously; that was by definition highly mobile and had gone with him. But there were no cables, no note pads, no books, nothing to say that a teenage boy had been there at all.

And then, there were the tools. Outside, on the patio and in the garden, they were all over the place, a typical builder's yard. In here, though, the place was like a museum; everything neat, ordered, polished and presentable. She half-expected to see a series of little cards, 'This chisel was donated by the Old Fogey family in memory of their granddad'.

Jacquie had never come across a killer with full-blown OCD before, even if her better half insisted on calling it AC/DC. And, she remembered with a shudder, as she thought of Tim Cathcart's body, there was nothing neat about the murder itself. You can't shatter a skull with the neat precision of laser surgery. Suddenly, she had to get out into the fresh air, to feel the sun on her face. Beyond the thick hedge that bordered the path at the back, she heard the paparazzi muttering behind their masks. One voice was louder than the others.

'Well, now one of their own's been killed, they'll be pulling out all the stops. You can bet on it.'

She wanted to crash her way through the privet, rip the stupid mask off his face and ask him why he didn't get a real job. But perhaps now was not the time.

'So, Dads, that's all you do. You can choose to save or copy and then just click and choose paste or insert. Got it?'

'Yes, mate. Thanks. I'll … I'll let you get on, then. What's the schedule for the rest of the morning?'

'I've got science later. I've got a list here, hang on …' Nolan ran out of the room and came back with a piece of grubby paper. 'I wrote it down. I need some …' he squinted at the paper and turned it this way and that. 'What do you think that says?'

Maxwell also squinted. 'It *says* bikernet of soder, but I think you mean bicarbonate of soda.'

'Yes, that's right, I remember now. She was going a bit

fast.' To Nolan's credit, his spelling was normally much more accurate, but bicarbonate was a bit of a big ask. 'And a lemon.'

'The answer's a lemon,' Maxwell muttered. 'Well, we've got those, so no need for a shop. What's the experiment, then?'

'We've got to put the lemon juice on the bik … stuff and write down what happens. Then, we have to see if we can find out anything else that makes it happen.' He frowned. 'It doesn't sound like much of an experiment to me.'

Maxwell was just relieved that it was something he could help with. He wasn't a watchword where cleaning hackers gathered, but even he had heard of Mrs Hinch. He made a mental note to check if they had any white vinegar and also to test the theory out with yoghurt. Would blueberry do the trick or did it have to be live? When he had started teaching, this kind of arcane knowledge was not being taught, for some unknown reason, but who knew back before the Flood that bats would start giving people colds?

The laptop pinged and Nolan poked his father in the ribs. 'Email, Dads,' he said.

'Thanks, Nole. I have to get back to this, anyway. Tell me when you want your lunch.'

'We can have lemon and bikernet, perhaps.'

'Why not? Come here a minute.' Maxwell held his arms out and Nolan ran into them. He would never turn down a hug.

The laptop pinged again.

'Another email, Dads.'

'Yup. A Maxwell's work is never done.' He unwrapped his arms and turned to the laptop. 'Give me a shout when you're hungry.'

'Dads!' Nolan yelled, almost in his ear.

'Very droll. Now off you trot, sooner I do this, sooner it's done.'

Nolan went out, shaking his head. Some of the things adults said were really too weird for words – all his friends said so.

The first email was from Sylvia, a quick greeting and

then a list of things and their rough location in the house. There wasn't anything to give any problems, some more clothes, a few books and then, at the end of the list, a couple of woodworking tools. 'These last things are very sweet,' Sylv had added at the bottom. 'Apparently they're very old and were in the shed when they moved in. Marcus and Guy are taking up woodworking as a hobby and Marcus remembered seeing them there. When he saw the price on Amazon, he insisted that we had those, not bought new. He is such a thoughtful boy, old beyond his years in many ways. He says there are some old bits of wood as well. If it isn't too gigantic, or too old, can you also bring a bit of that, for practice. And that's it, I think. If you give me a call when you've assembled it, perhaps we would be allowed to fetch it, or Jacquie could arrange to have it brought over.'

Maxwell pursed his lips and leaned down, single forefinger extended. He tapped 'reply' and then typed 'will do' and tapped 'send'. Not for him unnecessary capitals. If he had done more, Sylvia would have supposed that he had been abducted by aliens.

The next email was one he had been dreading for weeks. At the start of lockdown, a roster of staff had been drawn up to be present in the school to accommodate the children of key workers. He knew he was on it – he had to be, there were no exemptions – but he had always hoped that he would be so far down the list that normal service or the summer holidays would arrive before his turn came. But no – he was out of luck. From being in double figures from the top only the other day, he was suddenly there, in the frame. Apparently, Helen Maitland had tested positive, the good news being that she seemed to be having only a minor case of the lurgy, as he knew she called it. He did have a small chuckle when he read that, as Helen was not someone who would have a severe case of anything – and a pandemic laying the world by its heels would not stand a chance. Not such good news was that the inoffensive Thingee One, the morning receptionist, was currently in ICU and when she came out – the email was at pains to say 'when' – it would be to the bad news that her mother had died in the next bed to her. Maxwell closed his eyes. He was a resilient man, God knew, but when the hell would this all end?

But for now, he had the long-dreaded Day In to contend with. Another Plocker bubble would need to be arranged. It was actually allowed for staff to take their own children in with them, but he was not going to inflict that on his child. Then he needed to concoct a few activities to keep the little dears happy for the day. He knew that there would be no second-guessing which kids would be there but one thing he could be sure of – they were going to be a mixed bunch, to say the very least of it. He tapped a quick reply so that the depleted office staff knew he had received the email and would be there in time for breakfast club the next day. Then he texted Mrs Plocker to ask if they could rebuild their bubble. Her reply was so ecstatic that he arranged for her to pick Nolan up before supper that evening. Then he would have carte blanche to talk murder with the Mem, without worrying about little wandering ears. This social secretary lark could get very wearing.

He opened the Jack the Ripper document and made a mental note to remember that he had named it Jack the Ripepr, so he could find it again. There was doubtless some way to rename it, but who on earth could be bothered to do that? He just didn't fancy it any more. The day had got away from him, academe-wise so he went down to take in the washing. A woman's work was never done.

Down in the garden, filling his arms with sweetly smelling laundry, he listened with half an ear for any signs of life next door. Mrs B. was not a natural outdoorswoman, her usual habitat being other people's houses and – of course and always – up at the school. In the meeting before lockdown, the caretaker of the building had announced that a skeleton staff would be kept on to keep the school running at a base level, but he didn't say how that would be achieved. The other staff would be furloughed. Mrs B. had no doubt chosen that, with her responsibilities next door suddenly off the scale, so she wouldn't be there. She couldn't be visiting her charge. She would have refused all blandishments to go home and be the skivvy for her feckless family. So, somewhere behind those silent walls, she was entertaining herself as best she could. She had taken the washing in and Maxwell, looking at the crumpled mass in his arms, wondered if he could somehow introduce the subject of ironing, then decided that perhaps this was not the time to remind her of how much time she had on her hands.

Washing distributed in the right rooms if nothing else, he gathered Nolan and the cats for lunch. Metternich had taken a sudden aversion to any fish-based food, having eaten nothing else for as long as anyone could remember. Bismarck, never one to be left out, had disposed of his furball in the most economical fashion by chucking it up on the furball vomit coloured rug in front of the cooker. Nolan was getting excited about his experiment and was surmising that perhaps it could blow up the whole house. Maxwell dispensed chips, fish fingers, Gourmet duck in vegetable sauce and Iams Anti-furball mixture (the latter too little, too late) in random order and sat down at the table staring ahead like a man who has looked into the future and hasn't liked what he saw there. His vision had been of a road, stretching on and on and on, straight as doom. And at the end of it, two figures, one so bland it was hard to concentrate on his face and the other looking like a nodding dog in a car window, its enormous head suspended precariously on its unfeasibly long neck. There was a speech bubble over their heads and in the speech bubble, in huge capitals, was the legend – You're All Going To Die.

'Dads! Dads!'

Maxwell came out of his reverie with a jump. Nolan was looking at him anxiously and was shaking him by the arm. 'You were mumbling, Dads. Are you all right?'

'Sorry, matey. I was just having a think.' He looked down at his son's plate, which was empty all except a slight smear of tomato sauce. 'Goodness, you were hungry. Well, shall we do this experiment, then?'

'Shall we film it?'

Maxwell looked hunted. He was no great shakes at taking anything other than still pictures and they were in the lap of the gods.

'I'll set it up, then you just have to press the red button.'

'That sounds simple enough. Let's get everything on the table and then you can do it live, one take. We'll need bowls, bicarbonate of soda, a lemon – you'd better let me cut that in half – some vinegar and some yoghurt.'

Nolan looked at him with narrowed eyes. 'Do you already know what will happen, Dads?'

Maxwell donned his most innocent expression. 'Goodness, no. I just chose those things because they were handy.' He never broke a promise to a child, but straight out lying was another thing altogether.

All things considered, the experiment went well. A squirt of lemon juice hit Maxwell in the eye, but like all cameramen in dangerous settings, he carried on filming. Everything behaved as it should, the yoghurt alone being a little underwhelming. But, all in all, there was a gold star, right there. Everything was wiped up and tidy by the time Jacquie got home. The day had been an emotional one and she was not that sorry to hear that Nolan had been re-bubbled. She had always tried her best to keep the worst of her job from him, but doing that was a whole lot easier when he wasn't actually within earshot.

Maxwell did as he always did in times like these – he microwaved a lasagne, poured her a gin and tonic that would fell an ox, and sat next to her on the sofa, rubbing her feet while she ate and sipped.

'The trouble is,' she said, handing him her empty plate and cradling her glass with both hands, 'the trouble is that Tim Cathcart was such a dick most of the time. He was only doing the night shift because Henry was trying to teach him a lesson. It was the naughty step, if you like. And it was … we all feel bad … but it was a nice change to not have his stupid one-liners all the time. But …' and she buried her nose in her glass.

'But now he's dead and you would all give your eye teeth to hear one of his stupid one liners again.'

Without looking up, she nodded.

'Regret is a painful thing,' Maxwell said. 'Without it,

we would be less than human, but we shouldn't dwell on it. There's something very wrong going on in Broadgate Avenue and I can see that you all have a devil of a job on to try and find out what the hell is the matter. So …' he leaned over and deposited her plate on the floor, 'so perhaps tonight isn't the best time ever to tell you what I have been asked to do. I was going to do it tonight, but …'

'What?' She took a gulp of her drink and almost choked on a lemon pip. 'This lemon is a bit mangled. What happened, did you stand on it?'

'It's a long story, but we must all suffer in the march of science.' Seeing her blank look, he said, 'I'll show you the video later.'

'Impressed. But, what did you want to do tonight?'

He explained about Sylvia's call and the really very reasonable list Marcus had sent. 'But I realise now, of course, what none of us knew at the time, that the shed is a crime scene, all over again.'

'It is, but SOCO have really given it a going over. There's nothing there that we could hurt, really. And everything has been dusted for prints so … look, let me just ring Henry, to check. It would be nice to have a blow out in the car, wouldn't it? We could pop down to the Front and get a bit of sea air. We've still got a few hours till it's dark and it's supposed to be one of those posh moons tonight, you know, the ones that look like every other full moon you've ever seen.'

He chuckled. 'Yes, I know the ones. The Mock Moon, one of them, isn't it? The Gotchya Moon, that's another.' He smiled at her and reached out his hand. 'The I'm Amazed Every Day Moon. Is that the one?'

She touched his fingers and smiled back, leaning her head on the back of the sofa. 'I believe it is,' she said. 'I do believe it is.'

As they drove, having got Henry's blessing and then the keys from the nick, Maxwell thought it was time to catch up on where things were. He had thought, when working from home had begun, that time would hang heavily on his hands, but in fact he was finding more and more that the evening would arrive and take him by surprise and with much still left undone. It was good to be driving somewhere, even somewhere as near as Broadgate Avenue.

'Did they find anything?'

'Did who find anything where?' Hedging was still a default setting, even after all these years.

'Come on, it's just us. We don't even have Alexa spying on us here.'

'I've told you to stop reading those urban legend websites.'

'She does though.' He sounded a lot like Chantal.

'Yes, she does. Granted. But even so.'

'I'm still here. Did SOCO find anything in the latest crime scene?'

'It was incredibly clean. I don't mean just clean for a crime scene, but clean for a shed. It had almost been polished. There wasn't a fingerprint or a speck of dust anywhere. There was dog hair at the first scene, but none here. Not even Bob's. Not even Marcus's prints, which is ridiculous, because it was where he spent a great deal of time, before. So whoever did this cleaned up after himself or …' She bit her lip, 'I don't know what to make of this, really.'

'Go on, heart of darkness. If you can't share loony theories with me, who can you share them with?'

'True. Well, that SOCO guy I told you about, the one who fancies Henry and thinks no one knows?'

Maxwell chuckled. 'The man has impeccable taste. Yes, I think I've seen him at various Christmas dos and whatnot.'

'He's a bit strange, but harmless. He is really, *really* pernickety. In real life, as people persist in calling life, he is close to having full blown OCD but he manages it really well. It's almost a perfect condition for anyone in SOCO, of course – no one wants anyone on that team to be slapdash, after all. He came to me after they had finished with a very interim report, and one thing stuck out. He mentioned it specially and it obviously confused him as much as it did me.'

'Have you ever thought of going on the stage?' he

asked her, suddenly.

'Good heavens, no. You know how I go in front of a crowd.'

'It's just you've got me on the edge of my seat. What did he tell you?'

'He's not sure he …'

'*What did he tell you, woman?*' The words were delivered through gritted teeth.

'He said that the one small blood splash he could find – just one, after all that violence – was on a surface that was already clean and polished.'

Maxwell pulled a face. 'That's odd.'

'As far as any of us can remember and from the first SOCO of the shed – which was only quite cursory, of course, the crime being committed upstairs – it was just the usual dusty old shed. Clean enough for Marcus to use for schoolwork, but that's all.'

'That is strange. Who would clean a shed?'

'If she'd had time, I would say Mrs Bencher. But she didn't, not really. And I don't think that even she would want to control things to that extent. She liked the Ancasters well enough, but didn't get involved in their lives.'

They drew up in the drive at Number 67, to accompanying shivering curtains at Number 66. Millicent Morrison had had a day of calming down her father and silently hating her husband and it was taking its toll. The sound of any car slowing down and stopping was now almost more than she could bear. The yapping of the paparazzi was one thing and you could zone that out if you tried. Some of them had been there so long they seemed like old friends almost. One of them had even come to the door to ask for the loo, but she was wise to that one – give them an inch and they'd take a mile, pictures on the front page, street of death, all that nonsense. So she'd sent him packing. She peered through the nets but it was just that nice pretty policewoman with the older man who had driven off with the child what seemed like a lifetime ago. If Millicent Morrison had ever wished for a more exciting life, she never would do anything so foolish again.

Maxwell was struck at how different everything looked. Without the lights, the tent, the flapping tape, this could be any house in an ordinary street. He stood looking up at the bedroom windows while Jacquie locked the car and came round to join him.

'Isn't it peculiar,' he said, 'how clouds can look like faces.'

'Please don't start that again,' she said, unlocking the front door. She glanced behind her. 'Yes, okay. I can see … a lamb, maybe a dragon. A dog smoking a pipe.'

'Hmm?' Maxwell was confused. 'No, I mean, in the reflection, the clouds made it look as if there was someone looking out of the window.'

'Oh, I see. Well, no one is. Everything has been locked down tight, no one, not even someone who had a key, could get in. Now, do we have that list?'

Maxwell fished it out of his pocket. 'It's mostly clothes. Some books – hmm … yes, they're for course work and that kind of thing. He was reading, and I'm rather impressed with young Marcus, *Monmouth Harry*; an oldie but goldie. Rattling good yarn. That's up by his bed, apparently. And … special mug … woodworking tools and some waste wood. Apparently, he and Guy are taking up woodworking.'

'Sending him to Sylv seems to have been a good call all round. Is she going to apply to foster, do you know?'

'I wouldn't be surprised. They all seem really happy together.'

'Right … look, Max, no offence, but … shall I do the clothes and book?'

'I can still do stairs, you know.'

'I know. But you've been to more crime scenes than the normal person, if I can use the term normal anywhere near you. But you haven't been to an ex-crime scene. I mean, a crime scene where everything has gone bar the sadness, the dried blood. The … well, there's usually a smell. If you don't mind, I'll go up and pick up some clean folderols for Marcus, his books and whatnot and you can get his mug. I'll see you in the shed for the woodworking bits. Do you know what you're looking for?'

'Absolutely no idea. But I think he wants the old school woodworking things and they should show up nice and clear. He doesn't want drills and that kind of electronic stuff. I expect Guy has all those.'

Jacquie went upstairs with a smile for the husband who had once tried to knock in a nail and come off the worst. But he was probably right; men *did* have those things, even if they never came out of the box. Upstairs surprised her. The cleaners had obviously been in; in these odd times, they probably had less private work to do and so could give the police more of their time. It looked quite pristine, even the mattress. The bed had not been made but the bedding, laundered and folded, was stacked at the foot. The stain on the carpet would only be visible if you knew it was there. Impressive. Bearing in mind that Chez Maxwell there was still a stain on the sitting room carpet where Nolan had upended a jar of stewed prunes when they were having a first go at weaning, she made a note to ask the cleaning crew what they used, because she needed some.

Maxwell found the mug in the spotless kitchen. It was in a cupboard, sadly flanked by 'The World's Best Mum' with a picture of Bob grinning gormlessly printed on it, and 'Dad in a Million' with crossed hammer and saw behind the writing. The mug with 'Marcus' on was plain otherwise but it was obviously a favourite. The handle had been glued on at least once. He left it on the counter and then unlocked the back door and went down to the shed. The sun was limbering up to set away to his left and he was reminded of the old saying, 'red sky at night, the hayrick's alight'.

The shed was marked by blue and white tape but the door, to his surprise, wasn't locked. Ducking under the tape, he went inside and was immediately struck by how very clean it was. Much cleaner than when he had seen it last, on his computer screen. He remembered then that Marcus reached out and brushed a spider off his webcam. No spider would be allowed to stay in this pristine space. It even smelled lovely, like pencil sharpenings. He switched on the light, because despite the flaming sky outside, the shed was very gloomy. On the wall, outlined by faded black lines, were various arcane woodworking tools which Maxwell remembered from his own, very short, woodwork classes at school. A diligent student in almost every other way, he had never managed to complete a single item in woodwork. His designs were usually given an A; the finished article didn't have a grade, because there was never a finished article. In the end, he had been allowed to go to the library on Thursday afternoons, when his classmates whittled, smoothed and gouged; it was undoubtedly true that both he and Twinks Mulrooney, the woodwork teacher, were the happier for it.

He looked around for a box and found one stashed under the bench which Marcus had been using as a desk. He piled some tools in and added some blocks of wood from a shelf. They were offcuts cut off so long ago that the ends were as mellow as the sides and they felt dense and heavy, perfect for some fledgling woodworkers. He smelt them, but they just smelt of dry wood. So, where was that lovely pencil shavings smell coming from? He couldn't believe, in this day and age, that Marcus used a pencil and in the unlikely event that he did, that he had sharpened a pencil just minutes before he had left the shed for the last time. He looked around and, in the gloom, he saw the back of a garden chair gleaming out against the grey of the weathered wood. He touched it and smelled his fingers – yes, this was the source. He pulled the chair out and took it outside. He could see when it was out of the shadows that across the back, someone had taken a layer of wood away, the old grey layer that accrued on any teak furniture left out in the weather. He fingered it ruminatively and was still there when Jacquie joined him.

'Sorry,' she said, jogging down the grass-grown path. 'I got a bit indecisive when it came to underpants.' She smiled. 'Some of them had become a bit disreputable and I thought he would appreciate that remaining his secret. Teenagers can be a bit sensitive.'

'Tell me about it,' Maxwell said. He had had enough sensitive teenagers in his life to stretch from here to the moon. 'What do you think of this chair?'

'Nice. But surely Sylvia has enough garden chairs. She can't possibly want this one – look, it's been left out and gone all grey. Like ours.' The jibe was an old one and he ignored it.

'Yes, but look, here, on the back. It's all clean and new.'

'Perhaps Roger Ancaster was doing a bit of renovation. Sitting out in the garden in the nice weather. Let me just let you into the shed. I've got the keys here somewhere.'

'Why would he? They've got a faux wicker dining set and also a swing seat up the garden. And what do you mean, let me in the shed? I've been in, that's where this chair was.'

'It was unlocked?' Jacquie was horrified.

'I was a bit surprised but … if SOCO have finished, surely it's just a shed, isn't it?'

'It shouldn't have been unlocked, though.' She bent to look at the lock. 'It's been picked, look.'

Maxwell couldn't claim to be an expert when it came to locks, but he dutifully looked. 'Hmm, yes,' he said politely.

'I say!'

They both looked up as someone hailed them from beyond the back gate.

'Yes?' Jacquie said. 'Can I help you?'

Her voice was met with a storm of barking and whoever it was in the lane shushed his animal and then stood up. 'I'll just tie up the dog, hang on a minute. He can be a bit much when he meets strangers.'

After a pause, broken by muttered colloquy between man and dog, he pushed the gate open and walked towards them up the path.

'I was surprised to see anyone here,' he said. 'It's a crime scene, you know. A lovely couple were murdered in their beds, or so I'm told.'

Jacquie looked at the man, though it was hard to see much. He wore casual clothes to suit the weather, but from the neck up he was all but invisible. He had swim goggles on his eyes, a blue medical grade mask over his mouth, taped with micropore to his cheeks and across the top of his nose. Over all that, he wore a Perspex mask which curved below his chin. One false move and he could have been on the way to decapitation.

He peered at them. 'You're not wearing masks,' he

pointed out. 'And you're standing far too close together.'

'We weren't expecting to meet anyone,' Jacquie said, reaching for her mask and putting it on. Even with it in place, the newcomer made her feel rather underdressed. 'And I am police, Detective Inspector Carpenter Maxwell, to be absolutely precise.' She flicked her ID out of her pocket and held it up, for all the good it did, in the semi-gloaming and at least ten feet away.

'Precision is always best in these matters, don't you think?' the man said, archly. He looked at Maxwell from behind his modern bassinet. 'Why haven't you put your mask on?' he demanded.

'I don't have one with me.' It was a simple answer to a rather irritating question.

As far as either Maxwell could tell, the man's eyes grew huge with distaste and contempt. 'But what if you needed one in a hurry?'

Before the whole thing could degenerate into maskist name-calling, Jacquie stepped in. 'To be fair, Mr …' she left a gap, but it wasn't filled. 'To be fair, we weren't expecting anyone. As you rightly say, this is a crime scene. And as we are married, we can stand as near to each other as we wish.'

The man looked doubtful. 'I have never really been sure on the government guidelines as to that,' he said, 'but as you are a police person, I will take you at your word. I'm sorry to have interrupted you. I'll let you get on.'

'No, no, don't go. Since you're here, Mr …?' And again the gap was left yawningly empty. Jacquie was getting very disgruntled by the general public's desire for anonymity these days. With so many rules to inadvertently break, no one wanted to stand up and be counted. 'Do you walk your dog regularly along this path?'

'Morning, lunch time if I am at home, and evening,' the man replied promptly. 'I do believe that may be more than the guidelines, but as I live alone, I can't let that interfere with my dog's comfort. He's getting on and after a lifetime of being trained not to Go in the garden, it's not fair to expect him to change overnight.'

'If you're at home?' Maxwell said pleasantly. 'Are you

a key worker?' With all that gear on, he wouldn't have been surprised.

'No, sadly,' the man said. 'Although I always made sure I clapped for carers, only right and proper. No, I am freelance.' He began backing down the path, seeming to be unwilling to turn his back. Perhaps, Maxwell wondered, he was afraid that if he did, Jacquie would whip off her mask and they would both breathe on him.

'Have you ever seen anyone in this garden?' Jacquie asked, as though he was still standing in front of her, not clandestinely leaving.

'The family, when they …' Beneath his masks, he was discomfited.

'What about next door?' Jacquie asked.

'Mrs Bencher? Yes, I talked to her sometimes. Very keen gardener. She occasionally gave me cuttings. Last year, I gave her a root of mirabilis jalapa, but I did warn her it was very vigorous.'

'And on the day she died?'

'I have spoken to your people already. A slip of a thing, posted on the rear gate. I didn't see her that day.'

The sound of a dog yapping came from beyond the hedge.

'I must go. That means another dog is in sight and I don't want there to be an altercation. My old chap is rather out of condition, but he can get a little aggressive with other dogs. Nice to have met you. Good evening,' And with that, against a background of increasing yaps, he was gone.

They watched him go and heard, rather than saw, that the dog fight had been avoided. It had got a lot darker while they had been talking and they had to pick their way carefully back up the path and round the side of the house to the car. They had just got in when Maxwell remembered the tools and wood.

'I'll go,' he said. 'I should have remembered.'

Jacquie got out as well. 'I'll come too,' she said. 'I'd clean forgotten about locking the shed. And I think we'll take that chair with us. I have a thought and I'll need to speak to SOCO. Easier if we have it than leave it here.'

'Easier? What about chain of custody?'

'Ooh, listen to you, Mr *CSI Anywhere At All*! It's not going to be evidence, I don't think. It's just something I want to clear up, for my own sanity.'

The shed door was in total darkness when they got there and Jacquie used her phone to light the lock when Maxwell had rescued the box. It tricky to get the key in. The lock guard was screwed on slightly off true, and it wasn't easy to make the bulky key fit.

'There you go,' she said, looking up at Maxwell. 'It wasn't picked. It's just a real bugger to get the key in. I'm making a mountain out of a molehill. It was just some daffy SOCO forgot to lock up.'

'It's hard to remember everything when your eyes are full of Henry Hall,' Maxwell pointed out.

'Oh, no, it wouldn't be him.' Jacquie was absolutely sure. 'He never forgets anything, ever.'

TWENTY

As Maxwell opened his eyes that morning, to the background of the bird with a megaphone and all his chums, he realised that he had a sinking feeling in his stomach. He hadn't had that on a school day since he was about six, so it was something with which he wasn't entirely familiar. Then he realised – starting with breakfast club, it was going to be him and a couple of dragooned teaching assistants against the rising tide of key workers' children – they didn't want to be there when all their friends were at home, skiving, as they saw it, and even the best behaved were beginning to kick off. They rarely saw their parents and when they did, they were shattered after days spent at the sharp end of the pandemic. The more sensitive among them were in a constant state of fear for their parents' safety. However you looked at it, it was going to be a day and a half. He groaned and pulled the duvet over his head.

'As we're awake,' his wife's voice sounded less than amused and rather muffled as he had pulled the duvet over her head too, 'why don't we get up and face this thing head on?'

'Don't wanna.'

'Don't sulk. A nice leisurely breakfast is going to make us both feel better, isn't it? No coco pops in your hair. No obligatory frozen waffles. Look,' she pulled the duvet down and prised up an eyelid, 'what if I do pancakes?'

'And bacon?' The single eye rolled in her direction and she let go because truth be told it was a bit creepy.

'Of course.' She swung her legs out of bed. 'I'm not an animal. But unless you're down in ten, the whole lot goes in the bin and you face the hordes on an empty stomach. Deal?'

'Deal.' He rolled over and pulled the duvet back up again. 'There in ten. Got it.'

The smell of bacon finally got him motivated enough to become vertical and he made the deadline with seconds to spare.

'I feel bad about this, really,' he said. 'Going to breakfast club after a breakfast like this.'

'I think it's brilliant that the breakfast club is running in all this hooha,' Jacquie said. 'A bit of normality for the kids. And a guaranteed breakfast, as well.'

'It is the most important meal of the day,' Maxwell said, around a mouthful of pancake.

'So they say,' Jacquie said. 'Actually, that's what Tim Cathcart used to say, to excuse bringing a bacon sandwich into meetings. He was the most annoying tit in the whole team, but … he's dead and it's horrible.'

'Any man's death diminishes me, because I am involved in mankind, and therefore never send to know for whom the bells tolls; it tolls for thee.' Everyone could quote – or almost quote – the first five words, but it took Peter Maxwell to quote it all. 'John Donne.'

'John Did, dear.' They were big *Number Nine* fans Chez Maxwell and never missed an opportunity. 'But well said, even so,' Jacquie added. 'I heard some horrible pap yell something about us pulling out all the stops now one of us had been killed. As if we don't do that anyway.' She sighed. 'People are beginning to feel we're never going to catch him because he's just a wandering madman.'

'You keep saying "he",' Maxwell pointed out, in defence of all men. 'Are you sure it is a man?'

'The wounds were … well, we're eating, so I won't go into detail. But I somehow just don't see a woman managing it. Not the ferocity, women can be ferocious, we all know that. But just the *strength* needed. A skull is pretty thick, after all.'

'I don't want to put a dampener on your day, but do you have any idea at all?'

'Not a one. We know more about him every day. He's a whizz at cleaning, we know that. Apart from some dog hairs, which more and more look like red herrings … no, not literally, so you can stop right there … we have nothing. Not a fingerprint, not a human hair, not a scrap of DNA.'

'Of course, these current legislations are helping him no end, aren't they?' Maxwell mopped up the last drop of maple syrup and popped the pancake in his mouth.

'Are they? How? I would have thought that it would have made him more obvious as he made his way about, with fewer people around.'

'There's that, yes, of course. But have you *seen* some people? I mean, look at that idiot last night. Every bit of him wrapped and covered with so much plastic and gauze you could hardly see whether it was a man or a woman. You can't possibly identify someone dressed like that on CCTV. No one can do a description, because everyone looks the same. Voices don't sound right. We've essentially become a nation of lookie likies.'

'That's true. But of course, as we have no sightings …'

'Except I bet Mrs Bencher saw something.' He slurped his coffee and looked at the clock. 'Are you dropping me, or am I riding Surrey?'

'Have you been out on the bike lately? It's probably disappeared under that mountain of packaging in the garage.'

'It's not me who orders everything from Amazon. I wouldn't know how to begin.'

'Point taken, but have you?'

Maxwell made casting-his-mind-back faces and then shook his head.

'I'll drop you, then. What does that give us, ten minutes?'

'Hmmm. In the interests of accuracy, perhaps nine and a half. I'll go and do my teeth, possibly brush my hair. If I still can – working from home is a bad influence.'

Jacquie sat at the table cradling her cooling coffee. It

seemed odd to have them both going off to work. It was quite incredible how fast the unusual became the usual and she wondered – is this really how the world ends, not with a bang, but a whimper?

As Maxwell got out of the car outside the school, there was an unreal feeling to it all. Whenever he arrived as a rule, spinning to a halt in the staff car park and chaining his bike to a handy fence, the place was humming, sounding like a hive on a sunny day on a heatherclad hillside, the noise of people melding into a single sound. As he walked nearer, he would hear the occasional raised voice, a laugh, a slamming door but mostly it would be the tramp of many feet, the buzz of conversation.

Today, the building basked in the sun, but silently. It was looking very spick and span, so the caretakers were clearly using their time wisely. Windows shone, the steps showed no sign of hastily discarded gum or windblown crisp packets. All was neat and tidy and quite, quite soulless. The building had died without its blood coursing through its veins. Even in the holidays, it had never seemed like this, so echoing and bereft.

Inside, the reception desk had a sign on the sliding window, which invited anyone who had come this far to call an 0800 number where their call would be directed to a colleague. No entry signs were on almost every door. Yellow footprints had been stuck to the floor, the statutory distance apart. All the chairs had been removed, stacked in one corner, some police-tape lookalike stretched over them. As Maxwell made his way to the dining room for Breakfast Club, he made himself a promise never to watch a dystopian movie again – this was all too real. He almost expected a lurching zombie to come through the door to his Sixth Form block, one arm hanging useless by its side, one eye on its cheek looking hopelessly skywards. But not even that relieved the silence.

Inside the dining room it wasn't quiet, but even so, the level of noise didn't really represent the number of children there. He did a quick head count and made it about equal to a normal class contingent, which he knew could, on occasion, make a noise like Concorde, may she rest in peace, taking off. These children were chatting, certainly, but there was none of the raucous good humour – and occasional bad humour – that marked them as a rule. They were sitting strictly two to a table, one at each end, the only exception being two sets of siblings, who sat together, them against the world. It was a sad sight.

'Morning, everyone,' Maxwell said, raising his voice a little to combat the deadening acoustic of the dining room. When it had first been built, it was so full of echoes that someone scraping a knife on a plate could bring everyone to their knees, hands over their ears. So, eventually, the education authority had agreed to sound baffles and now it was so deadened that it was like having cheese in your ears.

Every head turned and some called back a greeting. Feelings were clearly mixed. Being taught by random staff in a group which was itself random, was not making for very useful education levels. Some staff had left multi-level lessons, so they could be taught across the board. Some had even videoed themselves giving a lesson which everyone could access in the IT block, which had been re-designed with distancing in mind. But some – Maxwell immediately populated that list in his mind – had just pinned up a couple of ideas in the staffroom and retired rejoicing to DIY, gardening or loafing as their personal tastes dictated.

Over the weeks, the general consensus had been to teach in the dining room, on the principle that they already had their bags with them, they were already sitting down suitably far apart and … there was actually no 'and' – it had become a simple matter of expediency. Trying to keep the group together yet apart to get to another location had proved to be akin to herding cats, so in the end, no one tried.

'When you have finished your breakfasts,' Maxwell continued, 'we will be going out onto the field. If it was good enough for Socrates (or was it Aristotle?) it's good enough for me. Do you all have hats?'

There was a muttered chorus of what Maxwell decided to call assent.

'Sunblock?' He had read the risk assessment and decided for now it made sense.

'Mr Maxwell?' One voice stood out and Maxwell turned to face it.

'Yes, Meriel. What is it?'

'I forgot mine. I'll have to go home.'

'No, you won't. Borrow some.'

'Ain't allowed, Mr Maxwell,' Meriel said, complacently.

'Not generally, Meriel, no. But as the girl sitting next to you is your twin, I think we can stretch a point. Right, anyone else? No? Okay, eat up, then, and we can get out in the nice open air where we don't need quite so many masks and what not.'

'Mr Maxwell?' The voice was muffled.

'Yes … umm, who are you? I can't tell behind the mask.'

'It's Martin, sir,' someone piped up. 'His mum makes him wear triple layers of masks and he can't take them off inside.'

Maxwell was tempted to ask how Martin's mum would know, but desisted. Let the woman have her moment of omnipotence – God knew, it was a short enough span. 'What's the trouble, Martin?'

The boy repeated his question.

'Nope. Sorry. Someone is going to have to … thanks, Coral. Can you translate?'

'He says, can we bring our breakfasts outside, please? He's not allowed to take his mask off indoors so he can't eat it in here.'

'Well, what a brilliant idea. Gather up your …' he looked around, 'your bananas and whatnot and let's get out there in the sun.' He thew the double doors wide and they trooped out, like the children of Hamelin, heading for the land of plenty.

Although she was getting used to it, Jacquie still had a slightly dystopian feel when she went into the nick. Going through the front door normally meant running the gauntlet of outraged neighbours, old ladies with lost dogs and the occasional serial offender leaning on the desk chatting to Genghis as if they were old friends. But now, with no entry signs all over the place, it was empty and quiet.

Upstairs, Henry's office was empty, with a large notice propped up on the desk saying that the DCI was working from home and could be reached on the usual number. And good for you, Jacquie thought, though it was slightly disturbing that even Henry, workaholic Henry, would take time out with a three-time killer on the loose. It did give her carte blanche, though, to make her calls to various other agencies, the need for which might not pass the Hall necessity test.

Firstly, she called the morgue and got Donald on the second ring.

'Yup?' From this, she assumed that the precise Philip McIndoe was not in residence.

'Donald? It's Jacquie.' With Donald, it was a fine line to tread when saying hello. Too formal and you'd get nothing, when he was in a certain mood. On the phone, though, friendly was fine as he had no space to invade.

'Oh, hello. What can I do you for?' That made it definite. McIndoe was certainly nowhere nearby.

'I needed to ask you something, something I am sure you have already done. But if you haven't, could you?'

'Er … okay. That sounds complicated, but I'm sure when you explain it will all fall into place.'

'Yes, sorry, that was a bit confusing. Basically, Donald, I visited the crime scene last night …'

'Are you talking about the Ancaster crime scene, the Bencher crime scene or the Cathcart crime scene.'

'Put like that, it sounds even worse. It was all of the above, I suppose, but the Cathcart one specifically. And Ancaster – there's another question about that.'

'Blimey. Do I need a pen?'

'We'll take things one at a time and then, hopefully, not. First thing – I'm sure you swabbed Tim's hands.' Somehow, using his first name made it sound worse. It made him a real person, not just another victim of violence.

'Of course.' Donald's little grunt of affront was something to watch for. He had been known to withhold details for hours when he got huffy.

'I knew you would have.' Jacquie smiled, hoping it showed in her voice. 'And that's gone off, has it, to the lab?'

'Went off yesterday, mid-afternoon, at a guess. We had some other things to send, so we got a courier, rather than wait for the evening run.'

'Brilliant. So … any results yet, do you think?'

'Dunno. Can you hang on while I go and have a look?'

In the days of Jim Astley, the phone in the morgue was old-school, attached to the wall near the door. This was mainly to prevent Donald and his predecessors from taking a handsfree with them and propping it up in any convenient place, often a body part. But Philip McIndoe had been like a whirlwind round the place, bringing it into the twenty-first century with a bang and the phone was now handsfree. But old habits died hard, so Jacquie knew without being telling that Donald had left the phone on the shelf and gone to check his emails.

While he was gone, she logged on to her own mails and read through – or was skipping a better word? – the plethora of reminders about hands, face, space until she felt like screaming. The number of ways that everyone could break the law these days was just breath-taking. She almost felt like going out and hugging the next person she saw, just for the hell of it. Except that that person would probably be Genghis, so she decided against it.

'Jacquie?' Donald's voice squawked from the desk and she picked up her phone.

'Yes, I'm here.'

'They've sent a preliminary report. It's quite long, so I'll forward it. I'll pop our prelims on as well – the full thing will be along later. Is that okay? I haven't amalgamated them yet.' Donald dropped his voice, despite being· alone. 'Dr McIndoe is a bit of a stickler, if you hadn't noticed. I'm having to scour everything down. *Every day*!' His outrage was palpable.

Jacquie, who in her ignorance has assumed that he

always did that, merely grunted in reply. There didn't seem anything else to do.

'Is it there?'

Jacquie glanced at her screen. 'Yes, it's just arrived. I'll let you get on, while I check it over.'

'Only, I didn't hear a ping.'

'No, I don't have a ping. I have the speaker turned off.'

There was a sigh. 'Yes. Dr McIndoe makes me turn mine off as well. He didn't like me using Spotify. He says it's inappropriate, for some reason.' Jacquie, knowing Donald's taste in music, could only agree. 'Anyway, I'll let you go.' There was something rather plaintive about Donald's voice, but she was firm.

'Yes. Lots to do. Bye, then.' Poor Donald, she thought, all dressed up, and nowhere to go.

She clicked on his email and opened the first attachment, which was the preliminary post mortem report. There was nothing she wasn't expecting there, so quickly closed it again. There was no need at this point to make matters worse by reading about Cathcart's injuries. The second one was less gory and more interesting. She skipped the list of material sent, with the long numbers full of forward slashes and digits which probably meant something to someone. The nitty gritty made her punch the air, though she didn't know why. It confirmed her suspicions, but got her absolutely no further forward. She was just digesting it to pass it on to Henry when her phone rang.

'DI Carpenter Maxwell.'

'Jacquie? It's me, Donald.'

She stifled a sigh. She had poked the dragon in its lair so more fool her. 'Yes, Donald. Everything has arrived fine.'

'I know that. I always put a read alert on, so I know you've got it.' Jacquie couldn't help look over her shoulder. It was a little like being stalked. 'You said you wanted to know something else, but you didn't ask me anything else.'

'Did I? Didn't I? I wonder … oh, yes, I know what it was. Who arranges the crime scene cleaners?'

'Now you've asked me. It's you lot, isn't it? When everything is sorted. There won't have been a visit yet.

Sometimes it's months. I know one of them, he's on my darts team. He says it can be gross after a long time. Especially in this weather. Not much to do in the middle one, I would think nature will sort that one for you. But in the house and shed, it could be ages. *Will* be ages, I should say. Why, has someone complained?'

'No.' Jacquie was confused. 'I was there last night, as I told you, but … Donald? Can you ring your friend? I don't want to get everyone aerated if there has been a mistake. Can you get him to ring me, please?'

'No problem.' Donald liked to be in the thick of things. 'Is it urgent?'

'Ish. If it's no trouble.'

'No trouble at all. I'll ring him now.'

'You're a star. Thank you so much. And for ringing me back. Forget my head, next.'

You're catching old from that geezer you're married to, Donald thought. But he kept that to himself.

The morning had gone better than Maxwell could possibly have hoped. Outside, spread out on the grass, the kids had soon become completely entangled in Maxwell's tales of derring-do. He had explained the rules to them. He would start with a topic and would tell them about it, no need for notes, there wouldn't be a test. If they had a question, they could ask it, but if the question took them off at a tangent, then that tangent was where they would go, like it or not. So, he had begun with telegraph poles.

'Eh?'

'Tall thing, Mustafa,' Maxwell explained. 'Made of wood. Over there. You've walked past hundreds of them in your young lives. I wouldn't recommend this or they might lock you up, but when they first put those things up in America, the Indians …'

He paused while Alistair, the Most Politically Correct Boy in the School, put him right.

'Native Americans,' Alistair said.

Maxwell beamed behind the mask. 'I knew I could rely on you, Alistair,' he said. 'The Native Americans didn't know what they were, but if they put their ears to the polies, they could hear the wires humming – singing, as they called it'

'Didn't it frighten them, sir?'

'It probably did, Katrina, yes. But they'd already learned how to handle the white man's guns and horses. Which leads me on the *Winchester 73*. Anybody,' and he knew what the answer would be 'heard of an actor called James Stewart?'

'Wasn't he in *It: Chapter Two*?' somebody asked.

'Almost certainly not, in that James Stewart died in 1997. And you, Bonnie, are too young to be watching *It*, no matter what chapter it is. But while we're talking about clowns …'

Rather spookily, the bells still rang throughout the school to mark the divisions between lessons long forgotten. Like Pavlov's dog, he could almost hear the rumble of feet and the shrill of voices as every session was marked and ignored. Finally, though, it was the lunchtime bell, slightly longer than the others, and the student body began to stir, sitting where they had been lying, standing where they had been sitting, stretching, yawning, reaching for their packed lunches, warm now from being out in the sun, crushed from being in a bag which had become a pillow.

According to the rules, Maxwell let his charges go in one by one to get cold drinks from the machine and then, with them all disposed in their ones and occasional twos around the place, he stood up, brushed the grass from his knees and clapped his hands for attention.

'Ladies and gentlemen, this has been enormous fun.' And, to his surprise, it had been. 'I am popping inside now to check on any messages in my office and in the staffroom. If you need me urgently, I will be in one of those places. This afternoon, we will be convening in the shade of those two trees over there.' He pointed to two oaks which had somehow avoided the general scorched earth policy of the builders back in the day. 'When the sun comes round, it will be too hot out here. For the rest of the day, we will be exploring scientific advances since … well, since who knows when. I may not be too hot on the subject after Faraday, so I will be largely relying on you.'

'I have to leave at two,' one lad called. 'It's my mum's shifts.'

'I totally understand,' Maxwell said. 'I have a list here of everyone who has to go early. Please do not insult us both by pretending you are on it when you aren't. But take it as read that it's okay, so just go when the time comes. Any other questions while I'm here?'

There seemed to be nothing, so he beat a retreat indoors. A nice packet of Wotsits and a Dr Pepper and he would manage until he got home. The teaching assistants who had been rendered pointless by Maxwell's methods were sitting in the staffroom, feet up but they jumped to attention as he went in.

'Ooh, do you need us?' one of them said, suddenly guilt-ridden.

'Not really,' he said, mildly. 'Though if you want to pop outside and watch that mob while I'm not there, it might save us from a lawsuit down the line.'

They both dashed out, grateful to be let off the hook.

Maxwell opened a window and sat near it, partly for the look of the thing, partly because the smell of maturing banana peel in the bin under the sink was a little overpowering otherwise. He ate his Wotsits and popped open his can and was just meandering nicely into the Land of Nod when the sound of a hoover jerked him rudely awake.

After a few false starts, he sat upright and saw something that had become as rare as a sighting of a phoenix. Mrs B., in all her overalled glory, was making her way across the untenanted acres of staffroom floor, led by the business end of her Henry.

It was hard to know which of them had the greatest shock. Mrs B. certainly turned as white as a sheet and fumbled for the arm of a chair before collapsing into it. Maxwell recovered first and dashed over, stopping short as he saw the alarm in her eyes. When, if ever, would that end, he wondered.

'Mrs B.!' he said, sitting opposite. 'I didn't know you were back?'

'I had time on my hands, what with Jessica and everything. I didn't know you were here either. What's happening to Nolan? He's surely not at school, is he? Not with all these viruses in the air? Is Mrs M. at work? What about all those murders, then? Do they know who done them?'

'I expect you did. It was a bit of a surprise to me as well. He's with his friend, you know, Plocker. Certainly not, though I understand they're still open, as we are. There are, aren't there, but it's best not to believe everything. She is. I know. No, they don't.' There was something very comforting to be back in the old routine. Then, he added a rider, which the elephant in the room insisted he ask. 'Any news on Mrs Troubridge?'

Tears welled in the woman's eyes and slowly spilled over and soaked into her mask. 'I rung this morning,' she grated. 'It's a disgrace, how long they take to answer the phone. I know I shouldn't complain but, well, it's different, ain't it, Mr M., when it's your own?'

Breaking with tradition, Maxwell just answered the final question. 'It is, Mrs B. Very different indeed.' He waited for the rest. He knew it would come in her good time.

'It took ages, but when I got through to the ward, it was a different nurse, not the one I've had before.' She took in a shuddering breath. 'I had to prove I was allowed to ask. I had to give her Jessica's date of birth, address, my date of birth – oh, Mr M., you wouldn't believe the palaver!'

'But, in the end, she talked to you?'

At his gentle prompting, Mrs B. nodded and dropped her head, the tears dropping now on her clasped hands. 'In the end, yes. She did.'

Silence was the only way to go from here, so he waited until she was ready.

'After all that … after all that, she went away to check. I could hear her feet, clacking away. I could hear people talking. Then, somebody picked up the phone and asked who I was. So, I said and … and he said, "Didn't they ring you? She died, about half past seven."' She lifted her head and howled. 'And that was it, Mr M. "She died" as if that's all she was. A dead old lady, at half past seven.' She held her arms out, this woman who had never asked for anything, who had never asked for a hug in all her hard-working, put upon life. And in an instant, Maxwell was across the two metre divide and held her, while they cried, for poor Jessica Troubridge, one among so many, who had died at about half past seven.

TWENTY-ONE

Jacquie wasn't missing Henry Hall that much. She had got through so much work she was starting to think about heading home, then remembered that Maxwell was at school until at least four, so she decided instead to go to the vending machine and grab a sandwich. While she was there, trying to decide between a rather manky-looking chicken and sweetcorn – something she never had at home as Maxwell considered sweetcorn in bread an affront to civilisation – and a slightly less-manky-looking egg and cress, her phone rang.

'Is that Jacquie?'

She didn't have calls that informal from unknown numbers on her work phone as a rule, so was wary. 'Who's speaking, please?'

'This is Chris. Friend of Donald's.'

'Of *course*. Sorry, he said you'd be ringing back. You're one of the crime scene cleaning crew, is that right?'

'One of a very small crime scene cleaning crew just now, yes.' He seemed a jolly sort of chap, bearing in mind what he did for a living. 'How can I help you?'

'Sorry to have bothered you, but trying to get through to any central point these days …'

'Tell me about it. I quite understand. I'm just in the office checking the emails, so I've got the schedules in front of me, so fire away.'

'That's amazing, Chris. Thank you. I just want to know when you went to clean at 67, Broadgate Avenue.'

There was a silence. 'Is that the married couple?'

'That's right, yes. And, of course, very sadly, a policeman the night before last.'

'I don't hardly need a schedule for that. We won't be there for a couple of weeks yet.'

'So … you definitely haven't been there.'

'No. Definitely not. You lot would have our guts for garters if we went in this soon. You might need to check something. And believe me, when we've been in, there's nothing to check. Guaranteed.'

'My mistake, then.'

'Can I ask why you're asking?'

Jacquie knew that the real questioner here was Donald, but she saw no harm in quenching their curiosity. 'I was there last night and … long story cut short, really, the place is spotless.'

'Where they died, everything?' The man was clearly amazed.

'Yes. There isn't even a stain on the rug.'

'It's not some over-zealous family member, is it? A neighbour? Sometimes people do shove an oar in. We've had it happen to us sometimes. Although they don't usually make much of a job of it. Getting bloodstains out isn't a job for just anyone.'

'I'm quite sure it isn't.' Jacquie knew professional pride when she heard it. 'Well, if you're sure, I'll just have to spread my net.'

'Sorry not to have been more help.'

'No problem. It's as helpful to know who it isn't as to know who it is. Or at least, almost as helpful. Thank you for getting back to me. And good luck in your next darts match, whenever that might be.'

'This year, next year, sometime, never,' he said, ending the call.

Jacquie walked back to her desk, sandwich forgotten, walking in step with the old skipping rhyme. She had an email flashing as she slid back behind her desk. It was an update on the forensics, still minus final DNA, which took longer.

'Addendum,' it began. 'The three small sawdust fragments and associated resin from victim's right palm and thumb now confirmed as coming from the wood of the teak tree, *Tectona grandis*. Also present were minute traces of preservative, suggesting that the sawdust and resin in question come from a piece of garden furniture, possibly older as the preservative element was minimal.' Written at the bottom, in blue, was 'Hope this helps. D.' Jacquie smiled to herself. She could add another parameter to their murderer's profile. They now needed to look for someone who was a really excellent cleaner. Now she put it into words to herself, it sounded less exciting. But any news was good news at this point, so she punched Henry's number into the phone and waited for him to answer. He'd had the morning off – hopefully he hadn't got an overdose of Dettol in the interim.

Maxwell and Mrs B. were deaf to the bell that went to signal the end of lunchtime. The teaching assistants poked their heads round and saw that Mad Max was in a clinch with a cleaner and decided that discretion was the better part of valour and went out to the shade of the oaks, where they started a game of Six Degrees of Separation. Because most of the kids didn't know Kevin Bacon from a hole in the ground, they chose Arianna Grande and it went surprisingly well.

Back in the staffroom, Mrs B. finally cried herself to a standstill and extricated herself from Maxwell's embrace. They had both found a good howl very cathartic and now were re-established in their original seats, noses blown and eyes wiped.

'Have you spoken to Jacquie?' Maxwell asked.

'No. I didn't want to bother her. And I knew you wouldn't have your phone.'

There was no argument to be made there.

'So I thought I'd come up here, take my mind off things. The house … well, she'd lived there so long, it's as if she's still there. I'll have to have a clearout, I suppose, but not yet. It's not decent.'

'Do you know …?' Maxwell remembered how he had felt when people started asking him about his mother's will, minutes after she had died so stopped himself from asking the obvious. 'Do you know if she had any thoughts on her funeral?' he asked, as a slightly better question.

'Oh, don't get me started on that, Mr M.! She talked of almost nothing else, some days. Depending on the mood, she wanted to be buried in a cardboard box under a tree somewhere, burned and scattered out at sea or what amounted more or less to a state funeral. So, who knows which one it was when she wrote it down.'

'She wrote it down?' Maxwell was surprised that Mrs Troubridge was that organised. As he had always found, she just set out to do things with no planning and just expected the world to get out of her way.

'She had the solicitor round, just before lockdown. I don't know what was said,' Mrs B. primmed her mouth virtuously. 'I've never been one to pry.'

As someone who had bowled the woman over several times over the years by the simple expedient of opening a door suddenly, Maxwell doubted that, but let it go.

'She did leave a note, all signed and that, to say I could stay in the house while all this was going on. She got the ambulance men to sign it.'

'It shows she trusted you with the house. That's nice.'

She sniffed and her eyes welled up again. 'She knew I didn't want to go home. It's bad enough when they can all go to the pub all hours, but cooped up …' She shuddered. 'I couldn't stand it.'

'It will be lovely to still have you next door, if only for a while.'

'Thank you. Same to you.'

They sat silently for a few moments, each lost in their own thoughts. Maxwell knew that they both knew very different Mrs Troubridges, but they had one thing in common; she was loyal and loving and once she had decided you were her kind of people, then you were set with her for life. The fact that she could include Bismarck, Nolan and Mrs B. in her broad church perhaps proved, more than anything else, what a really amazing old dear she was.

''Course, Jessica isn't the first one to've died on me,'

Mrs B. said, suddenly. 'First one to upset me like this, though. I don't know how old she was.' She made the statement into a question and Maxwell shook his head – he had no idea either, except perhaps 'very'. 'But I reckon she had years in her yet. No, first ones to die on me, it was the Pettifers.'

It wasn't like Mrs B. to reminisce. Her present had so much going on in it as a rule, what with feckless husband, even more feckless sons and a daughter who seemed set fair to repopulate a small town with children by various men, that she had no time for the past. But Maxwell, of all people, knew the peace that dwelling on the past could bring, so he gave her her head. He would just interject the occasional interested grunt and see where they ended up.

'Not that old, they weren't. He was a bit older than her, I suppose.' She looked upwards, calculating. 'She had their last when she must have been knocking fifty, mind. Not so common then, it wasn't. Not like those pop stars now, having kids when they're fifty-odd and pretending it's all normal. Not right, I don't reckon.'

It was time to join in, briefly. 'No, indeed it isn't.' He picked a name out of the blue. 'That Janet Jackson. Tcha!'

'Mr M.! I wouldn't have thought you were a fan.'

He laughed. 'I'm not. I just remember you being just as outraged when she had her baby as you are now.'

She smiled back, the tear tracks still on her cheeks. 'And why not? Anyway, Mrs Pettifer, she had four kids in what you might call the normal way, almost grown up the youngest was, when she had little Theo. They didn't like it a bit, but they didn't have much to complain about. They'd all left home or as near as never mind when he come along. My word, that's a long time ago. My old mum was their cleaner then. I used to go with her sometimes. It was nice to play with a baby.' She looked up at Maxwell, suddenly. 'I'm an only one, you know. Not many people know that. Have you got any brothers or sisters, Mr M.?'

'I've got a sister.' This conversation was taking much the shape of his morning's lesson, going wherever the wind took it. 'We don't see much of each other. She often lives abroad with her husband's job.' He made a note to self to email her as soon as he got home – it had been too long.

'Well, anyway, my poor old mum, she got rheumatics in her knees and had to give up most of her jobs. I was older then and looking for work, so I took some of them on and Mr and Mrs Pettifer was one.'

'Did you never think of …' Maxwell almost said 'a proper job' but mercifully stopped himself, in the nick of time judging by Mrs B.'s narrowed eyes.

'If the internet had been around when I was at school, Mr M.,' she said scathingly, knowing she had him by the short and curlies when it came to technology, 'I might be Steve Jobs now, only not dead, o' course. But at the time, it was cleaning or barmaiding and I chose cleaning. It's not done me so bad. I've got some savings – which I would thank you to never mention, if you don't mind, knowing my gannetting lot – and I've made some friends.'

Maxwell smiled. 'You have indeed, Mrs B.,' he said.

'Don't be so soft,' she said, flapping her hand at him, but anyone could have told that she was as pleased as Punch. 'But Mrs Pettifer was special, because I'd known her so long, see. Theo still lived at home when I was cleaning there. But there was never much to do. I used to say to her, "Mrs P.," I'd say, "do you clean up before I come, because if so, you shouldn't. It's what you pay me for." And she'd say no, but I always wondered. And more now, because I've worked for some pigs in my time. Ooh!' she looked up, aghast. 'Present company excepted, Mr M., of course.'

'Of course.' Maxwell knew that the next thing would be the story of the cleanee, as he and Jacquie referred to them as, who, gospel truth, Mrs M., as I live and breathe, would use the wet room as a loo and push any solids down the drain with his heel. And indeed it was. When it was over, she was back to Mr and Mrs Pettifer. During the wet room story, he had wandered across to the window and glanced out, but everything seemed happy and content under the greenwood tree, so he resumed his seat.

'At first, it wasn't that obvious. Mr P. got a bit forgetful and in the end, they had to stop him driving. Mrs P. had never learned, so I used to take her shopping and that, for a change, because he started to get quite aggressive with her, ordering her about. When I got there, sometimes, he'd made her cry. A few years after he started to decline, he went off one day and didn't come back. She was frantic. But he was found a few days later, he'd wandered out onto the Dam and just curled up behind a wall up there and just died. It was the best way, in many respects, but a shock.'

'I should think it was,' Maxwell said. 'Do you remember that case up on the Dam, where the old chap drove the wrong way in the car park and ...'

'Went over the edge? Course I do. It was Amelia's parents. Now ... what was her name? She married that ... ooh, horrible bloke. All hands. Wait a minute ... Beacher? No, Bencher. That was it. She was murdered, you know, the other day. But of course you know – it would have been a case for Mrs M., I expect, though it's clear the husband did it.'

Maxwell tried not to sit there with his mouth open, but feared he had failed in his quest. 'Did you clean for them as well?'

'Oh, no. I'm afraid they were a bit fur coat and no knickers. Liked to make out they had money, but I don't think they did. I always thought he did it on purpose, before anyone found out. Very proud. And poor Amelia. Very proud.' She sat there, shaking her head and considering how pride cometh before a fall, though she probably wouldn't have phrased it quite like that. Though, with Mrs B., who could tell? Since her surfing days had begun, she was a fund of unconsidered trifles.

'How did you know them, then?' He was working it out and thought that possibly the two Mrs B's were about of an age.

She looked at him as though at the village idiot. 'Because, they lived just along the road from Mrs P. When Mr P. died, they were lovely to her. They'd come and visit, take her out. Really nice, they were. I think for a while, they hoped that Amelia and Theo might make a couple. There were a few years between them, but nothing to matter.'

'But Amelia met ...' Maxwell suddenly realised that he

knew far more than he should, then he remembered it was Mrs B. and he could say what he liked – they had no secrets from her. 'Charles.'

'That's it. Charles. What a piece of work he was. Amelia and I are of an age, more or less …' Maxwell secretly awarded himself a Brownie point 'and so we'd see each other, out and about, you know. Before I met the first Mr B.'

Mrs B,'s marital history was an arcane and secret thing and Maxwell found it best to just tag along.

'That Charles, all the girls hated him. He was always a bit handy, but if he got you in a corner, he took liberties above and beyond. I give him a black eye once and I'm not ashamed to say. But Amelia, she was besotted, and they got married. I think he thought there was money, so he must have been disappointed to find there wasn't.'

Maxwell made a note to tell Jacquie this, although Charles Bencher seemed to have been cleared as far as the police were concerned. With so few cars on the road, anyone on a journey like his would have stood out like a sore thumb.

'But anyway, Mrs P. was never the same. She lingered a year or two but when she died it was really a release. The kids – the eldest ones, not Theo, he never left her side – had all moved away, didn't visit much. They had kids of their own and they'd never even met their grandmother, most of 'em. It was a shame. Theo was working by then, very creative, he was. Arty, you know what I mean.'

'What did he do?' Maxwell was going through the motions, still assimilating the fact that Mrs B. knew Amelia and Charles Bencher.

'I don't know. An artist, maybe? I know he used to keep the house beautiful. Decorating, that kind of thing. A bit dated now, it would be, very Eighties. One wall with big patterns, that kind of thing. Once he had finished a room, that was it. He didn't like things moved. And clean! I stopped going after a while, because I felt bad taking their money. They didn't have much. But I still went to see Mrs P., just as a friend, like, and to please my mum. She worried about her, on her own, but her rheumatics …' Mrs B. made a rueful face. 'She couldn't get out much, at the end.'

'Mrs B.,' Maxwell said, 'Have you ever read the poem *Sons of Martha*, by Kipling? If not, you should.'

'They shut the road through the woods,' Mrs B. suddenly and unexpectedly said, 'Seventy summers ago. Weather and rain have undone it again, and now you would never know there was once a road through the woods, before they planted the trees.' She laughed at Maxwell's face. 'They learned me that at school. I say that to myself, sometimes. It's nice.'

'Indeed it is,' Maxwell agreed. You could never go far wrong when you had some Kipling in your head.

'So anyway, Mrs P. died. She had cancer, poor soul. Very quick it was, though.'

'So, Mr and Mrs Pettifer lived in Broadgate Avenue?' Maxwell thought he had better check because with Mrs B. it never did to assume facts.

'Yes, of course they did. I said that, didn't I?' She thought for a moment. 'Well, perhaps not in so many words, but yes, they did. At that house where that couple died. Number 67.'

Now, Maxwell's mouth really did hang open and he wasn't ashamed to show it.

'Mrs M. will have found out all about the house, though, won't she? There was a real fuss when Mrs P. died. She'd left it to all the family, you see, in equal shares. It wasn't the right thing to do, not really. One of the lads – Brian, was it? Bernard? Can't remember – he had four kids, so there's five shares in one household, right there. And poor Theo, it was his home, still. And he couldn't afford to buy the others out, though if you knew what those houses fetched in the mid-Eighties, you'd weep!'

'Mid-Eighties. So … who bought it, do you know?'

'It was snapped up, that I do know. Now … let me think. I know they asked me if I would clean for them, but I was just getting married and expecting my Dawn … Leadbetter, that's it. And of course, they was murdered as well.' She laughed. 'Mr M., I do believe I know almost as many murdered people as you do!'

'I doubt it,' Maxwell said, absently. 'What happened to

Theo?'

'I don't know. I see him sometimes, around town. He doesn't seem to have done too badly for himself. He looks quite respectable. But I know he was all over the place at first. Well, o' course, all he had was a fraction of the house sale, I reckon it must have been split a dozen or so ways, and that wasn't much. He got a flat in town, I think, but he was always hanging round Broadgate Avenue. I know Amelia found him a couple of times in her garden. But he stopped doing that, in the end. He was just sad, poor lad. A bit lost.'

Maxwell could feel a pricking in his thumbs. Something evil this way comes.

Mrs B. suddenly slapped her knees and got up. 'I've done nothing this afternoon, Mr M.,' she said. 'You'll talk the hind leg off a donkey, you will! I must get on.' And she and Henry meandered off into the corner of the staff room, where the biggest spiders in the world lurked, grown fat on forgotten crumbs.

Maxwell looked out again and under the oaks, everyone seemed to be having a raucous time. He wandered out and sat at the edge of the crowd, unremarked. He didn't know a single name of the many being bandied about so after a while, mimed making a phone call to one of the assistants, who gave him a thumbs up before adjudicating whether it was possible to link Bob Marley with Arianna Grande in any universe. Maxwell made his way back to the main building, happy that they had even heard of Bob Marley in the first place. Or his ghost.

He had got used to the odd echo in the school now, so didn't feel fazed by it as he made his way to his office. He knew he should have his mobile with him but settled for knowing exactly where it was – it was in the pocket of the passenger side door of Jacquie's car, put there temporarily when searching for a restorative fruit pastille on the way to school that morning. So he needed a landline and hoped that they hadn't been temporarily disabled in some insane cost cutting measure by County Hall.

He picked up the receiver and dialled nine. The

reassuring burr was very welcome and he tapped in Jacquie's number, which he had finally managed to learn. It didn't matter how often people told him that mobile numbers were the same length as landline numbers, they still weren't as easy to remember. But finally, he had Jacquie's down pat, even if he couldn't remember his own.

'The person you have called knows you are waiting. Please leave a message after the tone. If you would like …'

Drat! Of all the times for Jacquie to be on the phone to someone else. It wasn't every day, after all, that he could ring and give her the name of a murderer, no matter how tentatively. He left a message.

'Hello, heart. I've just had a long chat with Mrs B.' Oh, hell. He couldn't tell her about Mrs Troubridge on the phone; that would be horrible. 'I think I may have a name for you. Not definite, of course, but it might be good to look up Theodore Pettifer. Not sure of the spelling, but how many can there be? He does something arty according to Mrs B. See you later. It's …' he looked at the clock which seemed to have stopped weeks ago 'some time this afternoon. I'm heading off to Broadgate Avenue, it's not far from here. Just for a shufti. I'll see you there, shall I? Mwah.' And he rang off.

'So, how much further does this get us?' Henry said. He was in what he obviously fondly thought of as smart casual, but in fact it was far too tweedy for that. Nonetheless, he was relaxing a bit more, and that had to be good.

'I don't know whether it gets us further, as such,' she said. 'But it is odd, isn't it? Someone has been in and cleaned. And I mean *really* cleaned the place up. There wasn't a mark anywhere, no stains, no nothing. Even the specialists would have trouble getting it that clean. It would have taken ages. They'd even put clean bedding on the bed, ready to make it up. And the lock … I told you about the lock?'

Hall nodded. She certainly had something, it was simply a matter of deciding what.

'And another thing. When Max and I were there last night, picking up the bits for Marcus, Max thought he saw a face at the window. He said it was the reflection of a cloud, but that's because he thought that's what it had to be, because the house had to be empty, do you see? So he rationalised it. But what if it wasn't a cloud? What if it was actually a face, looking down from a bedroom window?'

'But you went in, then.' Henry was playing devil's advocate. 'Surely you would have known if anyone was there?'

'Not necessarily. I went into Marcus's bedroom. I only noticed the cleaning in the master bedroom because the door was ajar and it should have been bloody on the threshold and wasn't. There are two more bedrooms, a bathroom and an ensuite. Anyone could have been hiding there.'

'Hmm.'

She could tell he was far from convinced. 'And in the shed, don't forget. Your SOCO stalker said about the surface under the blood being clean. And it wasn't that clean for the first sweep after the first murder.'

'But still … it doesn't give us a name. Not even a lead. I don't think putting a man on overnight will go down well in the circumstances, do you?'

'I'm not asking for a man, guv. I don't mind going myself.'

Hall exploded. 'Don't be bloody ridiculous, woman! Four people are dead, struck down from behind. What makes you think you're immune from that?'

She blinked. He rarely raised his voice and never to her. 'I … I don't think that. But knowing what the perp's MO is …'

'And stop talking like some copper on the telly. It doesn't make the idea any less stupid. If anyone is going, I am.'

'Oh, really?' she snapped back. 'And you are immune, then, are you?'

They had approached to far less than six feet apart. In any cop show, in the next ten seconds they would be in a clinch, ten more and they would be naked writhing to annoying background music. But this being real life, Hall simply threw his hands up in the air and gave in. 'Okay,' he said. 'You ring Max. I'll ring Margaret. We'll meet in the car park in ten. Grab a couple of cans of something from the vending machine on the way out. It could be a long night.'

She looked at him and grinned. She hadn't thought it would be anything like that easy. She dialled Maxwell's number and wasn't surprised when it went to voicemail. 'I've had a bit of an exciting day, discovery-wise,' she said. 'So I can't pick you up, I'm afraid. I hope you don't mind getting home by yourself. If that doesn't work, drop me a text and we'll sort something. Nole is okay with Plocker for tonight, so no worries there. I'll ring the landline later, you old dinosaur. Love you.'

And, grabbing her bag and her jacket, she went off to catch a murderer.

TWENTY-TWO

axwell had slightly underestimated the distance to Broadgate Avenue, but the day was pleasant, a bit cooler than earlier, and with his jacket over his shoulder, like the pelisse of one of his plastic Light Brigade, and a bottle of water in his pocket, he felt quite light-hearted as he strolled along. He could only picture the scene at the nick, when Jacquie got his tip. They would find the guy in minutes – after all, he was still local and his name wasn't exactly commonplace – and this walk would be pointless. But when they arrived, just to dot their eyes and cross their tees, he would be sitting, nonchalantly, at the Ancasters' faux wicker dining set, taking the evening air. Life was good – it wasn't every day a man solved four murders, or possibly six, while sitting comforting their next door neighbour's carer. He was glad he had been on minder patrol today. Every cloud had a silver lining, after all.

When Jacquie got downstairs, Henry was waiting in the lobby.

'We're going to have to postpone our little visit,' he said. 'There's an all cars – and that means all bodies – call out down to the Front. Apparently, there's been some kind of flash mob stunt, all fuelled by social media, of course, and the place is teeming with sunbathers, skinny dippers, you name it. Not a mask between them and some crazy conspiracy theorist is banging on about the whole pandemic being a Tory plot. We've got to get there, asap.'

Jacquie had never actually heard Henry say asap before, so could tell it was serious.

'Don't get your car. We'll go in mine, sod the distancing regs.'

There was a steady stream of coppers exiting the building, all heading for the Front. Some of the more athletic were jogging – with the traffic chaos which must be pertaining down there, it was probably quicker. Cameramen had appeared from nowhere, the local radio had sent a representative and the BBC news stringer was tagging along, anything to make the Tories look bad was okay by him.

Jacquie rode along with Hall and felt she should have a shotgun across her lap. 'What do we do when we get there, guv?' she asked. 'We can't bang that many heads together, can we?'

He sighed. 'You're right. We can't. And if I had my way, we'd just leave them all to breathe on one another and let nature take its course. But we have to be seen to be doing something, God help us, and this is all we can do. Muster some numbers and go down and drag some of the stupid bastards into a Maria.'

He took the final turn onto the seafront and the scene that met them looked like a Breughel representation of hell. If Leighford had seen the same number of visitors on any normal summer's day, the shopkeepers would have died happy. The crowds milled slowly about, shoulder to shoulder, no masks or any attempt to comply with any regulation. On a makeshift podium, a scruffy-looking man with a megaphone was yelling disjointed phrases at the crowd, who every now and again let rip with a cheer. On the water's edge, a rim of nude bathers looked like scum washed up on a rough tide. The police charged with collecting them up and ushering them into vans were not quite sure what to grab, because whatever they chose, they would be headlines the following day.

Behind Hall's car, a row of police vans were honking and hitting their siren buttons in frustration. Some of the crowd looked slightly startled to be there; they were locals who had been in the habit of going for a gentle constitutional before going home to watch that nice Mr Whitty and Vallance, see what the news of fresh disasters was for today. And suddenly, there they were, in the middle of an insane mob of yelling people. The locals were trying to go one way. The rabble were trying to go the other. In the end, both pedestrians and cars and vans were in the gridlock to end all gridlocks and no one was going anywhere.

Maxwell subsided on the faux wicker with a sigh. He almost wished he had his phone with him. He had seen Jacquie check her step count and it would be intriguing to know how far he had walked. The sun was warm and he moved into the shade, sipping his water and looking forward to the arrival of his wife. He tilted his head back and let his mind wander. Life was going to be strange without Mrs Troubridge next door. It wasn't as though she was any trouble as far as the day to day went, but she had been involved in so many of their crises big and small, they would miss her. And who would move in? It would be nice if Nolan could have a friend next door, as Maxwell had, but a family of screaming children might not be a good fit. He sighed. Always another problem …

'It's no good, Henry,' Jacquie said, leaning away from the unpleasant sight of someone's beer belly in an inadequate tee shirt pressed against the passenger window. 'As soon as this bloke has unpeeled his gut off this door, I'm going back to the nick, getting in my car and driving round to Broadgate Avenue. Yes, yes, I know.' She held up a hand. 'Don't start about immunity. Lecture these idiots on immunity, not me. This is totally insane and to have a Detective Chief Inspector and a Detective Inspector trapped in a car in the middle of it is the most insane part of it. We've been here over an hour and not moved a yard. So, I'm off.'

    She wound down the window and poked the encroaching belly hard with her pen. She ignored the stream of invective and pushcd the door, hard, muscling her way out. She stuck her head in through the window. 'I'll let you know how I get on,' she said and turned to force her way through the crowd.

She wasn't making very good headway until suddenly, she felt the press behind her lessen.

'I don't think we are doing much good in a car, no,' Hall said in her ear. 'Let's push together and see how we do. Head for Arundel Street, look, up there ahead. We can cut through that way and get to the nick in no time.'

'But, Henry – your car!'

'Is likely to be in its component parts by morning. I never really liked it. Come on. Push!'

Maxwell woke to find that the pleasant sun had turned to a less pleasant dusk. He glanced around but was still alone, or at least, he was as far as he could tell. He listened as hard as he could but there wasn't so much as a whisper of a vole in the undergrowth. Obviously, the feline population in Broadgate Avenue were of the same persuasion as the killing machines of Columbine. Even so, moving carefully, he got up from his seat and moved down the path to the shed. He tried the door and, not very much to his surprise, he found it open. Either it was the strangest lock on earth, or he was not alone at Number 67, Broadgate Avenue.

He flung the door open and stood foursquare in the opening, relying on the element of surprise. It was empty, the interior gloom tense and expectant. He checked behind him and slid in through the open door, closing it behind him, and pulled Marcus's homework chair across to the far wall and sat on it, facing the only direction his attacker could appear from. He folded his arms and waited.

While the little light lasted, he looked around. The spaces where the woodworking tools had hung looked odd. It must be a trick of the light but surely … he got up and felt carefully. His first impression had been right – replacement tools hung there, not identical but as near as made no difference at all. Someone had noticed they had gone and had put some back, so that the shed still looked the same. Somehow, this fact sent more of a chill down Maxwell's spine than any other and he pressed himself back into the chair, making sure the wall was between him and anything or anyone outside. It began to dawn on him that being stuck in a shed without any means of communication with the outside world, probably in close proximity to a hammer wielding maniac was not the best situation in the world to be in. Also, Jacquie was taking an age to get there. He had got out of the habit of wearing a watch in lockdown but he hadn't missed it all day, ruled by bells. But now he began to wonder what the time was. When he should give up waiting for Jacquie. When he should try his best to get out of this shed and make his way back to the street, with luck without getting his skull bashed in.

Then his heart nearly stopped. What if Jacquie *had* arrived? What if she was, even now, lying on the path, dead? Studying history had not made Maxwell imaginative. As a rule, everything that happened happened for a reason, but did that apply to hammer wielding maniacs? There was no real precedent as far as he could remember. He began to ease himself away from the wall and flex his knees, ready for action, whatever that action needed to be.

Then he heard it. Footsteps approaching the shed, with a determined stride. It wasn't Jacquie, that much he knew. But perhaps she was with someone. Or had sent someone. Or …

It took far longer than Henry's estimate, but eventually, they were at Jacquie's car. There was total gridlock heading down to town, but by turning left, they should be able to take a fairly circuitous route to Broadgate Avenue without too many detours. In the car, Jacquie fished out her phone.

'I'm sorry, Henry. I must just ring Max again. I don't expect he has even looked at his phone today. He's really not ready to join this century yet.' Signal wasn't great in the car park so it took a few seconds before the screen said 'Calling'. And when it did, they both heard Maxwell's phone ringing loud and clear. Henry fished it out of the door pocket and held it up with a wry expression on his face.

'I don't know why you even try,' he said. 'Why not just send him out with a couple of pigeons and a basket? It would be more reliable.'

Jacquie rang off and then held up a finger. 'I've got a voicemail,' she said. 'He's probably rung me from school, or home. Hold on.' She pressed the phone to her ear. Sometimes Maxwell made remarks in fun which were not for others to hear. Henry saw the colour drain from her face and leaned forward, anxiously. She held the phone up, pressed 1 to replay and put it on speaker.

'I think I may have a name for you. Not definite, of course, but it might be good to look up Theodore Pettifer. Not sure of the spelling, but how many can there be? He does something arty according to Mrs B. See you later. It's … some time this afternoon. I'm heading off to Broadgate Avenue, it's not far from here. Just for a shufti. I'll see you there, shall I? Mwah.'

'Theodore Pettifer?' Henry said. 'Who the hell is Theodore Pettifer … hang on. Hang on.' He squeezed the bridge of his nose between thumb and forefinger, pressing the wire of his mask into the skin and not even noticing. 'When I saw Metcalfe, he said a suspect for a while in the Leadbetter killing was called Potter. Potter or something, he said. What if it was Pettifer? It will be in the record. Let me …' And he went to open the door.

Jacquie blessed Henry's total recall, but this was no moment to wait. 'Call it in while I drive. He's there, with a murderer. I *know* that the guy's in the house. He's probably been there all along. The dog hairs. The fact he was there … I've *met* him, Henry. He was at the house last night.'

Henry slammed the door just in time as Jacquie backed out of her parking space and was at the exit, drumming her fingers in exasperation at the solid mass of traffic in her way.

'Calm down,' Henry said. 'When the lights change at the top we'll be able to squeeze through. Try the flashing lights. If they don't work, the siren. But calm down. We'll not help Max if we pile up somewhere on the way.'

'Oh, hello.' The newcomer looked round the door and opened it all the way. 'I hope you don't mind my intruding, but I saw the door ajar and I thought to myself, "Paul Mitchell," I said to myself, "Paul Mitchell. That's a crime scene, that is. That door shouldn't be open. And now here you are, sitting here, so … I assume you are with the police, are you? Not a hammer wielding maniac? Ha ha.'

'No, not as such,' Maxwell said, his heart returning to its usual speed.

'Not a hammer wielding maniac as such?' the man asked, stepping back.

'No, not with the police as such. I'm waiting for my wife. She's a Detective Inspector here in Leighford.'

'I met a nice little police sergeant the other day. Guarding the gate at the back. That's how I know about the crime scene. Was that your wife?'

'Umm … no, my wife is a Det …'

'She was questioning people coming past. What our jobs were, everything. I'm an accountant, so she wasn't very interested in that. Who is?' He chuckled. 'I'm not, for one.'

'They have to do that,' Maxwell said.

'Cyclist came past, nearly took Phaedo's nose off, didn't he Phae?'

The invisible dog outside gave a single bark, then pushed its nose around the door, a very handsome if slightly elderly golden labrador.

'Quite an altercation.'

'Cyclists can be annoying.' Maxwell wasn't sure whether he believed that this man was really called Paul Mitchell. He offered his name so early in the conversation and so obviously, could it be that simple? 'Well, I suppose I had better go and wait for my wife out in the road. She's later than I expected.'

'It's probably that riot on the seafront.' A new voice made them turn. 'Don't know how many hundreds of people from all over the South Coast, all congregated to hear some bloke talk about how this is all a government conspiracy. News blackout at the moment, but it's going to be all over the papers by tomorrow.'

'How do you know, if there's a news blackout?' Even in extremis, Maxwell needed the facts to add up.

'Oh, hello,' the newcomer said. 'We met yesterday, didn't we? With your wife? Didn't I say when we met yesterday?' the man said, his face invisible behind his habitual double mask. 'I'm a freelance cameraman. A stringer sometimes, but they use my images more than my words, but that doesn't matter; it's the pictures that pay the money, not the copy.'

'A paparazzo?' Maxwell's mind was racing.

'Not a word I like much, but if you say so,' the masked man said. 'Look, shall we go outside? It's a bit claustrophobic, don't you find, all of us in here? Very gloomy, by this time of day.'

Maxwell was torn. He really wanted to get out of the shed, but not with this man. He wasn't sure whether being a paparazzo would class as something arty, but the chances were that he took other photographs as well as news images. On the other hand, the labrador owner was there and surely, no one would bash someone's head in with a witness there? Or … was the lab owner the murderer? Why else would he offer so much information about himself on a first meeting?

He made up his mind and followed the men outside. On the path, two dogs were squaring up to each other, but not with much enthusiasm. Phaedo, the labrador, had his hackles up and his top lip was pulled back to show his teeth. The other dog, something which would once have been called a mongrel but now doubtless had a posh name, was drawing back, with his tail between his legs.

'Phaedo!' the accountant said. 'Leave it.'

'Leave it?' the masked paparazzo was appalled. 'Do you mind? Vlad isn't roadkill. He's a pedigree cockerpoo.'

'Isn't that something of a misnomer?' Mitchell said. 'A pedigree mongrel?'

'Mongrel?' The photographer was outraged. '*Mongrel*? May I tell you that my family have had cockerpoos for decades. Highly bred, very loyal. Incredibly obedient. Watch. Vlad. Vlad. Heel.'

Not taking his eyes off the bigger dog, the cockerpoo backed off until he was pressed against his owner's leg, which he spackled with a mix of soft top hairs and shorter bristles from his undercoat. The man stooped and brushed at his trousers.

'They do shed, that's their one failing.'

Maxwell's ears pricked up. Dog hair. There were dog hairs at the scene.

'Labs are the same when they get to Phaedo's age,' the accountant said.

'I'm more of a cat person, myself,' Maxwell said and both men looked at him as if he had farted in church.

'Well, as long as it's all safe here,' the paparazzo said, 'I think I'll be on my way.'

'Me too,' said Mitchell. 'Phaedo is very pernickety when it gets near to supper time. He doesn't like being late. As if it isn't enough that he will only eat poached chicken. We're hostages to the damned creature.' He patted the animal's head, to show no hard feelings.

Vlad led the way down the path, heading back to the lane. 'Don't get me started on feeding,' his owner said, over his shoulder. 'This one has to have a special diet and it's driving me mad. He won't eat anything else.'

And the cat person watched the dog people go.

The traffic began to move at last, but slowly. Henry was able to vent his frustration by shouting at people on the phone. It was so unusual to hear his voice raised that Jacquie was quite disoriented. Eventually, his shouting bore fruit and he clicked his fingers at Jacquie, miming a pen. She pointed at the glove compartment. When he opened it, he had to forage beneath a pile of Hot Wheels but eventually found a pad with Minions all round the edge and also a pen with a dinosaur on the top. But any port in a storm.

'Uh huh. Uh huh. Uh huh. Where? Say again. Okay. Can you get someone round there, see if he's in? I *know* about the seafront. This is a murder case, not some idiots who should all be certified. Let me know if he's there. If he is, keep him there.'

Putting the phone back in his pocket and reading from the paper, he told Jacquie his news.

'Theodore Pettifer was a suspect in the murder of the

Leadbetters, insofar as he was questioned, but not under caution. He had lived in their house before they bought it, but there was no other connection, other than that he would browse in Mrs Leadbetter's bookshop. Metcalfe had forgotten about the house connection, or perhaps it would have made us look into him a bit more. I won't even ask how Max got to know about it, but it sounds as if it might be a good call. I've got someone going round to his house, see if he's there.'

'And if he has a dog.'

'Umm …?'

'Dog hairs at the scene.'

'Yes, of course. Dog hairs. Jacquie. Don't worry. He'll be fine.'

'Of course he will,' she said, beating on the steering wheel as a learner driver stalled at the next lights. 'I know he will. Only …'

'We'll soon be there. Just drive. And please don't …'

But he was too late. Jacquie's two fingers were in the air as she sailed past the weeping learner.

Out of the shed, Maxwell was stuck for somewhere to go. The dog hair clue had seemed such a good one, and a photographer was surely a creative person. But … the accountant had given his name far too pat. And the masked pap was known to hang around the scene. As he got nearer the house, Maxwell realised he had few choices as to places to sit, where he could watch every approach. In the end, he pulled one of the faux wicker chairs over to the patio doors which had the double advantage of making sure he had his back covered and also could catch the last rays of the setting sun. Now he could stop fretting about where Jacquie was, he could resume his watch and wait regime.

In the distance, he could hear a rustling and some heavy breathing and he sat as still as he could, every muscle tensed. The sounds got nearer but there was no one to be seen and it was a rather spooky thing until suddenly, he got his eye in and saw a string of tiny hedgehogs, following their mother who puffed and grunted at the front of the entourage. Behind them, the bigger male kept a weather eye out for anything that might hurt his brood. Like guided missiles, they came up the path and straight to a bowl , set in the corner of a flower bed. With ice in his veins, Maxwell saw that it was full of dog food, as recommended by no less an authority than Chris Packham, may his tribe increase.

The hedgehogs were tucking in and Maxwell was watching them with one eye and the rest of the garden with another when suddenly, the door behind him slid across and an arm like iron was around his throat, pulling him backwards, his back arched almost out of the chair. His hands came up to claw at the arm, but it was useless. It seemed to be encased in something unyielding. His head was pressing into something hard as well, something with a sharp edge.

'Hello, Mr Maxwell,' a voice above his head grated. 'Cute, aren't they, the hedgehogs? I've been fond of hedgehogs since I was a little boy. It hasn't mattered how much stupid building the idiots in this house do, the hedgehogs still come. They like dog food, you know. Lots of people put out bread and milk, you know, but that isn't good for them. Do you put bread and milk out, cat person?'

The arm squeezed harder and Maxwell arched his back again. Then the man behind him relaxed his grasp, just enough to let him breathe.

Maxwell drew in what breath he could and managed to gasp out a few words. 'Theodore Pettifer, I assume,' he said.

'My word, Mr Maxwell,' the arm pulled him back again. 'That's a feather in your cap, indeed. Six people I've killed, and the plods haven't even come close. Then the *hubby*,' squeeze, 'the *hubby* for goodness sake, of a plodess works it out, just like that.'

'I can't breathe,' Maxwell wheezed.

'That's the general plan,' Pettifer said and pulled harder.

'Don't you want to know how I worked it out?'

The arm relaxed a little and Pettifer gave the idea some thought.

'All right,' he said. 'Whycver not. I haven't ever strangled anyone, as a matter of fact. I'm more of a blunt instrument chap myself as you probably know. It's a lot more effort than the telly makes you think. So, let's just rest a while like this and you tell me. I'm assuming it wasn't Amelia Bencher.'

'I never had the pleasure,' Maxwell whispered, saving his voice.

'Nor did I,' Pettifer said. 'She was a cracker when she was younger, but she didn't give me a second glance. Mind you, I dodged a bullet there. She wouldn't have lasted as long as she did if she had been married to me.' He sniggered. 'I had form pretty young, as you must know if you know who I am.'

'Why did you kill her?' Maxwell asked. It was something that Mrs B. couldn't possibly know.

'Well, two things, really. The obvious one is that she turned me down in 1987.'

'My goodness. You do know how to bear a grudge.'

Pettifer hissed and pulled his arm so tightly that Maxwell almost passed out. 'It's not bearing a grudge,' he said. 'She was rude and unpleasant and she got what was coming to her. But the second reason was that she had seen me, that night.'

'How did you know?' Maxwell was learning to keep his remarks general.

'She told me. Or more or less, anyway. I was walking by and caught her eye. She was weeding. She was a keen gardener. I had given her a cutting of …'

'Mirabilis jalapa, yes, you said.'

'So, when I saw her, I went up to see how it was coming along. She said it was starting to come through, which is a bit late, but it might have still done all right, I suppose. Anyway, she said she had seen me next door.'

'That's it, is it?' Maxwell said. 'Did she accuse you?'

'She didn't have to *accuse* me,' Pettifer said. 'She said she had seen me. I know what she meant.'

Maxwell hoped she had meant more. It would be terrible to be killed for a social nicety.

'Can I ask,' Maxwell said. 'Why did you do it? Why did you kill all these people?'

'I didn't hurt the children,' he said, suddenly and Maxwell felt the spit spraying from behind his Perspex mask. Even when killing someone, he took proper precautions.

'I think that was very much appreciated,' Maxwell said.

'I was a child, you see,' Pettifer said, and relaxed his hold so that for the first time in minutes, Maxwell could breathe properly. 'I loved this house, this garden. We had dogs, always, cockerpoos, mainly. And the hedgehogs to watch. We had a pond then, filled in now by some vandals. Frogs. Newts. Dragonflies. Oh, dragonflies as long as my arm, or so they seemed. It was a paradise for children. So … I didn't harm the children. It wasn't their fault.'

'I'm sure the police will bear that in mind,' Maxwell said, and was rewarded by the iron forearm across his throat.

'It won't really be an issue, will it?' Pettifer said. 'By the time they extricate themselves from the chaos on the front, you'll be dead and I'll be long gone. At least strangulation doesn't take much cleaning up after.' He squeezed a little, just as if he were practising. 'It took me ages to get the blood out upstairs.'

'Why did you clean up so well?' Maxwell asked, panting. 'They had done the SOCO and found nothing. Well, apart from the dog hairs.'

'Dog hairs? What do they matter? The Ancasters had a dog.'

'Not like your dog, though. Apparently, you can tell the difference.'

Pettifer thought for a while. 'Vlad's old,' he said. 'He may need to be put down. I'll see how that goes.'

'So, why did you clean up?'

'It was my mother's bedroom. I didn't want to leave it messy, did I? She hated mess. She had a cleaner though she didn't need one. She just wanted everything to be perfect. And it *was* perfect. Until people started messing with it.'

'The Leadbetters?'

'Yes. They put this horrible extension up. I had to stop them before it got worse.'

'But why wait so long? Before you killed anyone else.'

'When the Leadbetters died, the boy was a minor. I wanted to buy the house, but the trustees didn't want to sell, they let it to make more income. Then, when he needed the money as he got older, he put it on the market, threw the tenants out and sold it. I was abroad at the time, on an assignment and when I got back, it was done. And for a while, it was all right. Roger Ancaster was a builder, but he didn't do anything to the house. I thought it would be all right. Then, this bloody lockdown gave him all the time he needed and he went *mental*. New windows, new doors. These patio things which allowed me to creep up so easily on you. But in all these years, do you know what no one ever did? They never changed the locks on the side door in from the garage. I've been coming and going for years and no one knew a thing. I'd do some cleaning, sometimes. People can be such pigs, and I wasn't having it in my mother's house.'

'So … that was it? You killed six people because they changed your mother's house?'

'That's reason enough, you idiot. Wouldn't you do the same?'

'Not really. My mother moved several times both before and after I left home.'

Pettifer's arm relaxed. 'Didn't that make you really sad?' he asked, his voice soft and solemn. 'All your boyhood memories, gone, just like that?'

'My boyhood memories are in my head,' Maxwell said. 'That's where memories belong.'

'*My* memories are here,' Pettifer said, in his distress letting go of Maxwell altogether. 'This house, this garden is where my memories are. With the hedgehogs and the frogs and … Wait, you bastard!' Maxwell was not at his fastest, with his breath still coming short, but he was away off down the garden, past the hedgehogs, heading for the shed. He made it with what seemed like inches to spare, slamming the door in Pettifer's face. He had always mocked runaway criminals on the telly when they ran upstairs to the roof or into the bathroom, but now he had done the equivalent. He could hear Pettifer's hammer beating on the door and knew it wouldn't be long before he was through. It was now pitch dark in the shed and he stretched out his hands in front of him and walked forward until he could feel the wall. Surely there was something there that could serve as a weapon. The spokeshave or the granny's tooth wouldn't cause much damage. And a hammer against a hammer seemed to be of little use. He finally settled on a pair of loppers. He wasn't sure whether he was up to actually snipping off a piece of human being, but on the other hand, he had never been faced by a hammer before, so who knew?

Finally, the beating on the door stopped and Maxwell rushed the slightly lighter rectangle it revealed, loppers extended, rushing the doorway like a Norman up Senlac Hill near Hastings.

'Max?' Henry Hall was perplexed but relieved to find his old friend still in one piece. 'Loppers, Max? That's an unusual choice of weapon. Something medieval, perhaps?'

'Henry? I have never been so glad to see anyone in my whole life. Is Pettifer …?'

'Under arrest? Yes. We managed to get a squad car down from Arundel. They were on their way anyway, to help with … have you heard about the thing on the seafront? I suppose you haven't.'

'Pettifer told me.'

'How odd. Anyway, yes, they tagged along and they happened to be two very big lads, so we were very grateful. Jacquie is reading him his rights. Oh, hang on … sounds like her now.'

Running feet were pounding down the path and she was in his arms, holding him as if she would never let him go. 'Max,' she murmured into his chest. 'Don't ever, *ever* do that again.'

'What?' Hall said, who had hearing like a bat. 'Catch a murderer? Don't put him off, Jacquie. Given time, he might get quite good at it.'

TWENTY-THREE

'So, anyway,' Jacquie said, wrapping another cold towel around her husband's neck to try to reduce the swelling before he went in to give his statement, 'all the way to the nick, apparently all he could do was fret about the hedgehogs, about who would feed them. Whether they would take him out there once a day, to give them dog food. He was obsessed they would give them bread and milk. He's as mad as a tree, of course. But not so mad he won't be doing a whole load of time for what he's done.'

'No trial, I'm assuming,' Maxwell said.

'No. I mean, he'll have to appear before the magistrate, but there'll be no jury trial or anything. Nothing to upset Marcus, if that's what you're thinking.'

'Yes, I was, actually. Pettifer was quite proud of himself, because he didn't hurt the children. He has no idea what hurting means.'

'He thinks he had an idyllic childhood, though. Birds, dragonflies, that's all he talks about.'

'I know. I think there may be things suppressed. You could ask Mrs B., but she's a bit fragile herself right now.'

'Poor thing. Mrs Troubridge was very special to her. To all of us, really. I don't know how we're going to tell Nole. He's known her all his life.'

'I think carefully is how. But no sugar coating. He needs to know she's gone and why. I don't want him growing up thinking the world is made of candyfloss and fairy wings.'

'I don't see how any child brought up in this house can think that. You have a scene of death and destruction in the loft. I am a policewoman. And Metternich and Bismarck are killing machines on an almost industrial scale. Hardly a day goes by without some entrails or another ending up on the mat or worse. The boy is soaked in blood, metaphorically.'

'I wonder how he will remember his childhood?' Maxwell wondered.

'How do you remember yours?'

'How many words do I have?'

'Lets say a hundred. Maximum.'

'Okay, keep count for me. Starting now. My childhood was … school. Learning to read before I went and ending up in the corner because I was bored. It was … fireworks. My dad setting his hair on fire – that's one memory, by the way, he didn't set his hair on fire except on Bonfire Night. But he did do it most years. Umm … grey mince. My mother was a stranger to tomato puree. Realising that history was something so magical that once I discovered it I was never the same again. Music lessons – ugh. Football practice – double ugh. Friends for life who you never see once you change school. Christmas morning. Grey turkey – there's a bit of a pattern evolving there. Umm … how many words is that? Too many, probably.'

'Almost certainly. I stopped counting when you got to the bit about your dad continually setting his hair on fire. Whenever we are looking through the photo albums with Nolan, I shall be looking for signs of charring. But, burning hair and grey food aside, I doubt that he will see his childhood as much different. He will remember his wonderful parents, if I can be less than humble for a minute. He will remember his cats. He will remember Mrs Troubridge, for sure. He'll remember America. He'll remember pancakes. He'll not have to remember Plocker, because there is a friendship which will survive all things. But one thing he will never have to do to remember it is to kill. Because you, my love,' and she dropped a kiss on his forehead, 'have taught him that all you need to do is keep it up here, inside your head.'

Other titles by BLKDOG Publishing for your consideration:

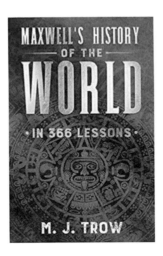

Maxwell's History of the World in 366 Lessons
By M. J. Trow

Peter Maxwell is the History teacher you wish you'd had. If you meet anyone (and you will) who says 'I hate History. It's boring,' they weren't taught by Mad Max.

Many of you will know him as the crime-solving sleuth (along with his police-person wife, Jacquie) in the Maxwell series by M.J. Trow (along with *his* non-policeperson wife, Carol, aka Maryanne Coleman – uncredited!) but what he is *paid* to do is teach History. And to that end has brought – and continues to bring – culture to thousands.

In his 'blog' (Dinosaur Maxwell doesn't really know what that is) written in 2012, the year in which the world was supposed to end, but mysteriously didn't, you will find all sorts of fascinating factoids about the *only* important subject on the school curriculum. So, if you weren't lucky enough to be taught by Max, or you've forgotten all the History you ever knew, here is your chance to play catch-up. The 'blog' has been edited by Maxwell's friend, the crime writer M.J. Trow, who writes almost as though he knows what the Great Man was thinking.

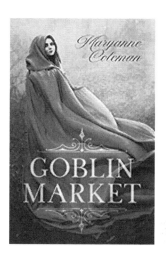

Goblin Market
By Maryanne Coleman

Have you ever wondered what happened to the faeries you used to believe in? They lived at the bottom of the garden and left rings in the grass and sparkling glamour in the air to remind you where they were. But that was then – now you might find them in places you might not think to look. They might be stacking shelves, delivering milk or weighing babies at the clinic. Open your eyes and keep your wits about you and you might see them.

But no one is looking any more and that is hard for a Faerie Queen to bear and Titania has had enough. When Titania stamps her foot, everyone in Faerieland jumps; publicity is what they need. Television, magazines. But that sort of thing is much more the remit of the bad boys of the Unseelie Court, the ones who weave a new kind of magic; the World Wide Web. Here is Puck re-learning how to fly; Leanne the agent who really is a vampire; Oberon's Boys playing cards behind the wainscoting; Black Annis, the bag-lady from Hainault, all gathered in a Restoration comedy that is strictly twenty-first century.

Prester John: Africa's Lost King
By Richard Denham

He sits on his jewelled throne on the Horn of Africa in the maps of the sixteenth century. He can see his whole empire reflected in a mirror outside his palace. He carries three crosses into battle and each cross is guarded by one hundred thousand men. He was with St Thomas in the third century when he set up a Christian church in India. He came like a thunderbolt out of the far East eight centuries later, to rescue the crusaders clinging on to Jerusalem. And he was still there when Portuguese explorers went looking for him in the fifteenth century.

Was he real? Did he ever exist? This book will take you on a journey of a lifetime, to worlds that might have been, but never were. It will take you, if you are brave enough, into the world of Prester John.

Fade
By Bethan White

There is nothing extraordinary about Chris Rowan. Each day he wakes to the same faces, has the same breakfast, the same commute, the same sort of homes he tries to rent out to unsuspecting tenants.

There is nothing extraordinary about Chris Rowan. That is apart from the black dog that haunts his nightmares and an unexpected encounter with a long forgotten demon from his past. A nudge that will send Chris on his own downward spiral, from which there may be no escape.

There is nothing extraordinary about Chris Rowan...

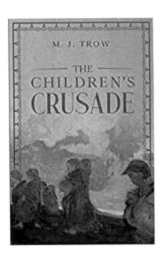

The Children's Crusade
By M. J. Trow

In the summer of 1212, 30,000 children from towns and villages all over France and Germany left their homes and families and began a crusade. Their aim; to retake Jerusalem, the holiest city in the world, for God and for Christ. They carried crosses and they believed, because the Bible told them so, that they could cross the sea like Moses. The walls of Jerusalem would fall, like Jericho's did for Joshua.

It was the age of miracles – anything was possible. Kings ignored the Children; so did popes and bishops. The handful of Church chroniclers who wrote about them were usually disparaging. They were delusional, they were inspired not by God, but the Devil. Their crusade was doomed from the start.

None of them reached Outremer, the Holy Land. They turned back, exhausted. Some fell ill on the way; others died. Others still were probably sold into slavery to the Saracens – the very Muslims who had taken Jerusalem in the first place.

We only know of three of them by name – Stephen, Nicholas and Otto. One of them was a shepherd, another a ploughboy, the third a scholar. The oldest was probably fourteen. Today, in a world where nobody believes in miracles, the Children of 1212 have almost been forgotten.

Almost… but not quite…

The poet Robert Browning caught the mood in his haunting poem, *The Pied Piper of Hamelin*, bringing to later readers the sad image of a lost generation, wandering a road to who knew where.

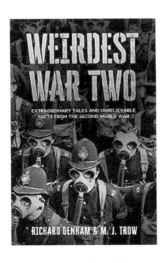

Weirdest War Two
By Richard Denham & M. J. Trow

Was Britain's Thermopylae really fought over a tennis court?

What happened in Canada during the invasion of Winnipeg?

How did the Night Witches terrify and torment the Axis?

Was Hitler actually sent to spy on the Nazis by the army?

Who was the schoolgirl who helped win the Battle of Britain?

Truth, they say, is the first casualty of war. You will have to decide how many such casualties occur in this book, the third in the *Weird War* series. Amber rooms worth a fortune, the spear that pierced Christ's side, deadly female snipers and Lucille Ball's spooky teeth, it's all here for the discerning buff of 1939-45.

Whether it's official Nazi propaganda dreamed up by Josef Goebbel's Ministry of Enlightenment or the 'scuttlebutt' of the US navy; tall stories from the officers' mess or attempts to escape from the grim reality of total war, the Second World War provides a fascinating glimpse into the mindset and ingenuity of a generation.

Have we now exhausted our supply of weirdness? With new information coming to light all the time from the classified archives in the corridors of power, we wouldn't bet on it!

www.blkdogpublishing.com

Printed in Great Britain
by Amazon